NOVELS BY LISA M. MATLIN

The Only One Who Knows
The Stranger Upstairs

THE ONLY ONE WHO KNOWS

THE ONLY ONE WHO KNOWS

A NOVEL

LISA M. MATLIN

BANTAM
NEW YORK

Bantam Books
An imprint of Random House
A division of Penguin Random House LLC
1745 Broadway, New York, NY 10019
randomhousebooks.com
penguinrandomhouse.com

Copyright © 2026 by Lisa Matlin

Penguin Random House values and supports copyright. Copyright fuels creativity, encourages diverse voices, promotes free speech, and creates a vibrant culture. Thank you for buying an authorized edition of this book and for complying with copyright laws by not reproducing, scanning, or distributing any part of it in any form without permission. You are supporting writers and allowing Penguin Random House to continue to publish books for every reader. Please note that no part of this book may be used or reproduced in any manner for the purpose of training artificial intelligence technologies or systems.

BANTAM & B colophon is a registered trademark of Penguin Random House LLC.

Hardcover ISBN 978-0-593-59998-3
Ebook ISBN 978-0-593-59999-0

Printed in the United States of America on acid-free paper

1st Printing

First Edition

Title-page art: cbpix/Adobe Stock

BOOK TEAM: Production editor: Kelly Chian • Managing editor: Saige Francis • Production manager: Sam Wetzler • Copy editor: Laura Jorstad • Proofreaders: Julia Henderson, Barbara Jatkola

Book design by Diane Hobbing

The authorized representative in the EU for product safety and compliance is Penguin Random House Ireland, Morrison Chambers, 32 Nassau Street, Dublin D02 YH68, Ireland. https://eu-contact.penguin.ie

For my mum,
The only person brave enough to live with a writer.
Thank you for handling the deadlines and mood swings like an absolute champ.
My books are 10 percent talent, 90 percent your love, support, and snacky-do-dahs.
x

For my sister,
Who knows all my secrets and still hasn't sold them for profit.
Yet.
Hi darls! — Thank you for quoting the same three movies with me (which is often).
And for stopping me from spiralling every time I lose my mind (which is also often).
x

For my brother,
Not everyone is fortunate enough to have a brother who answers their questions with your patience, kindness, and genuine enthusiasm. I'm deeply grateful that I do.
(I'm still working on that superyacht.)
x

In the darkness of your room
Your mother calls you by your true name
You remember the faces, the places, the names
You know it's never over, it's relentless as the rain

> —*Bruce Springsteen, "Adam Raised a Cain"*

THE

ONLY

ONE

WHO

KNOWS

THEN

I can never think of my father without a knife in his hand.

He's sitting at the dining table, wet waders on, dripping salt water. I'm watching TV on the floor while he sharpens the knife behind me. I keep looking over my shoulder at him, terrified he'll catch me looking.

My father had many kinds of silence, and I'd learned how important it was to analyze them all. Fish can tell a storm is coming days in advance. Can sense a change in the pressure system long before there's any sign of rain. We were like that. So sensitive to any changes in my father's moods. For us, our father was *the storm* and *the sea.* Perhaps if we were quick enough, vigilant enough, we could swim for calmer waters.

But most of the time, I remained on the floor, silent and frozen stupid, wondering, What do you want from me, Dad? What will make you stop? Name your price, I'll pay.

Maybe then he would see how willing I was. How obedient. How goddamn good.

His silence after my mother left us was something different, something new and dangerous. Sometimes when I close my eyes, I can still hear him sharpening that black blade.

If there was one thing he was proud of, it was his fishing knife. He made it himself. The handle, the blade.

"See this?" He'd point proudly to that sharp, black tip. "This was an old padlock I found near the train tracks. The thing about steel, Minnow, is that it can live a thousand lifetimes. It might look like nothin' at the start, but you gotta wear it down, put it through the fire..."

He turned it over and over, marveling at it like I wasn't even there. "Then you can turn it into anything you damn well like."

And I sat there and thought, That's what he does to me.

Holds me to the fire and watches me burn.

CHAPTER 1

Here's what the TV producers of *Morning, Sunshine!* want you to know about their three co-hosts:

Joy Marriot is a grandmotherly TV veteran of fifty-seven years.

Lynny Stewart is her hooting sidekick.

Melanie (me) is the new kid on the block. The timid voice of reason to Joy's *opinions* and Lynny's nonstop shrieking.

Here's what they *don't* want you to know:

One of us tiptoes out to the staff parking lot to enjoy an early-afternoon pounding from the sports reporter who is definitely *not* her husband. (Lynny.)

One of us released a Paleo cookbook three years ago and pledged 15 percent of the profits to a cancer charity. They're still waiting for the money. (Joy.)

One of us is staring at a terrifying text from her fiancé and stuffing her palm against her mouth to hold back the screams. That one is hanging on *by a fucking thread.* (Me.)

I sit stiffly on the edge of the white leather couch, angling my phone away from the bustling set designers as I read my fiancé's text over and over. The studio lights are bright and burning hot, but I've never felt so cold. Somewhere in the darkness the director yells, "Showtime in five minutes, people!"

I stare at my boots, hyperventilating. I cannot sit through *two entire hours* of this live taping and pretend to give a damn about this morning's news when my own life has just gone to hell in one text.

Everything is a blur of noise, color, and movement. Aqua skirt. Red hair teased to maximum height. Skin stretched so tight it looks like it hurts. Joy.

Bright pink and plunging blouse. Lemony perfume and a shrieking laugh. Lynny.

My co-hosts sink onto the couch beside me, crossing their legs like synchronized swimmers. Their stilettos gleam under the studio lights, the heels so thin and sharp, you could use them to play darts.

My shirt is seashell white and buttoned so tightly at my throat, it hurts each time I swallow. My culottes are hideously ugly and the color of iced coffee. My suede ankle boots are blocks of concrete.

White. Camel. Neutral. That's me. I'm the one brought in once a week to, in the producer's words, "connect with the Gen Y crowd."

It's not working. The ratings are appalling, and the network has no money. I only got this job because I knew the right people, and no one else could stomach Joy's on-air bullying like I do. But I'm an expert at blending into the wall and the couch until the threat disappears. Survival instincts I carried over from childhood.

Underneath my neutral shirt and neutral bra is a stinging rash with raised red bumps. Hives, my doctor said. *Have you been stressed lately?*

Joy sips at a coffee as bitter and boiling as she is. She's the first of us to reach for a tissue when a Z-list reality star brims with dutiful tears. The first to pat their knee and cut to a commercial while staring grimly into the camera, only to reappear smiling three minutes later. How can you trust someone who shuts off their emotions like a light switch?

Lynny opens her cavernous mouth wide while the makeup artist applies another coat of gloss. She's forty-two, shrill as a whistle and easily bored, and I'm pretty sure she loves gossip and screwing the sports reporter more than her four children.

Look at them, these two brightly colored fish. Seventy years of showbiz experience between them. They gleam. They preen.

And they scheme.

You have to hand it to these pretty, dirty bitches.

"Two minutes!" someone yells out, and I jump. My co-hosts stare at me like they've just remembered I'm here. That's me. I'm so agreeable, so *neutral*, I might as well be the couch.

Lynny practically shoves the makeup artist away and inches over, her whole body an exclamation mark. Instinctively, I place my phone face down in my lap. My entire body trembles.

"Melanie, dear!" she yells, as if she's surprised to see me. I've sat beside her once a week from 5 to 7 A.M. for nearly four months now. "And where were *you* this morning, missy?"

I missed the morning briefing. All of it. I stumbled into the makeup chair five minutes ago, stumbled out again, sat on the couch, and received the worst text of my life.

She doesn't wait for me to answer, that's how short her attention span is. "How's that *gorgeous* man of yours?"

Oliver is my fiancé of three months, boyfriend of seven, a meteorologist on a rival network, one that actually has money. He proposed to me right on this couch, live on air, despite me telling him repeatedly that I hate surprises. My fiancé loves grand gestures, but it was at that moment I realized that none of them were for me.

I hesitated for long enough that Lynny cried out, "Melanie! Put the poor dear out of his misery!"

"Okay . . ." I finally stammered. "Sure."

Oliver drove us home in steaming silence and didn't talk to me for two days. That was not the first red flag I ignored.

"He's *good*!" My voice cracks and I blurt something to cover it up. "Busy. We're both so busy lately."

We are indeed busy. *I* am, anyway. I left him again this week.

"You hold on to that one," Lynny says, giving me a playful tap on the arm. "He's a keeper."

Like hell he is. But it's one thing to want to leave. It's another thing entirely when it's eleven o'clock on a Friday night and your fiancé is screaming at you, again, because you looked at the Uber driver too long, and your dress is too short, and you're suddenly, startlingly aware that your confident, assertive fiancé is actually a controlling shithead who's stealing pieces of you little by little and you've allowed it.

Maybe you weren't even fully aware. I wasn't. But that night, I looked into my fiancé's eyes, and I saw my father. And I stumbled outside, exhausted and desperate, because I don't fight. I don't flight. I just freeze, and yes, I hate myself for it. In the movies, the woman packs up her shit, leaves the house, and drains the joint account. Begins again.

But it's been three days since I left, and all I've done is survive. I left in a daze and spent the last two nights in a hotel, lying on a double bed, staring at nothing. *I didn't even think to take Jessie.* That's how crazy I was. How crazy it makes you. It must have been how my mum felt. I think I finally understand how she could leave us behind. *I understand now, Mum. I understand and I'm sorry.*

"Thirty seconds!"

Smears of color. Hot lights. Cold hands.

All I can think about is the text I sent Oliver this morning as I sat on the edge of the hotel bed. *I'm coming back to get Jessie.*

And his response:

You're not taking Jessie.

I feel like I'm choking. He bought Jessie, our golden retriever, as an engagement present. He's walked her twice in three months and snaps at her when she gets underfoot. Poor Jessie is always flustered around him. So am I. I suspect now that Oliver just wanted the image of Jessie and of me. A compliant wife and a golden puppy for the shitty tabloid interviews he wanted us to pose for. And I wanted somebody who didn't see my chronic people pleasing as an open door.

You're not taking Jessie.

"Good morning, sunshines!"

Shit, we're live. I glance into the camera, my face tight and terrified.

Joy wriggles in her seat, booming, "Some *breaking* news this morning..."

I feel like I've dunked my head underwater. Color, movement, lights, *you're not taking Jessie.*

But then I hear something clearly, Joy reciting, "Beasts from the deep!"

I raise my head, staring at the flickering images of a grimy beach town.

My heart freezes. I know this place.

Joy booms, "A second shark has been spotted off a Victorian beach in four days. A great white shark was spotted just meters from the shore in Kangaroo Bay, a small fishing town on the East Coast."

Lynny chimes in, "The last fatal shark attack took place off the coast of Sydney in 2021. A local man, Keith Walsh, was swimming in shallow waters when he was attacked by a great white shark..."

"...Melanie?"

The studio is silent as Joy calls my name. Her voice is round and soft, a bubble.

"What?" My voice is rough and heavy, a brick.

She raises an eyebrow, and her nostrils start to flare. I'm always deferential to her, off camera and on. Simpering, even. Sometimes I think that my entire personality is just a bunch of coping mechanisms. I spent our last show waiting to get a few words in, and when I finally did, Joy held up a ring-heavy hand and scorned, "Hush dear, the *grown-ups* are speaking!"

"Oh, Joy, you're so *bad*!" Lynny cackled.

Gentle ribbing, the producers said, defending them. It's not personal.

It is. I've spent a lifetime allowing myself to be emptied by people like these. Sometimes they're little thefts: "I know you said you're busy this weekend, but you can cover this shift for me, yeah? It's just that it's my mum's birthday and..."

And my needs are more important than yours.

Little by little they'll take. You may not even realize you've been robbed.

Sometimes they'll thrust a fist down the back of your throat, grabbing greedily at organs. My father did this. I imagine him, bloodied up to his elbow, angry with effort, fist squeezing my lungs. And me, mouth wide open and compliant as he snaps them free from my trachea. He inspects them, all spongy-pink and crucial and *mine*. *You won't need these,* he says. *Why are you crying? Little bitch.*

Why did you allow it? Because speaking up came with a price tag you couldn't afford to pay.

Dad won't like it. Oliver will be pissed. Joy will have me fired.

So open your mouth, wide. Let them empty you. What are you now? A hollow, filled with everything the thieves didn't want.

That's how they turn girls into ghosts, Mum cautioned. *Don't let it happen to you.*

But I did.

The studio is deathly quiet.

"Uh . . . we seem to have lost Melanie for a minute here, folks!" Lynny chortles, but I can finally hear the uncertainty in her voice. The alarm. Good.

"Cut to commercial," the producer snaps, "now!"

The moment they've cut the studio feed, Joy's mask slips. She glares at me and for the first time, I glare back. *Look* at me. *Really* look. See what I've done for you? For everyone? What I've allowed myself to become? Me in my bland and severe clothes so no one will see me. Me with my timid, little-girl voice so no one will listen.

Am I *fucking neutral* enough for you yet?

Enough. Shakily, I get to my feet, and someone hisses in the dark, "Is she drunk?"

I reach behind me for my microphone, a skinny black snake running from my chest to the small of my back. I yank it out, and feedback shrieks.

Nobody moves. No one knows what to do with me and my very uncharacteristic outburst. What a plot twist this is. Meek little Melanie clings to the rules, while everyone else breaks them. My father, my fiancé, my co-hosts . . . my mother.

I am compliant. Complicit. Obedient. *Good.* I could not have been *more fucking good.* But it didn't matter, did it? It never does. The more you give, the more they'll take.

Joy bolts upright and grabs for my arm. "Sit down, you little bitch!"

I wrench away, darting behind the camera into the dark.

You're not wearing that.

You won't need these.

You're not taking Jessie.

Sit down, you little bitch!

I grasp the mic pack, launch it like a baseballer, and hurl it at Joy's face.

CHAPTER 2

It misses her head by inches.

No one moves. But this time, I do. I run. Down the stage steps, right past the twenty-something camera operator, who has no idea where to aim the camera. I bolt into the darkness, out the doors, and into the early-morning light. It's not even 6 A.M. yet.

I wrench my car door open, fling myself inside, and lock it. I stare at the steering wheel, and then unbelievably, I start laughing.

I can't go back to my sterile house with my sterile fiancé in Northton, or my once-a-month lunch friends. They're nice enough girls who work in the industry and understand the pressures, demands, and overtime, but after two years, we've never quite made the jump from "How's work going?" to "I think I want to leave my fiancé," or "My doctor wants to up my Zoloft."

I can't go back to that hotel and stare at the walls again. I'm afraid one day I'll look in the bathroom mirror and see my mum's face instead of my own.

I glance at the double doors of the studio, but nobody has come for me. Yet.

I speed out of the parking lot as the sun begins to rise.

I CROUCH BEHIND THE NEIGHBOR'S privacy hedge, poking my head around the corner, looking up the street. The diamond-shaped leaves tickle my cheek, and the hems of my culottes are wet with morning dew. I parked two blocks away. Now I wait for my fiancé to leave for work, crouched behind a hedge like a madwoman.

The front door opens, and I reel back, breathless. I wait until I hear an engine hum to life, and duck to the ground as his car rolls past. I catch a glimpse of the back of his blond head, and the cuffs of his shirt on the steering wheel. My throat tightens as I scan the back seat of his Land Cruiser. But Jessie isn't with him. Thank God.

I watch Oliver drive off to work, wondering how the hell it came to this. When his taillights are long gone, I run.

I sprint up the road, my house keys rattling in my pocket. I yank them out as I run up the driveway until I'm panting at the front door. Heart pounding, I shove my key in the lock, darting panicked glances behind me.

But the door doesn't open. Stunned, I try it again and again, shoving the key in and jiggling it every way, swearing under my breath the whole time.

It won't open.

I step back as the realization hits. *He's changed the locks.* I've been gone for *two days,* and he's already locked me out. I pay rent here—he can't do that. But that's how it is with him: crossing lines, while I stand there, pretending they aren't broken. Was, I tell myself. That's how it was. Not anymore.

Jessie sticks her golden head through a gap in the blinds. Her eyes light up when she sees me. Her tail flaps back and forth so hard, it rattles the blinds. I crouch down in front of her and press my palms against the window.

"He's locked me out," I tell her breathlessly. "The *bastard* has locked me out."

Her tail falters, caught mid-wag, as if the hope in her heart just shattered. I jump up and wrench the door handle again; when it doesn't budge, I slam my shoulder against it.

Jessie whines again, softer this time. *Don't leave me here with him.*

It's like I'm seeing my nine-year-old self in her eyes. *Mum, don't leave Heath and me with Dad.*

QUICKLY, I SCRAMBLE OVER THE side fence, landing hard on the cobbled white stones of our tiny back garden. I dart around the side of the house until I come to the sliding glass door that leads to our dining room. We always leave it open for Jessie while we're out, so she can wander in and out of the yard until I get home.

The door's closed. I grab for the handle. Locked. Jessie meets me at the sliding door, her eyes wide, wet and pleading.

The kitchen window . . .

I try to wrench it open, but it doesn't budge. On top of the outdoor dining table is a god-ugly concrete vase housing a limp ficus. A gift from Oliver's overbearing mother. Eerily calm, I scoop it up, stagger forward, and grunt, "Watch out, Jess!"

Obediently, she backs away. When I can no longer see her, I hurl it at the kitchen window, and it explodes in a hail of glass and sound.

I move quickly, ducking under the remains of the broken window, my suede boots crunching on the glass. Beneath the dining room table, Jessie's golden head slowly emerges.

Jessie.

I half run to her, cramming her into my arms. She whines softly in excitement, spinning in her sweet golden dance, gently licking my face, my ears, my forehead. Thank God. I've got her. It's going to be all right. It will.

"Let's get the hell outta here."

I hurry to our bedroom, Jess padding softly right behind. I grab the sports bag in my side of the closet and rip my clothes from the hangers in my haste to get them inside the bag. I don't even know what else to take. What *do* you take when you're fleeing your shitty fiancé? I have no cash in the house, thankfully; that's all locked away in my bank account. I pause for one second. *Oh my God. Mum.* A memory flashes in my brain with a jolt. My mum standing over me with desperate eyes.

Always have a bank account in your name only, she insisted. *Promise me!*

I was eight, maybe nine years old at the time. Too young to understand why her voice was high and insistent and why she grasped my hand so tight that it stung.

But I kept that promise. I'm leaving with my own money. Not much, but enough to live off for a few months. I'll be all right. Unless Joy decides to sue me. Surely, there's a payment plan for attacking someone live on the air. Laughter bubbles out my mouth. This is crazy. All of it. Go, go, go!

I rush to my bedside table. Under a pile of ankle-length socks is a single photograph lying face down. I flip it over and take a quick look, though I know this photo by heart.

The boy is ankle-deep in the water, tanned and barefoot and months overdue for a haircut. His smile is huge, revealing two missing front teeth. The happy little girl is in his arms, naked except for a nappy. Hanging from her fists is the tail of a massive King George whiting, its tapering head bumping her ankle. She can't be more than a year old. Mum took that picture of Heath and me nearly thirty-five years ago.

I place it gently in the front bag pocket, dump my socks and undies in, and zip it up.

And then Jessie and I run. Out the bedroom, past the lounge room with its smoke-gray couch, and straight to the front door. I wrench it open, peer out, heart fluttering more with excitement than fear.

Coast is clear.

"Let's go, Jess!"

And we're off! Running wild down the street, my backpack slapping against my shoulder, Jessie bounding beside me. It hits me that she's never left this house without a lead on. Funny how much I relate to that.

I yank the car doors open, throw my backpack in, and harness Jessie into the back seat.

Seeing her so excited, I pull her into my arms, holding on tight as the weight of everything crashes over me.

I know damn well that I'm fired. And homeless.

But it's strange . . . because here, with my arms wrapped around my dog, I feel like I've gained more than I've lost.

I climb into the driver's seat, shut the door, and speed off, flipping the house off as I drive away.

It's barely 6:30 A.M., but Northton's already bustling. Cars doing illegal U-turns, wealthy millennials power walking to the office, lost in the success flex like Oliver. His mum's the senior editor of a gardening magazine, and his dad, a Qantas pilot. Meanwhile, my mum worked at the general store on the weekends, and Dad ran a fishing charter. Only I never told Oliver this. I never told him anything at all about my past. So he made one for me. "From now on, your parents owned a dental practice, okay?"

I nodded, complicit as always, because when I left home at eighteen, I had no idea what the hell I was doing. I was lost for years, drowning. And when I met Oliver, confident, assertive Oliver, I pulled myself aboard his life raft and let him steer.

Northton. I shake my head and flip it off, too. I don't belong here. It's time for me to scurry back to the dirty streets where I was born.

Goodbye, Northton, with your trendy terrace houses and lunchtime lip fillers. I always hated you.

Goodbye, my fiancé, who walks like the world owes him applause. Who doesn't lead but dominates, because winning isn't enough for him. He needs you to lose.

I glance in the overhead mirror, inspecting myself.

Goodbye, Melanie Holmes.

CHAPTER 3

My real name is Minnow, like the fish. Minnows are small and silvery, typically used as live bait. If we were quick enough, Heath and I scooped them out of the shallows with our bare hands. We'd cup them gently, marveling at their silver bodies, squirming in the sunlight. One morning, Dad snatched a minnow out of Heath's palm, plunged a hook through its bottom and upper lip, sewing its mouth shut, and cast its bloodied body back into the water. He couldn't understand why we cried.

I've been driving for almost three hours. Here on the East Coast of Victoria, the land is flat and thirsty and the color of straw.

Jessie wags her tail at a cluster of Friesians sheltering under a ghost gum. It's hot already and it's only 10 A.M. I count the roadkill as I drive, *eight, nine, ten*. Kangaroos, mashed and meaty on the side of the road.

There's no sign saying WELCOME TO KANGAROO BAY because the truth is, you're *not* welcome. This is a grizzled-old-man town, run by our filthy fathers, and they hate you so much it gives them ulcers. They want to stomp through their streets, animal-like and mean, smelling of rage and beer. They want to gather in pissed-off groups at the pub, complaining about the *farken tourists,* and overcharge you for tickets to their snapper charters, smiling like they're doing you a favor.

Our fathers are hot blood, heavy stomachs, heavier fists. Our mums, exhausted and desperate. Dads remain, mums flee, but I never thought mine would. My mum was soft hands, vanilla fabric softener, and *I love my girl* and *You're so clever, Heath!*

We used to collect wildflowers for her on lazy Sunday afternoons, then rush home to present them, wilted and crushed in our fists. You'd think we'd given her the whole world.

I pass a group of teenage boys in knee-length wet suits, surfboards tucked under their arms. Sporty tourist cars are parked carelessly on nature strips, and there's a long, snaking line in front, desperate to get to the five beaches ahead. I tap my finger on the wheel thinking about this morning's news report: BEASTS FROM THE DEEP: ANOTHER SHARK SPOTTED IN KANGAROO BAY.

Beaches only close for an hour after a shark sighting, and it hasn't seemed to put the tourists off. But then, nobody thinks it'll be them.

Until it is.

I slow the car as we cruise through the main street. You can spot the tourists, because they're the ones smelling like sunscreen. The rest of us just burn.

They dress in primary colors, sunset pinks and pineapple yellows, like flocks of pretty birds. They sit primly at the scratched wood tables outside the Roo Bay pub, grimacing at the watery globs of bird shit.

The pub dog, an ancient kelpie, sniffs at their ankles, and a woman in lemon shorts crouches to pat it. The dog loses interest, ambles to a magpie carcass, rolls in it, bloodied feathers sticking wetly to its coat.

I drive past the general store where Mum worked, the tackle shop, and that one building that seems to change business every year. It's empty now, windows smashed in, graffiti smeared on the boarded door, U WANNA C MY TEETH?

I must be breathing too hard, because in the rearview mirror Jess gives me a questioning look.

"I grew up here," I tell her quietly. "Fast."

We all did. This town isn't kind to its kids. We grow here, ungoverned inside the town's dirty fist until we fit neatly into our fathers' shadows. Then the legacy of violence begins again. We'll spend Friday nights at the Roo Bay pub, red-faced and aggressive, complaining of hand cramps and you: the *farken tourists*. And our children will clench their teeth when we stomp home, smelling of beer and blood.

Traffic crawls to a stop. At the end of this road, up a hill so steep, you have to press the accelerator nearly all the way down, is surf beach number 1. Golden sand, crashing waves, and rated one of the most dangerous beaches in Victoria. That clear cool water sure looks inviting, but it can suck you under in a riptide like someone's grabbing you by the hair and pulling you down. It happens quick.

That's Kangaroo Bay. You'll drown in our beaches and our dads will snicker when we pluck your corpse from the sea. Even the woods will slurp greedily at your bone marrow.

There's a meanness here. A darkness in this town.

This is cruelty's breeding ground.

The tourists don't see that. They see sun-bleached piers and shining water. They don't see the shadows below.

Surf beach 1 is the most popular, the only patrolled beach out of the five. It's where from November to March my brother volunteers to pull half-drowned tourists from the sea. When he was a teen, he won the state award for Surf Lifesaver of the Year. Mum and I cheered from the front row. Dad didn't come. *Let the fuckers drown,* he said.

The trophy was as tall as my torso: A surfer riding a golden wave that crested over his right shoulder. For years it was displayed proudly on the windowsill.

But not long after Mum left, I saw it, shining weakly under Heath's bed. The golden surfboard broken in two. I never said a word about it. I knew why Heath discarded his trophy and left it to rot in the dark.

Because there was one person my brother could not save.

I glance at the car clock: 10:13 A.M. He'll be there right now, sitting atop the sentry chair, scanning the water. I turn instead, driving silently away to the back roads of town.

I've only been here a few times since I left for good at eighteen. The closer I get to my childhood home, the more I keep checking the overhead mirror to make sure I'm still thirty-four and not that barefoot and frightened child.

I tighten my grip on the wheel. You're supposed to go home

victorious. *Look at me now. I'm not who I was. Not who you wanted me to be.*

But the familiar dirt roads scoff, **Bullshit, Minnow. You're the same scared kid.**

If there's one place you can't hide from yourself, it's on the streets of your hometown. And there's one place in Kangaroo Bay that knows me right down to my bones. Knows I'm a coward. Knows that when it's time to speak up, I won't.

The woods on Soldiers' Road.

I grip the wheel so hard, I feel it in my biceps. I haven't been to the woods for years, but I'm back there every night in dreams.

And nightmares.

I park on our front lawn, kill the engine, and stare at my childhood home. The unhappy house sits miserably on a tiny, flat block, patchy with sand. The rusted roof tiles are the color of lung tar, and the painted weatherboards are the ugliest shade of blue I've ever seen.

But the garden beds are lovely.

I unhook Jessie's harness and let her out, crouching in front of a bunch of daffodils tucked snugly into fresh black soil. Mum's favorite. I wait there as Jess explores the yard, smelling the roos, the wombats, the sea, maybe even the faint tinge of blood on the ground.

I retrieve the spare key behind the water tank and unlock the front door, trembling. Yeah, I'm still that scared kid. I thought I'd healed from it all. Turns out I was just distracted.

I step inside into semi-darkness. The heavy paisley curtains are drawn, and the house smells of fish and hot oil. But the sink is clean, the navy carpet newish. For a long time, I stand there at the door, flooded with emotions and memories as past and present me collide. I'd forgotten that you could hear the waves everywhere in this house. You eventually stop hearing them. Same with the sand. Hard little crumbs of it, everywhere. Deep in the cracks of the kitchen tiles, in the sheets, on the bathroom mat.

Funny what you forget.

Mum vacuumed twice a day until she stopped altogether. It was around the time she stopped speaking. I didn't notice, not at first. She was always quietly frantic, preemptive: *Be very, very quiet while Daddy naps. Shhhh! Here's your orange juice, darlings. Don't spill, don't spill!*

One day, she handed me a glass of juice, looking at me like she didn't remember who I was. My mother had turned into a ghost. A ghost doing the dishes. A ghost cutting our sandwiches. A ghost sitting alone for hours and hours in the dark, staring at nothing.

And then one day when I was about ten years old, the ghost vanished and never came back.

I glance at the kitchen bench, blinking in surprise at how clean it is. Always there was a fresh snapper or whiting there, eyes bright, mouth bloodied. Or a dozen maroon-red arrow squid, chopped into slimy rings.

One morning before school, I slung my bag over my shoulder and paused at the front door. On the kitchen counter was a plastic tub, the air above it, gory. And inside it, a bloodied row of kangaroo hearts.

I tiptoe past the sagging couch, my eyes fixed on the closed door down the narrow hallway. Dad's room. I wait for him to come storming out, my jaw clamping so tight my teeth hurt.

My bedroom is opposite the laundry. The stench of Dad's unwashed fishing clothes used to drift into my room like they were being carried by a slow-moving tide. When Mum lived here, my bedroom sheets smelled of vanilla and cherry blossom. After, they reeked of blood and brine.

I sit straight-backed on my childhood bed, and Jessie hovers at my door looking embarrassed, like she's not sure what to do with herself. Same. I pat the bed, and she hops up.

Slowly, I open the third drawer of my bedside table. It's still there. The bundle of newspaper clippings. I pull them out, rest them on my knee, and read.

Local man missing

February 8, 2000

Police are appealing for public assistance to locate a man missing from Kangaroo Bay, Victoria.

Peter Greenwood, aged 52, is the owner of the fishing charter Deep Sea. *He was last seen fishing at beach 3, Kangaroo Bay, at 11 P.M. He is of Caucasian appearance, about 175 cm tall, with a stocky build and black hair.*

Family and police hold concerns for his welfare.

Anyone who sees him or has information about his whereabouts is urged to contact local police or Crime Stoppers on 1800 333 000.

Missing Kangaroo Bay man Peter Greenwood had allegedly been threatened before vanishing

February 15, 2000

A 52-year-old fishing charter operator who vanished earlier this month was allegedly threatened a week before disappearing. A man acquainted with Peter Greenwood allegedly attacked him at his Kangaroo Bay home.

The man is considered a suspect in his disappearance.

The man obviously wasn't much help. My father has been missing for over twenty years. I was there the day Dad was threatened, playing in the front yard when the man rushed past, jaw set, eyes burning. He grabbed the screen door handle, rattled it, swearing. Dad appeared, voice pained and pleading. He reminded me of a frightened animal. I watched the man reach out with heavy hands, shove my father backward through the screen door. Watched Dad's head hit the floorboard with a cartoonish thud. The man stormed off, screaming threats, and Dad lay motionless as if playing dead.

A week later, he went night fishing. I did not see him leave the house. Did not see him return.

I stroke Jessie's head, remembering. I'm about ten years old, sitting opposite a policeman, his eyes soft with sympathy. *We're gonna do everything we can to find your dad, okay? That's a promise.*

I curl my body around Jessie's, remembering the kindness in the policeman's voice and the free bottles of Coke he gave me as I sat there, shaking.

But mostly . . .

I close my eyes.

Mostly I remember praying to God that my father would never return.

CHAPTER 4

I hate this boat.

I freeze at the dock, staring grimly at my father's fishing charter. *I hate you back*, it says, unconcerned. In the fading sunlight, the bone-white logo glows: DEEP SEA FISHING CHARTERS.

There are two teens in front of me, three behind, and one sleepy-looking blond kid and his dad, fishing rods slung over their shoulders. It's just after 8 P.M.; Jessie and I slept for hours, limbs tangled, breathing deep and steady.

It's a pretty evening, all golden bright and still. Three pelicans gather in an impatient knot near the dock, eager for the fishermen to hurl them slimy scraps.

I'm so nervous I keep wiping my palms on my jeans. Somewhere up ahead is my brother. I can't see him, but I hear him call out in his easy way: "Got your fishing license, mate?"

I tap my foot impatiently. Here he is. Cotton shorts because he hates jeans, oversized hoodie that looks warm, dark blue with the DEEP SEA FISHING logo.

"Got your—" Heath glances up at me and freezes, mouth falling slightly open.

"Hey," I blurt eagerly. I want to step forward and throw my arms around him, but something tells me not to. I wait instead, wiping my palms on my jeans again. God, what if I'm wrong? What if my brother doesn't want me here? How many times has he saved me over the years? And look at me now, running straight back to him, hoping he'll save me once again.

It's been a few years since I've seen Heath. I came back four years ago for Jonah's birth, sat rigid on the waiting room chair, thinking about the new addition. We don't add to the Greenwood name. We subtract. Mum. Dad. Me, in a way. Heath extended the bloodline when I wanted it to drip down to nothing. But my nephew arrived, squalling like a winter wind, and it was right.

Heath's a father now, but to me, he'll always be that overburdened teenager, drowning in slow motion. He stepped up without being asked, skipped meals so I wouldn't have to, blocked my bedroom door with the dining room chair when Dad came home drunk and vicious.

It made Heath serious beyond his years. He doesn't laugh or trust easily, and he's slow to let his own needs show.

He's forty-one now, and although he doesn't look older, he looks harder somehow. His neck, chest, and shoulders are solid, and his face has that weathered look that only men who work on the sea seem to get.

The little boy in front gives us a curious look, and I can feel the man behind me becoming impatient. But Heath doesn't notice. Or care. His eyes soften, filling with tears, and I exhale with relief. He doesn't say a word. Instead, he wraps his arms around me, his left hand cradling the back of my head. This is Heath. An open palm to my father's fist.

He slowly pulls back. Neither of us know what to say. There's a lot of blood under this bridge.

"Got your fishin' license?" he finally asks, smiling.

"I'm not fishin'," I tell him. "I just wanted to see you."

I step forward until my shoe touches his boot. "I might need to stay with you for a bit..."

He nods once, places a hand on my shoulder, guiding me toward our family boat.

He does not ask why I'm back. Of course he doesn't.

We're good at keeping secrets.

I CLIMB ABOARD THE *DEEP SEA*, teeth clenched. Dad's been gone for over twenty years, yet my body still watches for him. Everywhere. Trauma lingers.

This boat, like his fishing knife, wasn't just his possession. It was part of him.

Heath welcomes the tourists aboard. "Ya gonna catch a big one today, mate?" He smiles over his shoulder to the blond kid, who nods eagerly.

How different things are now. Dad tolerated the tourists, though most never booked with us twice. Sometimes they'd pose proudly with their catch, and he'd snatch the fish up, plunge his knife through its belly, and rip the guts out with his bare hands. I'll never forget the horrified looks on their faces. He always did enjoy taking what was rightfully yours.

Other times he'd hang around the railing, telling inappropriate jokes to the pretty women while their uneasy partners looked on, wondering if they should say something.

I stand behind the captain's seat, breathing in all these time-machine scents. Water. Brine. Blood. Every now and then, Heath's anxious gaze falls on me. I give him a tight smile, and I know he understands. The secret language of siblings.

When Dad owned this boat, it was blood-splattered, smeared with fish innards and squid ink. He painted it in rough coats of navy and black until the boat looked like a giant oil stain on the ocean.

But then he shot through, or got himself killed, depending on what you believe, and all we were left with was the mortgage payments and this goddamn boat. I urged Heath to sell it and pay off a good chunk of the mortgage, but he wanted to keep it. He makes his living off the sea, like our father, and his before him. One day, Jonah will usher tourists aboard this boat, hatefully or happily, I'm not sure yet.

"Surprised you're going out tonight," I tell him. "Thought you weren't doing the night charters anymore."

"I'm not," he says softly, nodding at the tourists. "But it's nearing the end of the school holidays and . . ." He hesitates, lowering his voice. "It was hard to say no."

What he means is, the money was hard to turn down. My brother's no fool; if there's money on the table, he's taking a seat.

I hesitate before asking carefully, "How's Jonah? Tara?"

"Good, good." Heath's reply is automatic, his smile tight. "They're up in New South for a bit."

I hesitate again, not sure whether to bring up his longtime girlfriend's frequent absences. Tara was a *Deep Sea* customer, just passing through. Ten years later, I suspect she still wishes she were only passing through. She doesn't like it here, doesn't like the men who move through it like sharks in the shallows. The men own the town in all the ways that matter. You don't get in their way, and if you do, you either leave town quietly or you don't leave at all.

Not for the first time I wonder if, in her mind, Heath belongs among those men. I love my brother, but I know he bends the rules just enough to get what he wants without breaking anything too important. There's a glint in his eye that says, *Don't ask too many questions,* and a smile that makes me say to myself, *You owe him this.*

I know it's wrong, but when it's your brother, sometimes you look the other way. I suspect he does the same thing with me.

I lean back, limbs loosening. I feel my brother here, in the boat. See him in it, too. The hull gleams, the ropes are neatly coiled. I watch him run a hand along the railing with a small nod, inspecting the rigging with a focused eye. For my father, this boat and this business were a chore. For Heath, it's an honor.

He looks over his shoulder directly at me and asks, "Ready, Min?"

I nod and he calls out, "Hold on, everyone! Gets a bit bumpy out there."

With a jolt, we surge forward and the ocean rushes past. It's a good feeling. Like you're flying on your feet. The engine thrums in my fingers, my teeth. It's the first time I've relaxed in days. Weeks, even.

The sun is sinking fast. By the time Heath pulls the throttle back, loosening his grip until we come to a slow stop, it's gone completely, leaving us in sudden darkness.

I watch him as he makes his way to each client, speaking to them in his patient way. He crouches in front of the blond kid, shows him how to thread the silverbait through the hook.

"All right." Heath claps both hands, grinning. "Rods in the water!"

It's funny how quiet it gets when everyone casts over the side of the boat. Their backs are to us, silent and hopeful.

"The boat looks great," I tell him. "You've done a lot to it."

"It's yours, too," he says, stopping to peer at me. "You know that, yeah?"

"No," I say firmly. "It's yours, Heath." Silently, I add, *It's for protecting me when no one else even thought to. Let me give you this. I have nothing else.*

"We'll see about that," he says, before adding softly, "You here by yourself?"

". . . Yeah."

He nods, once. He's never met Oliver, and now he never will. Thank God.

I look out at the water. It's still and silent, hard to see now. I lean back in my seat, open my mouth to say something.

And then, from across the water, a scream rings out.

I freeze. This isn't a shout of joy or even alarm. It's a scream of horror.

Heath whirls around, searching the dark water. It's deathly quiet now, just the soft lapping of the water and the murmur of the little boy from behind me, "Dad . . . what's going on?"

Heath leans across the railing, squinting through the darkness. I see the outline of the pier and, next to it, a boat decorated with a skull and crossbones.

I squint. "That the *Easy*?"

The *Reel Easy* shares a long rivalry with the *Deep Sea*. The two fishing charters used to butt heads back in the days when our dads were running them. But my dad disappeared and Steven Newton, owner and captain of the *Reel Easy*, reluctantly retired, handing the baton to his son, Luke. My brother's former best friend.

Heath marches up to the skipper's seat and reaches for the marine radio. "You there, Luke?"

Nothing.

"Luke?"

Another scream rips through the air. It's coming from the pier. Heath hangs up the radio, and calls out sharply, "Rods up, please."

Silently, they begin reeling in. "What's goin' on?" the kid's dad asks, nodding at the *Easy*. "They in trouble?"

"Not sure." Heath bustles around the boat, tying everything up, pressing the winch to bring the anchor up. When the anchor is aboard, he rushes to the skipper's seat. "We good?"

The tourists nod. The little boy sits on his father's knee, eyes wide and afraid.

"Hold on tight," Heath calls out.

We speed through the water, silent except for the roar of the engine. It's dark now, the sky lit only by a few handfuls of stars. I grip the rail as the spray hits me hard in the side of my face. Icy water splatters my hoodie, my sleeves soaked through. The wind digs in, freezing the spray on my skin. By the time we reach the pier, my teeth are chattering with cold.

The *Reel Easy* rests quietly beside the pier, motionless except for the gentle bob of the tide, the deck empty and still. I scan the pier, but there's nothing there but two seagulls perched on a railing.

When we're parallel to the pier, Heath kills the engine, calling out for Luke, who never responds. For a long moment, we're all silent.

My stomach tightens as I look the *Reel Easy* over, expecting Steven Newton to come stomping up to the bow. He paid no attention to me as a child, but he paid too much attention when I was a teenager. Eyes lingering too long, lips wet and slightly open, *hungry*. A lot of the dads here were like that. Harassing waitresses at the pub, winking at daughters not even grown, telling them filthy jokes that made them blush with shame.

Luke knew what his dad was like but did little to stop it. "Harmless," he said in his lazy way. "He's just havin' a bit of fun, Min."

But it wasn't harmless to me. I never forgave Luke for that. I was around fourteen when I finally told Heath about the harassment, and two things changed. One, I was never cornered by Luke's dad again. Two, Heath and Luke's sinking boat friendship broke down completely. I've always felt guilty about it, but Heath said it wasn't my fault at all. The truth is, their friendship had fallen apart two years earlier.

"Luke?" Heath calls out again. "You there?"

Silence.

Behind me, someone whispers, "What is that?"

The little boy steps silently forward and clasps the rail in his right hand. His father watches him, uneasily. Shivering, I lean over the railing, staring down into the dark water. Something's wrong.

And then out of the darkness, a fin.

"Oh my *God!*" someone cries out.

The father rushes forward to the boy. "Ben! Get away from the rail!"

I fix my eyes on the fin. It's sharp and black and jagged and God, it's fast. The *Deep Sea* explodes with movement and muffled yelling.

"It's a great white!"

I shake with cold and adrenaline, leaning farther forward until the rail digs into my abdomen. My brother yanks me back with one hand and yells out, "Luke! Are you there? Luke!"

There's blood in the water now, gallons of it, a red oil slick. And there's something else . . .

Heath sees it, too. His hand drops, and his body goes still.

"What *is* that?" a tourist calls out. "What the *hell* is that?" yells another.

There's something floating on the water. A bloody mass of flesh, drifting eerily in the current. The man beside me grimaces, presses the flat of his hand to his stomach like he's going to be sick.

"That a seal!?"

A dozen shrieking seagulls appear from nowhere, flying a foot from the surface, flapping their white wings, diving into the black water for scraps of flesh. And then someone screams, "Oh God, it's coming again!"

That black fin breaks the surface and the man beside me screams right in my ear. Heath grabs the back of my hoodie in his fist, yelling something, but it's lost in the noise. God, its *teeth,* so white in the darkness as it snatches at the flesh in a frenzy, ripping, tearing, blood gushing like spilled paint. I'm rocked by the sheer violence of it.

Its tail smashes the surface and then it sinks below. It's so quick, all of it.

Someone screams, "Where is it? Where is it?"

I try to peer over the rail, but Heath pulls me back.

The man behind me is shaking so hard, I can feel the tremors from his chest. "Is it gone?" he asks breathlessly.

We all wait in loaded silence. All I can hear is the sound of my own heart beating, and the seagulls squabbling for bits of leftover flesh.

And then a voice calls out, "Heath!"

Luke Newton is standing on the third rung of the boarding ladder, hooked over the gunwale. He's half bent over, loosely gripping the rail, laughing. "You *see* that shit, bro?"

Heath relaxes his grip on my hoodie, and I peer over, looking down. But the shark is gone.

"Musta been a seventeen-footer!" Luke calls out. "Sure was a big bastard."

I lean on the rail, watching the scraps of flesh float by in the current. Luke stops laughing and peers at me in surprise. "That *you*, Min?"

It's so quiet now that I barely need to raise my voice. "Yeah," I tell him, "it's me."

He breaks out into a smile, nods at the water. "The sharks are happy you're home."

"They don't *look* happy."

"What?" he calls out in mock confusion, spreading his hands out wide. "You didn't enjoy the show?"

He laughs again, and it feels like no time has gone by at all. Luke's laugh is the *holy shit, can you believe it!* type. Everything was a joke to him. Sometimes I think it got on Heath's nerves. Luke's an only child, his parents hands-off and indulgent. He's one of those *dare me* boys. *You dare me to jump off the pier? You dare me to eat this entire onion?*

Luke was restless and easily amused, tagging along everywhere Heath went, even if Heath didn't want him there. Heath was coiled up tight, watchful and clever, with a tendency to overthink. The plan maker. And Luke was always there, charging in behind him like Wolverine.

He'd follow us to our house, playing endless games of Uno, and he'd slip me extra draw 4s when Heath wasn't looking. Then Dad was home, steely and silent. Heath and I braced ourselves, quietly packing up our game, swimming upstream and away from his murderous current. But Luke . . . Luke would call out, "Hey, Mr. Greenwood!" and to our horror, he'd plunk himself beside Dad at the dining table, oblivious and chatting so cheerfully that Heath and I would flinch.

In the past few years, Heath's barely said a word about Luke. Now he won't even look at him. He just stares off, jaw tight, when Luke calls out, "He's gone. You scared him off, bro!"

Heath ignores him and turns instead to the little boy with pained eyes.

"It was a seal, yeah?" the kid's dad calls out to Luke, looking to Heath for confirmation.

"Uh . . ." Luke hesitates, eyes fixed on Heath. "Not sure, mate. Couldn't see much to be honest."

"No," Heath says quietly. "It wasn't a seal."

The father's face drains of color. He pulls his son into his arms as something slick and bloated drifts by in the dark current, turning slowly as the water pulls it along. He presses a soft palm over his son's eyes because the shapeless mass in the water wasn't an animal at all.

It was a woman.

CHAPTER 5

The steak is cherry red, dripping blood. The waiter sets it down on the pub table, wordlessly slides it my way. His hands are buried in tattoos, and there's a thin strip of dried blood on the back of his left knuckle.

It's 10 p.m. at the Roo Bay pub. A handful of locals are embraced in its dark warmth, dirty hands clutching their beers like they're worried someone's going to steal them. I recognize them from childhood, sharkish old men, like predators at rest. One of them is Steven Newton. Luke's dad. I freeze and something twists in my gut. He smiles at me, but it isn't warm; it's sharp, eager. Heath whirls around, alert, but the older man stumbles out the pub doors, grinning. Outside, he joins two fishermen who are smoking aggressively, spitting loudly on the sidewalk.

Heath doesn't touch his chicken parma and fries. I steal a chip from his plate and stuff it in my mouth, waiting for a reaction. He smiles weakly, pushes his plate to me.

"You can have mine," he says. "I'm not that hungry."

I'm transported back in time to our dinner table, shoveling kangaroo into my mouth so fast I'm choking on it.

"Slow down, Min," Heath cautions from across the table. "You'll make yourself sick."

But I couldn't slow down. Hungry. God, I was always *so hungry*. We lived outdoors, the beach, the woods. Anywhere but home, where Dad was lurking. Hunger. It was always there like a toothache.

I'd scraped my plate and asked, "Can I have some more?"

He'd pushed his plate my way and said, far too casually, "You can have mine, Min. I'm not hungry."

I've never been able to get that image out of my head. God, how much that must have hurt him. Trying to provide and failing. I was absolutely ashamed of myself for asking for more to eat. Disgusted. It started off a complex relationship with food that's worsened through the years. I only eat when I'm starving.

You're punishing yourself, a counselor told me.

For what?

Asking for what you need.

The pub doors swing tentatively open, and a man, my age, ushers an annoyed woman inside. She looks around doubtfully, a toddler clutched to her chest. Tourist.

The waiter calls out, "After a table, mate?"

The woman's eyes are locked on the fading photos on the walls. Dozens of dead fish, bleeding heavily from their mouths, held up by delighted fishermen. The woman winces, holds her baby closer. "No," she says quite firmly. "We're good."

The man stuffs his hands into his pockets and gives an embarrassed nod before turning quickly to the door. Behind me, someone snorts.

The waiter gives them a tight-lipped smile. When the family are barely out of earshot, he mutters loudly, "Farken tourists. Wastin' my farken time."

Us. Them.

If there's one thing that unites a fishing town, it's burning hatred for the tourists. *There used to be more fish in the good ol' days, but then the farken tourists came and wiped out the population.*

Of course, in the same breath, our dads will brag that they used to catch hundreds back in the day. But they're not to blame, you see? It's the tourists. The tourists with their broken rods and dead worms for bait, it's all their fault. *Let the fuckers drown.*

We know they're full of shit. But our dads have dominion, and this town, these waters, are their bloody playground. We are the mums and daughters. We are scared and silent, and so very agreeable.

We have to be.

Some of us hate ourselves for it. Some of us scream in silence because no one will listen until we shatter. Others, like my mother, run on empty to keep everyone else full. When that doesn't work, they just run.

I used to blame the women in this town for looking the other way, for looking down. I don't anymore. Thanks to my father and Oliver, I know now why they had to run. Because if you don't, you're emptied, bit by bit. Voice first. Then your presence, the weight of you. You're still here, still breathing, but you'll feel it: the fading.

Ghosts.

I chew the steak slowly, blood coating my mouth. Heath is hunched over the table, scanning the pub while his food goes cold.

I stop chewing. "You right?"

He nods automatically, forces a smile. "Yeah . . . hell of a night."

"I've never seen one so close," I say, thinking of the shark's unblinking eyes, its pale underbelly, jaw jutting forward. ". . . Have you?"

He pauses. "Yeah, a few times. Comes with the territory."

"Do you ever get scared to go out on the boat at night? Knowing they're out there?"

"Not at all," he says, surprised. "Most of the time, I feel safer at sea than on land." He gives me a sidelong look. "It's the people you gotta watch, Min. You should know that."

He straightens up, slow and deliberate, spine locking into place. He eyes me, sharp and still, assessing. Not angry, exactly, just uneasy. "You attacked someone live on air?"

Shit.

"No, I didn't. And anyway, they cut to a commercial before that," I say, eyes downcast. "They didn't get it on camera." My once-a-month lunch friends texted me that. *There's a rumor you threw something at Joy Marriot? Good for you! She's a nasty piece.*

Mel, if the studio tries to fire you, just remind them of her charity fraud.

haha, yep, I'm sure they'll change their minds pretty quick!

"It's fine," I insist.

"It's not."

I straighten up, too. "We've done worse in this family."

"Yes, we have."

I'm sure he's talking about our father. But why does it feel like he's aiming that at me? And why does it feel like he's not talking about what I did to Joy? Wounded, I meet his eyes and let the silence stretch. I wait for him to bring up Amy Anderson.

Thankfully, he doesn't.

I reach for my Coke, take a small sip. "Is Tara coming back? Or has she . . ."

Left for good.

"Of course she's coming back," he says, frowning. "Why wouldn't she?"

I give him a pointed look. "You tell me."

My brother is the best person I know, but sometimes you have to squint to see that. He has some questionable connections and can talk his way out of anything. I've seen him bluff through situations he had no business surviving, and I'd bet he's got some stories he would never tell me. Strategic, I'd call him. But others might say he's "a bit of a wheeler-dealer."

"They'll be back after the school holidays," Heath says simply. "Don't you worry about that, Min."

I get the message: *Don't ask too many questions.*

I don't. If he's into something, or up to something, it doesn't matter. Not to me. I'll stand beside him, quietly, a silent endorsement. Not because I believe in whatever he's up to, but because I believe in him.

I'm sipping my drink when a man enters the pub. He scans the room, and when he sees me, he does a double take. His face tightens, the corners of his mouth pulling down as our eyes lock. I wonder if he's seeing my dad. I know I look like him. We have the same brown eyes, hooded and suspicious. Even when I force a smile in photographs, my eyes flatten into dark pebbles. *You look so angry in pictures,* Oliver used to snap, peering down at the selfies he so loved taking. *Let's do it again,* he'd sigh. *And try not to look like you hate the whole world, please.*

Terry Hargrave is the owner of the Roo Bay pub. He owns the

Titan, a forty-foot snapper charter he operated for thirty years. He has no kids and never married, and he'll tell you it's because he never found the right woman.

But I think he did. And I think it was my mother.

He's older now, his face deeply lined, with eyes that look like they've seen it all. He's a no-nonsense type of man, but he lacks the cruelty of the townsmen. I saw the way he was with my mum, how he softened around her. I used to wonder what our lives would've looked like had Mum chosen him, not our father.

A moment later, he's hovering above me, peering down.

"Hey, Minnie."

God, I hate that nickname. Minnie. Minnow. All my life people have been trying to make me smaller.

And . . . I realize now, I have *let them*.

The last time Terry came around to our house was the week before Dad disappeared. I think of the newspaper clipping in my bedside drawer.

A man acquainted with Peter Greenwood allegedly attacked him at his Kangaroo Bay home. The man is considered a suspect in his disappearance.

The man was Terry Hargrave.

Terry places a paternal hand out, resting it gently on Heath's shoulder, and I'm surprised when Heath sits up a little straighter as if the older man's hand has anchored him, steadied him.

It's no secret that the whole town thinks Terry killed my father. Including Heath. Maybe he thinks Terry did us all a favor. My dad was not a popular man. Territory is everything in fishing towns, and my father had a habit of overstepping. Skippers have *their fishing spot* passed down through the generations, and they'll defend it with their lives. On the land, they're nobodies. But on their boat, they are skipper, boss, and God.

Dad didn't give a shit about boundaries. He'd fish the best spots, even if they were yours. *Especially* if they were yours. Not to mention the lies he'd tell. I've been on the *Deep Sea* with Dad when we caught absolutely nothing, and he'd pull into the general store, windburned and snarling. But the moment he stepped inside, he was slapping backs, bragging *loudly* about all the fish he'd caught. He started poaching fishing customers, even Terry's, moored the *Deep Sea* wherever he wanted.

But it was the way he treated my mum that caused the damage between Terry and my dad. To my father, Mum was his to be emptied, drained. Same with us. Who was going to stop him? Terry, by all accounts. But in my opinion, it was too late. I'll always harbor a grudge against Terry for not stepping in sooner. He was the adult; Heath and I were the kids. We shouldn't have had to shoulder what we did alone.

"Heard you been up in the big city," Terry says with a trace of disapproval.

I nod, wondering if he knows about the attack tonight, but Heath hasn't said a word.

"You hear about that farken journo?" Terry asks Heath, eyes full to the brim with anger. "He rocked up here the other day, askin' questions."

Before Heath can answer, I lift my head. "Who?"

"Chris somethin'." He frowns. "Cooper. Works for the *Daily*."

I stare hard at the sweating Coke, tightening my grip on my fork at the mention of his name. *Chris bloody Cooper.* Of course he's already here, poking his pale fingers around my hometown.

"You know him, Min?"

"No. The *Daily*'s based out of Sydney. And anyway"—I brush my sweating glass with a thumb—"I doubt I'll be rubbing shoulders with anyone in that industry again."

"Good," Terry says. "And trust me, he won't be 'round here again, anyway."

Heath raises an eyebrow. "Whadya do to him?"

"To *him*?" He grins. "Nothin'." He licks his bottom lip, excited to deliver the dirty punch line. "'Fraid his car won't be the same, though."

Heath smiles, raising his beer in a mock toast. Egged on, Terry continues, "And in unrelated news—if anyone's needin' four new hubcaps, just sing out."

Muffled laughter fills the room, and I'm not surprised. When it comes to hard questions, the town has a way of clamming up. Or retaliating by defacing cars.

And worse.

I grip my fork tighter, remembering.

Two locals in the corner shuffle over, beers clutched tight in their hands. The second man is considerably drunker, stumbling into a corner table, swearing as his beer sloshes on the carpet.

"Didn't catch any fish today," the first man says darkly. I look up and he explains, "The bloody great whites. They're scarin' the fish off."

"Or eating 'em all up," the drunk man half yells. "The school sharks, all the baitfish, even." He frowns into his beer before looking up. "You catch much on the *Deep Sea* today, mate?"

"Didn't really get a chance to be honest," Heath admits, poking at the chicken parma with his fork. He still hasn't touched his food.

"What 'bout Luke?"

"Not sure . . . There was—" Heath breaks off, shifts in his seat. "There was an attack tonight."

I flinch when the drunk man slams a palm on the table. "What?"

"Yeah, I heard," Terry mutters. "Near the beach-three pier?"

The drunk man lurches forward, eyes glazed and feverish. "Great white?"

"That's what I heard," Terry answers for us, and I'm grateful he's stepped in. "Big one, too."

"How much do ya reckon you'd get for a great white?"

"Absolutely nothing, since you can't eat them," Heath tells the drunk man. "They're full of mercury."

"Plus they're protected," Terry adds. "The money's in the mako sharks, boys."

"Yellowfin's sellin' for sixty dollars a kilo at the mo," Heath says. "Highest it's been in a decade."

The drunk man drops his head, contemplates his beer. "Hope the big bastards haven't eaten 'em all."

"It's spawning season," Heath explains. "The great whites won't stay around forever. Give it a few months and they'll move on. They always do."

"I hate those bastards," the drunk slurs, nearly toppling over.

Heath stands up, grasps his elbow to steady him. "Might be time to lay off the drink, mate."

The drunk man pulls away roughly, beer spilling everywhere.

"Easy now!" Terry cautions.

I stand up, anxious. I can't be around men like these; my throat's too tight, my skin itches. My dad feels too close, and I need to leave. Heath follows me to the bar, a steadying palm on my shoulder. I reach for my pocket to pay, but he says lightly, "I got this."

I feel guilty as hell as Heath hands the cash over. Money. Shit. What am I going to do for money now? I'm a journalist but it's useless in a town like this. Worse than useless. It's a *problem*.

A hazard, even.

This town only respects men who are bloody and silent. I respect anyone who ignores the anxious voice that warns: *He won't like it if I speak up. I can't do this!* and listens instead to the smaller, steady voice that whispers, *Yes, you can. Because you must.*

Journalism: What better way to piss off my father and honor my mother?

But after ten years in the industry, all I've done is write thousand-word blog posts about feuding celebrities or the miracle of rose hip oil, and cast my eyes down when Joy belittled me.

Surely my degree is still worth something, even after I threw that mic pack at her head.

Chris... Cooper. Works for the Daily.

You know him, Min?

Of course I know that bastard. There are only two national newspapers in Australia. An industry so small it's incestuous. Plus, before he got the big job at the *Daily,* he was the assistant news editor for the *Mill,* a tabloid paper in Melbourne. The same one I interned at. I spent four months smashing out non-stories about D-list celebs while Chris smoked cigarettes with the editor in chief and smugly pointed out a rare spelling mistake.

It's 'accidentally', Melanie. Not 'accidently'. Make sure to use a spellchecker next time.

After that, I proofread my articles until my eyes burned. By the second month, he had nothing to criticize me for, and he'd sign off my work with a laconic, *Good to go.*

It was no secret he was gunning for a role at the *Daily.* I still remember his goodbye email:

All the best, Melanie.

Accidently yours,

Chris.

Dickhead, I thought, deleting his email. I've barely spoken to him since, preferring to avoid him at industry gatherings. He always seeks me out, though. Marches up, smooth and confident, shaking hands a bit too aggressively with Oliver.

He rocked up here the other day, askin' questions.

He has questions. And I have answers . . .

I'm full to the brim with secrets about this town, which makes me just as complicit as anyone here. Just as dirty.

I did what I had to do to survive this place, I tell myself, hoping it will drown the other word that always follows.

Coward.

Terry chats with Heath and the bartender in their shared language, while I think about meeting up with Chris Cooper. I feel like I'm betraying him. The town. Maybe even me.

Because I have secrets I need to keep, too.

What if I share a secret with Chris? Let him uncover one dark truth about this town? I'll use his connections to find a job . . . Heath and the town don't have to know.

Uneasy, I glance around the pub at these dirty men and their dirtier deeds. I've seen what they do to rule breakers. Outsiders have no idea, but I do.

My dad used to say, *You're either the shark or the food.*

I stare up at the sharks covering the walls, a fluttery feeling in my stomach.

God, I think, *they're everywhere.*

Horror as woman is decapitated in great white shark attack

The Daily
January 17, 2024
by Chris Cooper

Human remains have been found at a Kangaroo Bay beach on the East Coast of Victoria. The horrifying attack occurred at about 9 P.M. (AEST) on Monday around 400 meters from shore. The attack was witnessed by two local fishing charters and a handful of tourists.

Tourist Alan Wright said, "I saw a massive great white just chomping on this woman's body. A moment later, the body was in half."

Human body parts were left floating in the water. The remains have not been formally identified, but police have taken them to the Victorian morgue for forensic examination.

It is the second fatal attack in Kangaroo Bay in twenty-five years. In 1998, Bendigo resident Hannah Striker's car was found abandoned at beach number 4. It's believed the twenty-four-year-old was taken by a great white shark while swimming. Parts of her wet suit were recovered.

There have been an increasing number of shark sightings in Kangaroo Bay in the last three years. Police are telling people to exercise caution when swimming.

Kangaroo Bay locals have declined to comment.

CHAPTER 6

We hate the tourists. We hate everything that isn't us. We protect our own, until we don't.

But when that sun descends, the town is ours again. I watch sunburned parents shaking out towels, lugging a cooler with one hand, an exhausted toddler with the other. They leave empty bottles of soft drink and brightly colored buckets discarded in the sand. It's like they think the day is over. Truth is, it's only just begun.

They might own the day, but we own the night.

Colleen Holloway, a long-term resident with wiry hair tied in a severe ponytail, marches up and down beach 2, pointedly picking up rubbish as the tourists step around her, avoiding her eyes. She's a short woman, five feet at most, but there's a toughness about her, and she's built like a firecracker, compact and coiled. She had a soft spot for the women in this town, especially my mum. Colleen's son, Travis, was my childhood best friend. After school, Mum and I would sometimes walk to Colleen's. Trav and I chased grasshoppers in the backyard while Mum sat at the kitchen table, crying.

I remember Colleen's arm slung around Mum's shoulders, not gently, but tight. A grip that said, *It's okay, I won't let go.* But what I remember most is that they barely spoke at all. Now I know why. Sometimes there's nothing women can say to each other except, "Leave him before he kills you."

And leave him, Mum finally did. I just wish she'd taken us with her.

But Colleen stayed to fight it out. Growing up, I felt the steadiness of her presence in the background. Like a hand just barely touching my back, making sure I didn't fall.

I sit on the sand, my knees up to my chest, cap pulled low over my head. Jessie is beside me, happily watching all the comings and goings, coat warm from the sun. She can't stop wagging her tail at the seagulls. She's not quite sure what to do with all this blessed freedom. Me either, I suppose.

"This yours?" Colleen spits out, thrusting a beer can at a teenage tourist reeking of cigarettes.

He ignores her, stomps off, towel slung over his shoulder. She glares at him like she wishes she could throw the can at his head. I smile into my knee, remembering Joy and my thrilling outburst.

Colleen charges over to me, dragging her bin bag as the sun drops fast behind her. I get to my feet, looking over my shoulder to the sand dunes, scanning them for any sign of my brother. She squints at me and the realization hits. Her features soften, and her grip on the garbage bag loosens. "Minnow."

I smile. "Hey."

I stuff my hands into my pockets as Heath strides down the sand dunes, a white fishing bucket hanging loose from his fingers.

"Good to have you back, Min," Colleen says simply. But I swear her eyes moisten. She quickly turns her face away as if she's glancing over her shoulder, but I notice how she bends her face into it. I've always felt that Colleen wished she could have done more for Heath and me. That she carries some guilt about the mess of the past. But I don't feel that way. Her background presence was comforting enough, and I knew I could walk to her house and watch cartoons with Trav whenever I wanted. I was always welcome there. That was enough.

But after the incident with Trav . . . after he was sent away, I stopped going around to her place. Truth is, I felt guilty about what happened with her son. Responsible for it.

We say nothing, and the silence swallows us up. It's my brother who breaks it, arriving at my side, shoulders stiff, as if he can feel the tension.

"Hey!" someone yells out. Luke waves at us from a yellow-and-white-striped beach towel. A toddler sits opposite him wearing only a nappy, clutching fistfuls of sand, her eyes narrowed in concentration. Luke lumbers over, leaving the child by herself on the towel. He stands in front of me, lips twitching, hands on his skinny hips. Colleen eyes him warily.

I nod at the kid. "She yours?"

"Fuck no, thank God," Luke snorts. "My girlfriend's. She's got a bun in the oven, though. That one's mine." He pauses before adding, "I think."

Heath frowns, stepping back, looking like he'd rather be anywhere but talking to his former friend.

Luke doesn't seem to notice. "Those bloody sharks," he says nodding at the water. "I'm scared to swim these days."

"Not even a shark would take *you* on, Luke." Colleen smiles, but it doesn't quite reach her eyes. She only tolerates him, I realize.

"Damn right about that." He smiles proudly.

"Was it a tourist, you reckon?" she says, frowning. "I bloody hope it was."

"Not sure," Heath says. "There wasn't much left to identify."

I look down at the sand, remembering the small chunks of meat on the dark surface.

Colleen chews her bottom lip. "You been checkin' the nets?"

I raise my head. "The nets?"

"The curtains of death!" Luke announces dramatically. "Shark nets."

"The VFA put 'em up last month," Heath softly explains, pointing far out to the ocean. "Two meters under the surface, a hundred meters long. S'posed to reduce the chance of an attack."

"Well," I say, "they sure as hell aren't working."

"You can't prevent shark attacks," Heath says. "Not really. The nets can only do so much." He must notice Colleen's face, because he adds, "We check for holes every afternoon. And every second night we make sure nothin's stuck in the bloody thing."

She asks, "Is there, usually?"

"Yeah, stingrays, turtles, it's a bit sad really," he admits. "Not the big boys, though, not yet." He hesitates before adding, "But I'd stay outta the water, yeah? For now, anyway."

"Surprised they didn't close this beach today."

Heath shakes his head. "The attack happened near the pier in beach three. It's closed until tomorrow. And even if they *did* close it," he continues gruffly, "they'd still bloody swim in it."

"Think they know better than everyone," Colleen says, annoyed. "Bloody tourists."

"Not just them," Luke sniffs. "We're not gonna stop fishin'. And Lord knows nothin' will keep the boys from surfin'. Look." He nods up at the parking lot. Five men in black wet suits survey the surf, boards gripped eagerly in their hands. Heath stares at the man in the middle, the one with the buzz cut. I freeze, heart thudding.

Colleen squints up at her son, swearing under her breath. "Trav."

My brother doesn't say a word, not yet, but I can feel it, the disapproval. The shift in his stance, the way his mouth tightens as he looks from me to Trav. Trav to me. Does he disapprove of Trav only? Or both of us? The shape we took on when we were together? The darkness we brought out of each other?

Trav shields his eyes from the sun, looks down at his mother. Then me.

Colleen calls him again; I can't hear what she's saying. Can't hear anything but the blood rushing in my ears.

One of the last times I saw Trav, he was slouched beside me in class, chin tucked into his palm, when the cop came for him. Our fifth-grade teacher paused at the blackboard, open-mouthed, chalk dangling from her fingertips. My classmates and I watched with interest as the cop marched up to her, terse and vaguely apologetic. They had a hushed discussion that left our teacher solemn and staggering to her chair, palm pressed into her abdomen.

The cop hauled Trav out of class. He was sent to a juvenile facility for violent kids, and I'd long left town before he returned.

Travis Holloway.

The girl he nearly stabbed to death was our classmate Amy Anderson.

Out of the corner of my eye, I can feel Heath's and Colleen's searching gazes. But my attention is locked on Trav. In my mind, we're kids again. Nine or ten years old. He's kneeling in the water, mud sticking to his thighs. I'm standing over him, waiting. He reaches up, offers me something. Greedily, I take it.

I shake my head, snap out of it. Trav throws his board back into the van, leans against it.

Waits.

Silence.

Heath gives me a sidelong look, and I keep my eyes on the sand until Colleen snorts, "There was a fatal attack yesterday and he still wants to surf. God, he's crazy."

"Sharks witnessed the rise and fall of the dinosaurs. Did you know that?" Luke asks. "You gotta wonder how they survived all this time."

"You're either the shark or the food," I recite.

Heath flinches. I'm quoting my father and he knows it. How many times did he repeat that? Stomping around the house or reeling in an undersized snapper that he'd use for bait. *You're either the shark or the food.*

Luke steps forward, annoyed that the attention has shifted from him. I glance behind him to where the baby sits on the towel, looking up at the sky.

Colleen shields her eyes from the falling sun as if she's scanning the water for sharks. "It's spawning season, isn't it?"

"Yeah," Heath says. "Lots of sharks around is a sign that the ocean's healthy. That's good news, at least."

"Not good news for those poor bastards who keep getting eaten, though," I mutter.

Luke snorts. "Least it's not *us*."

Us. Them.

I turn to him. "You sure it's not? Any of the locals missin' lately?" I'm aiming for a joke, but he doesn't smile.

"Like your dad?" he asks darkly before adding, "Or maybe it's old mate Terry you should be asking about that . . ."

Heath stares levelly at Luke, who raises a lazy palm in a defensive *I'm just sayin'* gesture. "He did youse a favor," he says flatly. "Did us *all* a favor. He always was a bastard, your dad."

I can feel it even before I look up. The heat of Trav's gaze on me, a stare that lingers. Even without meeting his eyes, I know. The back of my neck prickles, and there's a jittery energy in my limbs. I can't decide whether to run toward him or away. My heartbeat is too fast, too loud in my ears. But there's a strange hope buzzing under my skin, excitement laced with dread.

"Be back in a minute," I finally mutter, slinking away. I say it so fast it comes out in one word, *bebackinaminute.*

The dune rises, steep and soft, the sand shifting beneath my feet as I climb the golden wall. I feel Heath's disapproving eyes on my back, but he doesn't follow.

My breath is uneven by the time I reach the parking lot at the top of the dune. I pause there, wind tugging at my clothes, heart tapping my ribs.

Trav is turned slightly away from me. He stands there alone, still and quiet, his full-length black wet suit clinging to him like a second skin. It covers him collarbone-to-ankle, highlighting the curve of muscle and the sharp lines of bone beneath. Not a boy anymore, a man now.

There's a quiet tension in the way he stands, alert, contained.

I step closer, thinking about Amy. She played dead after Trav poked holes in her abdomen. Staggered home, white-lipped, bleeding hard from her belly. Like Trav, she never returned to school. Her family moved away and nobody spoke of her, after. We don't speak of those who leave. Maybe we should.

He finally turns when I approach. Slowly. The sun catching the side of his face, grazing his cheekbone, gold and warm. Buzz cut, hard eyes. Trav.

I'm just feet away from him, close enough to speak. Close enough to be heard. But I don't know what to say. Not yet. I can't stop staring at the fist-sized tattoo on his throat: a shield nestled between an emu and a red kangaroo, Australia's coat of arms. Interesting choice. The kids in town were raised on kangaroo. *Free meat,* our dads called it. They'd slaughter them in our corrugated iron sheds, serve them up on paper plates, all lean and bloody. Tasted good to be honest.

We eat our own.

His expression is calm, but his eyes give it away. Focused. Too focused. Like he hasn't been waiting minutes for me to climb this sand dune. It's like he's been waiting a lifetime.

I wait for him to speak. He looks like he wants to.

I want to ask:

How are you?

You married? Kids?

Why'd you stab Amy?

Why'd you leave her to bleed out in the woods?

But I know why he did it. I just want to hear him say it.

His eyes flick to the back of my right hand. When he sees the tattoo there, he pauses, curious. It's a tiny anglerfish, jaws open, its fins like torn sails.

Trav looks away, hiding a smile. "Nice tat."

I stare down at his hands. Every knuckle, every finger, even the spaces between his thumb and wrist are buried in tattoos. Painful looking, lived-in. A compass spans the back of his right hand, its points clean and sharp. On his left, a Bell Miner bird, tail vanishing up his forearm. Compared with his tattoos, my anglerfish looks puny, juvenile. But he seems to like it.

He leans against the van, half smile still on his lips. I nod at the logo and phone numbers stretching across the sliding door, stenciled in faded navy: TITAN FISHING CHARTERS. CALL TERRY OR TRAVIS. "You work for Terry now?"

"Yeah," he says with a hint of pride, "I've been skipperin' the *Titan* for a few years now. Terry wants to focus more on the pub. Can't blame 'im," he adds, nodding at the sea. "Gets rough out there."

His voice is deeper now, fuller. Trav never talked much, not because he didn't have anything to say but because he measured every word like they all mattered. He was always watching, listening, letting others fill the air while he sat back, collecting details. I liked that. Still do. His steadiness, purpose. It reminded me of my brother.

"I don't need to ask what you've been up to. I heard," he says, shielding the last of the sun from his face to study me again. "Showed your true colors in the end, didn't ya?"

"We always do."

We pass a glance like a whisper, and I know we're both thinking about Amy.

Why'd you stab Amy?

Why'd you leave her to bleed out in the woods?

Just say it, Trav.

"Minnow!" My name comes drifting through the air. I pause, turning my head toward the sound. It's coming from the beach. "Min!"

Heath. It doesn't sound urgent, but it pulls at me all the same.

I say goodbye to Trav, and just as I turn to leave, he reaches out and gently touches my elbow. It's nothing really, just a touch. But my whole body notices. My breath catches, my skin starts buzzing. I don't want him to let go, but he does. Dropping his hand, like he's not sure if he's allowed to touch me. The silence after is thick, loaded. I don't pull away, but he doesn't push further.

The warmth of his breath grazes the back of my neck when he asks, "Did you see the attack, Min?"

"Yeah," I whisper, "I saw it."

He pauses. "Musta been awful."

I fix my eyes on the ocean, but all I see are blackbirds clambering up and down the sweaty branches of a ghost gum. All I hear is something unholy shrieking through the woods as I shiver under the tree's shadow. I'm hiding, mouthing a frantic prayer: *Don't let Dad see me. Please. He'll kill me, too.*

Quietly, I say, "I've seen worse."

CHAPTER 7

Found you, ya bastard.

Audi. White. Missing four hubcaps. I squint in the sun, peering at the motel car park.

Pine Bay Motel. Fifteen minutes from Kangaroo Bay. It's 2 P.M., Heath's on sentry duty at the beach. Jessie is lying on our cracked porch in the full sun.

It's fine. It's all fine.

Except I can't breathe. I rub my chest in soft circles. I'm not doing anything wrong, I tell myself. Chris wants a story, and I want a job.

I keep my head down as I creep across the lot, hands shoved in my pockets, shoulders forward, eyes down. Other than me, there's only one woman in the lot, sitting at the circular table outside her door, smoking a cigarette and staring intently at her phone.

I walk past his Audi and pause. There's something tucked under a windshield wiper. I glance over my shoulder and pluck it out. I hold it between my thumb and forefinger, blinking when I realize what it is.

A shark tooth.

I stare at it, rubbing my thumb over its serrated edges. I tuck it back under, snap a photo, and force myself to keep walking. Go, go, go, right to his door. It's fine. It's fine. I knock twice, then step back, darting a look at the woman with the cigarette who ignores me.

From behind the door, a muffled voice: "Who is it?"

I can feel him watching me through the peephole. Before I answer, he unlocks the door, and it swings open.

Chris Cooper. The cleanest man I've ever known. He's stiff-backed and solemn with reddish-brown hair. Light blue plaid shirt, rolled up to the elbows. White lace-up shoes, clay-colored chinos. Black watch with a gold face that says MASERATI.

I shake my head. In my town, everyone wears the same unspoken uniform—grimy hoodies with stained sleeves. Ten-year-old T-shirts in black, gray, or dark navy. Cargo shorts or torn jeans.

Nothing like this man and his casual opulence.

I look down at my own clothes. Jeans, tomato sauce stain on the left knee that never quite came out. Black hoodie.

"Melanie?" he asks, uncertain for once. "That you?"

"Was."

He stares hard at the tomato sauce mark like he's never seen a stain before, then raises his eyebrow when he notices the anglerfish tattoo on my right hand. "That new?"

"No."

"Well, well." He smiles. "What else have you been hiding?"

"Let me in, Chris."

He opens the door a fraction wider, hovering in the doorway, staring at me with a faint trace of amusement.

I step inside, my left shoulder brushing his. He smells like soap and not the masculine ones Oliver marinated in, bourbon and leather and sandalwood. Chris smells faintly feminine, pears and peaches. He always looks freshly showered, well groomed, as barefaced as an infant.

He looks harmless, but he's not. Journalists never are. They don't look *at* you. They look *inside* you. You're not human to them. You're a sack of secrets in meat.

Chris shuts the door with a loud bang that makes me want to hit him. I don't like loud noises. I imagine others raised in violence feel it, too—the way our nervous systems flinch, riddled with bullet holes no one can see.

We close doors silently, keep our voices low, hold our drinks tight enough to crack the fucking glass. But people like Chris, they get to slam doors with no fear of retaliation. They get to live while the rest of us survive. Except now . . . I think of the tooth tucked under his windshield wiper.

Us. Them.

"Forgive me for asking..." he says, "but what on earth are you doing here?"

"I grew up in Kangaroo Bay. What are *you* doing here?"

His upper lip curls. "That place?" He really means, *That shithole?* But Chris Cooper doesn't swear.

"How's your story going?"

"What story?"

"Oh, we're going to do this, are we? Bloody hell," I say impatiently. "Your shark story. Bit light on the details, though..."

He frowns.

"Lemme guess," I say. "The locals aren't talking."

He snorts. "You don't know the half of it."

"You don't, either," I say bluntly.

God, it's quiet. The TV is off, the blinds drawn; there's no electrical hum. Nothing to shield us from the strangeness of this meeting. He points to the table pressed against the back wall, and we sit down in silence. He crosses his ankles, leans back, and I wipe filmy sweat from my palm onto my thigh.

He stares at my empty ring finger, pauses. "How's Oliver?"

I tossed my engagement ring into the same drawer that holds my father's newspaper articles. The drawer feels like a grave now. Sometimes I find myself rubbing my ring finger with my thumb, delighting at its emptiness.

"Great."

His eyes travel pointedly to my ringless finger. "Let me guess," he says, clicking his tongue, amused. "He dumped you after your on-air freak-out?"

"No, I left him before that. But that's not why I'm here."

"What made you do it?"

"Do what?"

He folds his arms across his chest. "Throw something at Joy Marriot. Allegedly."

"I take a lot, Chris," I tell him truthfully. "I take a lot until I can't take any more."

"Fair enough," he says, and for the first time since I stepped inside, he looks at me with real interest. "Why her, though?"

"She's ripping off her cancer charity. I can prove it."

His face goes still, expression frozen between confusion and disbelief. Then his eyes widen and a lip curls back like a shark on the hunt. "So that's why the studio's keeping it quiet. Lucky for you."

"And you," I tell him. "Because you're going to break the news."

The studio called this morning. We've agreed to part ways, quietly. No termination, no lawsuit. Just a clean break. I won't expose Joy, and they'll make a brief LinkedIn announcement, wishing me well as I "pursue new opportunities."

I agreed.

I won't expose Joy.

Chris will.

There's a small, almost invisible tension in his jaw, a flicker of anticipation in the way he leans forward. His voice is careful. Measured. Like he's not desperate to know, like he hasn't smelled the blood in the air. "Melanie, dear, would you like to tell me a bit more about that?"

"Not yet." I pause. "And my real name is Minnow, by the way. Greenwood."

His eyebrows lift instinctively, like he's not sure if I'm joking. When he realizes I'm not, he laughs, but it's hollow, reflexive. A laugh that says, *Give me a second, I wasn't ready for that.*

"I reached out to a Greenwood about the attack," he says thoughtfully. "The charter captain?"

"Heath," I say unwillingly. "My brother."

"He wasn't very helpful."

"Why should he be?"

"The other captain was. Talked my ear off, but wouldn't let me quote him directly. Chatty fella, Luke Newton."

"Luke's a bit different from the rest of us."

I don't tell Chris I was there that night. I don't want him sidetracked. I need him to follow my lead, not his.

He runs a hand through his brick hair, his silence thick and disapproving. "Okay . . . well, do you have any other massive surprises you feel like dropping while you're at it?" He tilts his head, subtly, staring at my tattoo, like he's reevaluating me, reevaluating everything. "Why the name change?"

"It's not illegal to change your name."

"No," he agrees, eyes flicking up to mine. "But it's curious."

I gesture to his car, changing the subject. "What happened to your hubcaps?"

"I'll find them."

"They lost?"

"Like I said," he says sternly, "I'll find them."

"These people . . . You don't know what they're like."

"Then tell me."

"Checked your car lately?"

"I don't give a shit about the hubcaps," he says tightly.

"I meant the tooth."

"The what?"

I freeze. "You didn't see the shark tooth under your windshield wiper?"

His mouth parts slightly, and there's a pause where his brain is clearly replaying what I said. "Excuse me?"

"Go see."

He gets to his feet and heads outside. Through a gap in the blinds, I catch a glimpse of him standing over his car windshield. A moment later, he's back, agitated. Before he shuts the door, he peers outside, scanning the car park. "That wasn't there this morning."

"They don't like people asking questions in Kangaroo Bay."

"Why not?"

Because we have so damn much to hide.

"If you're going to stay here," I tell him, "you need to find somewhere else to rent, quick smart."

He looks at the navy carpet, frowns. "Yeah," he says, "all right."

"Listen," I say, leaning forward, "I'm a local, and I can tell you why there's so many sharks around the bay. There are higher rates of shark sightings and attacks in fishing towns. Same with Sorrento, Angelsea, Coogee Beach." I list them off. "Coogee had two attacks in the last seven years. Why? 'Cause it's a snapper town and the vibrations on the lines bring them in. The tourists still come down, and some of them are so stupid they jump in the water, thinking it won't be them. Then it is."

Silence.

"That's your shark story," I continue. "But I've got a better one. Two, actually."

He pauses, reluctant to let it go, but I'm telling him the truth. He can continue being stonewalled and threatened by the Kangaroo Bay locals, or he can pivot and take down Joy Marriot . . . and uncover an almost-thirty-year secret that will make national news.

"I can help you. But first—" I hesitate. "—you need to do something for me."

"Such as?"

"I need an income. Writing blogs, copyediting, whatever."

He leans against the wall, considers. "That depends."

My blood pumps so hard, I hear it throbbing in my ears. "On?"

"Have you figured out how to spell *accidentally* yet?"

"For shit's sake, Chris."

"And what will you give *me*?"

"Joy," I tell him. "And something else . . . something better."

His eyes are fixed on my face, trying to read ahead, but even he couldn't guess the bomb I'm about to drop.

"A name," I say. "A name that will solve a thirty-year-old missing person case."

He's playing it cool, but I can see the eagerness in his eyes. "What makes you think they'll talk to me?"

"They can't," I tell him. "They're dead."

CHAPTER 8

Victoria Police: Missing Persons List

I'm lying on my single bed with Jessie, scrolling through my phone. My mum is officially listed as a missing person, but the truth is she had a habit of leaving. I used to whine endlessly, cross-legged at the front door, waiting for her to come home. She'd leave for a few days, stay for a few months. I never knew where she went. But as I got older, her absence became more common than her presence.

She left for the final time on August 8, 1998.

There she is. Mum. Danielle Greenwood. Soft blond hair falling over her forehead. Spooked look in her brown eyes. A cheap sterling-silver chain hanging from her neck and a Christian fish pendant resting on her green T-shirt. I'd bought it as her Christmas present.

I was so excited for her to open that box. When Christmas morning finally came, I woke her up at 5 A.M., placing it on her chest. I remember her opening it so carefully, peeking inside, while I hovered at her elbow, breathless and squirmy. She held the pendant up and read the inscription on the back of the fish:

MERRY CHRISTMAS, MUM!

LOVE, MINNOW

Then she pulled me into her arms and cried.

"I love it, darling," she told me later, patting my cheek. She always had the softest hands. "I just wish . . ." She looked out the window, eyes far away again, and I knew I'd lost her. "I just wish I deserved it."

I think I understand now. How some gifts feel like wounds.

She wore it for me, I think. Never took it off. I wonder if she's still alive. Wonder if she'll ever come home.

Mostly, I wonder if she even *wants* to. Even when she was here, most of her was missing. That's what abuse does.

Don't let them turn you into a ghost...

I rub my thumb over her precious photo.

He's gone now, Mum. He's gone.

I wonder what the odds are of being the child of not one but two missing persons. Luke said that once. *Doesn't look good for you two*, he cackled. *You got somethin' you wanna confess?*

I scroll down, hover my thumb over Dad's picture. Black hair, shark eyes, mouth that seems to sneer, *Just hurry up and take the farken picture, will ya?*

Peter is the owner of the fishing charter Deep Sea Fishing...

And Peter Greenwood pissed off a lot of people in town, which is why they neither mourned him nor looked too hard after he disappeared.

I scroll past Dad's photo. Women, men, a handful of teenagers. And one face that I still see in nightmares.

Donny Granger, 28.

Easy smile. Short black curls falling over his forehead. Lumberjack beard, drowsy eyes. He looked like the sort of guy who hung out at the pub most nights, and dipped out every twenty minutes for a quick smoke. Friendly. Unmemorable. That's how I've always imagined him. Not that I really know. I only saw him. Once.

Missing since late July 1998: Donny Granger.

Donny left his home in Warrnambool in a white Mitsubishi Sigma in mid-July. He was believed to be traveling to South Australia to stay with a friend, but he never arrived.

I quickly send Donny's profile to Chris, then I turn the phone face down because I can't stand to see him a second longer. Can't stand that I never said a damn thing about what happened.

Sweat gathers at my forehead, and my chest feels too tight. I roll onto my back and pull the covers up to my shoulders. It's hard to breathe.

Donny had a son. I found that out later. A young son with the same curly black ringlets and open smile. Aaron. He'd be mid-thirties now. Fatherless because I left his dad to die.

I hear them again as I drift off. Blackbirds clambering up and down a ghost gum as I hide in the tree's shadow. Every twig crack feels like a warning. Something is moving through the underbrush, deliberate, dragging. A gust of wind stirs the eucalyptus leaves high above. I don't dare move.

Then, a scream. It rips through the bush, echoing off the trees, bouncing between the trunks. The blackbirds scatter, black wings slicing the air.

Then another scream . . . shorter this time. Choked.

Cut off.

Then silence.

I WAKE UP TO THE phone ringing. Jessie lifts her head, disapproving, before settling back to sleep. I grab the phone and note the time: 1:07 A.M.

"Chris . . ." I say, voice hoarse. "What the hell?"

I rub my eyes. I bet he's spent the last few hours researching Donny's disappearance. Not that he would have found any new information. The case has been cold for years.

I clear my throat. "You found a new place to stay?"

"Yeah," he says distracted, "Airbnb on Parson Street, Pine Bay."

"Good, got a job lined up for me yet?"

He sighs impatiently. "I can't just—"

I end the call.

Heath must be home now, but I didn't hear him come in. I'm wondering if I should get up and peek in his room when the phone rings again.

"Look . . ." Chris huffs, not even saying hello. "I could go to the police with this right now, you know."

"With what?"

I can feel him bristle on the end of the phone, and I find myself grinning in the dark.

"You know how to use WordPress?" he asks wearily.

"Yep."

"Great, you're hired. *Trident* mag needs another content writer. Freelance. Eight hundred to a thousand words, two hundred bucks a story." He pauses, adding, "You're welcome."

"Three hundred?"

He snorts, "No."

"Two fifty?"

"No."

"But—"

"Oh, for heaven's sake. Fine, yes, I'll get you two fifty."

"What sorta content?"

"Oh, you'll love it!" he says brightly, and I know he's taking the piss. "The art of sliding into someone's DMs. Why an eight-thousand-dollar TV is worth the spend."

"How many pieces a week?"

"As many as you want," he says impatiently. "You know what it's like. They churn these things out in droves. Just remember—"

"A-C-C-I-D-E-N-T-A-L-L-Y," I spell out before he can rib me again.

"Gold star for you."

I rub my forehead, and he adds, "Oh yeah, don't use your real name by the way . . . Or your other one."

I don't answer.

"Melanie?"

"Yeah," I say finally. "I'll take it."

"Delighted to hear it."

There's a heavy air of expectation on the line. I think of the water. The missing people. Donny Granger. The darkness in this town. All of it rushing together like a wave about to crash.

I speak quickly. "Meet me at four A.M."

His voice drops. "Where?"

Can't breathe. Can't breathe. "The end of Soldiers' Road. The woods."

". . . Why are we meeting there?"

I end the call.

THEN

He hates the ocean. Hates himself for loving it once.

God, he loved the water before that day. Just couldn't get enough of it. Fishing, swimming, surfing, diving. Before school and after, rushing off the bus, throwing his bag on the sand, plunging straight into that blessed water until the sky grew dark. Sometimes Dad had to drag him out by the ankles, laughing the whole time.

He's eight years old when it tries to take him. Waist-deep in the ocean, hot sun burning his shoulders.

A wave rose up so high it blocked out the sun. It looked like the entire ocean was folding in half. Panic swelled in his chest. His knees buckled as the wave dragged him toward its mouth. Loud. God, it was loud, that rising roar.

And then crashing down it came like a fist to the head.

The shock, the cold, the breathless panic as he's slammed under. He kicks his legs, terrified and confused, which way is the surface? Cold, cold, can't breathe. The wave, its cold angry hand plunges him down. Holds him there. Wants him to drown. Wants him dead.

Can't breathe. He kicks hard, stops. He doesn't know which way is up. Lungs ache. Can't breathe.

Images.

Mum peeling potatoes at the sink.

Dad knee-deep in the water, fishing rod gripped in his right hand.

Jesus, his mind screams out, Jesus. Help me.

He never could explain it. But a moment later, he's at the surface like someone's reached down through the water, grabbed his shoulders, and pulled him out. He looks around. But there's no one there.

On wobbly legs, he half bends over, vomits so hard his vision goes black. The salt water burns as it pours out. Feels like scraping teeth.

He empties his stomach, waits for the rest to come out, because he still feels it, coating his stomach, soaking his lungs. The water.

For days after, he avoids the ocean. Tries to forget. Can't.

He bums a smoke in the school toilets, a morning ritual, but when he brings the cigarette to his lips, he hears himself crying out in the water, Help me, Jesus.

He inhales, feels guilty as hell about it. Wonders if Jesus is watching him, disapproving.

But he can't avoid the bloody ocean. His dad makes a living from it, and his dad before him. They don't feel it. They don't understand the ocean and its legacy of violence. But he does. Now.

Look at the ripples on the surface: There's a struggle below. Life and death. Mainly death. Look at the southern calamari squid, humble and wary and hiding in the reeds.

But are they hiding from you? Or hiding in ambush? He's seen them snatch baby herrings into their beaklike mouths, stripping them to the spine. Given the chance, they'll even eat each other. You've got to watch anything that pretends it's prey.

They're usually the predator.

THE NEXT TIME DAD TAKES *him fishing, he hovers anxiously at the edge of the water, eyes shifting over the flat surface. There's violence in the calm, he knows that now. What else is in that dark abyss, waiting?*

Dad hauls out a sparkling mullet, reaches immediately for the knife, and for the first time in his life, he can't look.

"Open ya eyes," Dad commands. "It's just the way of things, son."

But it's not. Not this stretch of beach, not this ocean. This ocean is violent and restless. This ocean is so hungry, it hurts.

For years after, he's jittery and sick around it. Even at home he bolts awake from nightmares, vomiting in his bedsheets, salt water on his lips.

One night, he's lying awake on his pillow, and he swears he can hear the ocean rumbling inside.

The water. The violence. It keeps calling him back. The more he ignores it, the louder it calls. The only time he feels still is when he's sharpening his fishing knife. But inside, his pulse and thoughts are racing. Inside, there's a hum. A tight coil of anticipation that never unwinds.

And that call, that maddening call, looping through his brain until he can't hear anything else. Not the cartoons Minnow watches on Saturday mornings or Heath chopping kangaroo meat in the kitchen while their mother weeps in their bedroom.

He can't hear his own family, but when he does, there's hell to pay. When he does, he becomes the ocean. It throbs in his ears, spews out his mouth, raging, violent, endless. On those days, he can't tell where he begins and the sea ends. Doesn't care, either. In his mind, they're just one, salt and skin, breath and tide. On those days, he loves it. But lately, the call is louder, rattling in his teeth. More, it roars. More, more, more!

One day it'll stop, he tells himself. One day it has to.

But it doesn't.

All the days of his life, he hears the ocean.

Calling.

CHAPTER 9

The red-gold dirt snakes through the woods and the pale trunks of the ghost gums look like they're drowning in a river of gold-red blood. The woods have a thin, muddy smell like wet bark and something else. Something animal.

We called them the Wicked Woods because they're shadowy and endless, and everything in this town was wicked anyway. Including us.

Especially us.

The worst thing that ever happened to me, happened right here.

The second worst thing, too.

I kill the engine, and the hum of the road disappears, replaced by a heavy silence. There's no other car in the parking lot, no noise at all, just a deep hush coming from the tree line.

The Wicked Woods stretch out in front of me, dark, still, silent. They feel like they're waiting for something.

I open the car door before I can change my mind, stumbling out into the quiet dark. I shut it behind me with a dull thud and stand there for a moment, keys still in hand. I shift my weight, suddenly aware of how loud my breathing sounds out here.

Uneasy, I glance toward the woods. They're too close. The trees huddle together like they're whispering secrets. *My* secrets. I wonder if they remember what happened here. Wonder if they carry the weight of it like I do.

Wonder if they wake in the night, chest heaving, breath ragged, a dead man's name on their lips.

My stomach turns, the heaviness in my chest suffocating. I want to turn and run. I can feel the past pressing in on me, whispering things I tried to bury.

I stagger back, vomiting so hard I see stars. I crouch on the ground, palms on my knees, panting hard enough to blow about the dead leaves at my ankles. I remain there, bent over and shaking as the sweat gathers into a single spot at the tip of my nose and drips heavily onto the red dirt. Out of the corner of my eyes, a man walks foward. Dark-blue jeans, brown belt, white tennis shoes. I can't see his face. I try to stand up, but my vision swims.

A tidal wave rises from my stomach, rushes up my throat, pours out my mouth. I vomit again and up it comes, secrets and water and guilt. I close my eyes, sweat trickling down my nose and chin.

"God," Chris groans. "You all right?"

My legs shake. I don't know how much longer they'll keep me up.

"Melanie?"

He pushes something into my left hand. I close a clumsy fist around it and open my eyes. Water bottle. He crouches beside me, his right knee nudging mine. He unscrews the lid. "Drink this."

The bottle shakes as I hold it to my lips. I rinse my mouth out and spit heavily on the dirt while he quietly surveys the empty car park. No one really knows the woods are here. Or cares. Sometimes tourists stray down here, clambering noisily out of their little cars, while their sweaty kids trail behind them, whining the whole time. They only last a few minutes before heading back to the surf beaches.

"Thank you." I pass the bottle back to him, wipe my mouth with the back of my fist, and stand up shakily.

"Big night?" he asks sarcastically.

I give him a look. He knows where I was last night. Knows I was on the phone to him but doesn't know about the nightmares that followed.

"Come on." I swipe at my mouth. "Let's go."

I step forward, hoping my legs will carry me all the way down this dark path.

Chris doesn't move. "No," he says shortly. "I'm not taking another step until you tell me what the hell's going on."

Donny Granger.

The bile in my stomach rises. "You saw the . . . the profile I sent you last night, yeah?"

"Donny?"

My blood rings in my ears. I manage to nod.

"Yeah, I saw," he says, inspecting me. "What about him?"

"I know where he is."

He raises an eyebrow, silent for once. My eyes flick behind him to that narrow pathway in the darkness.

"I'll take you to him."

He hesitates, narrowing his eyes like he's waiting for the punch line.

"Do you want to find him or not?"

"I don't get it," he finally says, throwing up his hands. "Is he waiting around the corner or something?"

"Yeah, he is."

He stares at me.

I trudge back to my car, reaching into the boot. And I watch his face fall in shock when he sees what I'm holding.

A shovel.

MINUTES LATER, HE'S A FEW steps behind, feet crunching on the dirt.

"Quiet," I hiss softly, "you need to be quieter."

He gives me a suspicious look. "Are your mates waiting for me up ahead or something?" He pretends to scan the tree line, like he's waiting for the townsmen to come charging out. "Hope you're not thinking of doing me in, Melanie."

"Wouldn't be the first time I've thought about that."

He snorts, treading quieter now, eyes wide with anticipation. If he does find this guy, it will make his career. I know he's thinking of the story he'll write, the breaking news, the pats on the back, Donny's grateful, heartbroken family.

"When we find the body, we'll call the police," he says, serious now. "They'll come and declare it a crime scene. They'll want to know how you knew the body was here," he adds nervously, as if afraid to scare me off.

I don't answer, and he finally stops talking.

We walk in total silence. It's a clear morning, no wind. To our right is a lily pond, looking like something out of a children's book. The giant lily pads are the size of dinner plates and home to two softly croaking green frogs. It's beautiful but odd, completely out of place. Makes you wonder what else there is to find here. My chest feels too tight; I keep rubbing the soft place over my heart again and again.

Finally, we come to the fork, and a Bell Miner bird calls out in clear warning. Chris brushes past me, and I grasp a fistful of his shirt, slinging him back. "No!"

I must have snapped it, because he gives me a wounded look.

"Sorry," I mutter. I don't add that there's a place just ahead that I don't want him to see. A creek.

Two evil things happened in these woods. One, to Donny Granger. The other, to my grade-five classmate Amy Anderson. I'll only tell Chris about Donny. He can write up the story, take the credit, and get me a job. I don't want him finding out about Amy.

"Well." Chris raises an eyebrow, waits. "Which track?"

"Neither."

I veer off the track until I'm parallel to it. I face a sign, knee-high and faded.

IT IS PROHIBITED TO CROSS THE FIRE ACCESS TRACK

I step onto the fire track, and Chris shuffles into step behind me. I can hear the change in his breathing, the anticipation. He's stepping carefully, lost in dreams.

And I creep forward, lost in nightmares.

THE FIRE TRACK HAS BEEN swallowed by the bush. A tunnel of tea trees closes in around us, their flaking limbs arching overhead to form a scraggly steeple. It's impossible to walk without tripping over a mass of roots or fallen branches. I feel like I'd have to suck in my stomach or inch sideways like a crab just to move around.

And that's just the beginning. The deeper you get, the more the woods begin to close in. Vines twist around my ankles, and the undergrowth scratches at my legs like grasping fingers. Branches rake across my face, clawing at my clothes as if trying to hold me back. As if they're saying, *Don't go farther. You won't like what you find here.*

Behind me, Chris falters, crying out softly in alarm. I whirl around, afraid. Chris flattens his back against a tea tree as a wallaby bounces past, half hidden among all the gray-brown bark. I watch it rush by, snorting at his fear.

"You're all right," I tell him, wiping the sweat from my upper lip. "Skippy won't kill you."

He gives me a look. "Feels like something will, though." He frowns, looking up at the bony branches of the tea trees. "This place is creepy."

"It gets worse," I say cheerfully.

He rolls his eyes and for the next ten minutes, we weave around fallen tea trees, clambering over and under, swearing under our breath. At some points, I hold the shovel in front of my face to break the silvery lines of cobwebs, bashing at the low-hanging branches. All along, I'm fighting hard not to remember, but it comes back hard. I'm walking in my father's footsteps, taking the track he did. And like me, he wasn't alone . . .

God, I shouldn't have followed him. Why did I do that?

The Bell Miner's call echoes through the woods, high-pitched, metallic: tink, tink, tink. When I was a child, I loved their background hum. Each call like a tiny bell being struck. Now I just hear:

Go back.

Go back.

A moment later, I swear I hear my father's voice in their calls.

You fuckin' dog.

A fallen she-oak blocks the path. My legs shake so badly, it takes me three tries to scramble over it. I reach the other side, landing hard enough that pain shoots up both ankles.

I rest my back against the tree, lowering my head because it's spinning. Chris lands at my side with a thud, pushing the bottle into my hands again. "Drink," he insists, annoyed. "Staying hydrated will help..."

He rambles on about lactic acid and body temperature until I rip the bottle from his hand and drink.

Get through this.
Get through this.
Make it right.

I spit on the ground, and he grimaces but at least he finally shuts up. And for the first time I wonder if he, too, is uneasy as hell.

I pass the bottle back to him, and he screws the lid back on.

"Thanks," I say gruffly before stepping forward. "Come on, let's go."

Each step is a battle as the underbrush claws at my legs and branches tug at my sleeves. Every noise we make feels amplified: our breathing, our footsteps. A root sneaks out of the earth and I trip over it, steadying myself with a hand on a tree trunk. I catch my breath and continue. The deeper we walk, the more it feels like the woods are watching, whispering.

And then I see it.

The crudely made cross is just two black twigs entwined with blue string, long faded.

I come to an abrupt stop. I remember setting that cross down so gently. Hoping it would dull my guilt, but knowing all along it wouldn't.

I'm sorry.

At the time, I didn't know his name. But a few days later, a man's face flashed on the TV screen.

Donny left his home in Warrnambool in a white Mitsubishi Sigma in mid-July. He was believed to be traveling to South Australia to stay with a friend, but he never arrived...

That wasn't true, though. I saw him in these woods. My father walked him through this path, the tip of his black fishing knife pressed hard into the man's back.

Donny Granger.

He was the first, I think.

I doubt he was the last.

For years after, I found myself returning to his grave. I'd be walking home from school, my bag slung heavily over my shoulder, and instead of walking home, I'd end up right here. For hours and hours, I would sit beside this man's grave. Mostly I was silent, still. Sometimes I'd look up, shocked that I was sitting in total darkness. Then I'd stumble home, ignoring Heath's questions about where I'd been.

Why didn't I call out? Why did I just freeze like a coward? And why did he even do it?

The yearly appeals were the hardest. Donny's mum would face the camera, voice shaking, as she begged for information about her missing son. As the years went by, her voice became steadier, her eyes more direct and focused. Like she was resigned to the truth that he would never come home. Then she simply started asking for closure. "I cannot fully grieve until I know what happened to Donny. Give me that, at least."

Dad saw the appeal, once. I was sitting in the lounge room while he sharpened his knife behind my shoulder. He sat still, eyes fixed on the screen, face unreadable, blank like a mask. I know he saw Donny's face, but it washed over him without leaving a ripple.

The moment I sink the shovel deep into the ground, a voice taunts, *You can't do this. Your dad will be so angry. How do you even know he's truly gone? What if he's not? There'll be hell to pay for this. He'll be so angry, so angry . . .*

My head spins. Chris calls out something I can't hear.

You can't do this . . .

To be honest, I thought this would be easier. But the longer I remain, the more I feel like I'm retraumatizing myself.

I cannot fully grieve until I know what happened to Donny. Give me that, at least.

I lift my head.

Yes, I can.
Because I must.
And if I do it vomiting, I do it vomiting.
"Here," Chris says, reaching for the handle. "I'll do it."
"No." I angle it away from him. "I have to do this myself."
I grip the shovel and start digging.

CHAPTER 10

I've been digging for hours now and found nothing. Chris hovers beside me, passing me a water bottle like I'm a long-distance runner. My body burns, my hands sting. Finally, it's Chris's turn. He starts a new hole ten feet from mine. I brush the sweat from my forehead, leaving a streak of dirt on my face. I lower myself to the ground, watching him silently.

"Good day for it."

He scoops the soil up, pauses. "Huh?"

"Grave digging."

"I'm going to pretend you didn't say that," he says, throwing the dirt to the side. He straightens up, stretches his back. "This whole thing . . ." He doesn't finish the thought. But I know. This whole thing is nuts. All of it.

"Yeah," I say, "I know."

But maybe . . . maybe if I find Donny and give his family closure, maybe it'll heal me. Maybe that ghost world of mine will finally stop following me. *Coward.*

He drops the shovel, cracks his neck, pausing. "I've been wanting to say something all morning . . ."

He pulls his phone from his pocket and stares down at it, frowning. This can't be good. I get to my feet and reach for the shovel.

"You see the *Mill* today?"

I raise an eyebrow. "Can't say I read that shit anymore." I throw the dirt to the side. "Not since I left. Surprised *you* do, to be honest." I look up. "Why?"

He hesitates, and my heart drops. Oh shit. Of course. If there's one thing the *Mill* loves more than pert stomachs or botched cosmetic surgeries, it's D-list breakups.

Like mine.

"Let me guess..." I say wearily. "My fiancé announced the tragic end of our relationship today?"

He nods, embarrassed. "Sorry," he says automatically. "I didn't realize..."

"Yes, you did."

"I didn't want to ask."

"Yes, you did."

Chris clears his throat. "You want me to read what he said?"

I shrug. "Sure."

"Sorry," he says again, and he actually does sound sincere. "Someone sent it to me. You know how it is."

I do. Everyone in the business is in a bitchy group chat, and there's always some shit-stirrer starting messages with, *Have you heard...*

Dan from the ABC is having angry bangs with Maya from Channel 10?

Amanda from Channel 7 got her boobs done in Turkey?

Oliver the weather guy and Melanie from Morning, Sunshine! *split up?*

I stare into the hole. "Go on."

Chris stands solemn at my side. "'After much thought and careful consideration,'" Chris reads, "'Melanie and I have made the difficult decision to end our relationship. We go forward with love and friendship for each other as we venture toward new horizons...'"

New horizons!

I snort, plunging the shovel back into the soil. "That it?"

"Uh...no." Chris hesitates. "He added a hashtag."

"Go on, then," I say, tipping my head back to the sky. "What does it say?"

Chris clears his throat. "'Hashtag thesunkeepsrising.'" He clicks his phone off. "I take it you didn't have a hand in writing that heartwarming statement?"

I give Chris an exasperated look. No, I didn't write that shit. But Oliver definitely did. It reeks of him. I can imagine him, sitting up until late, thinking, *How can I make this sound better? How can I still be the good guy here?*

"Are you going to release a statement of your own?"

"No."

From somewhere far away comes Chris's voice. "Do you think you'll get engaged again?"

"Right now, I'd rather die."

"Why'd you say yes, then?" he prods.

God, my hands sting. My back, my neck. My heart feels like it's rotting in my rib cage.

"Why would I tell you that? So you can get the scoop?" I loosen my sweaty grip on the shovel and face him. "So you can go back to the *Daily* and the *Mill* and tell them all the shit I said about Oliver?"

"I wouldn't do that."

"I think you would."

I tilt my head all the way back to stretch my neck. For a long time, we stay that way.

Until he speaks. "Linda dumped me."

Slowly, I lower my head and stare at him. I've met his girlfriend a handful of times. Schoolteacher. Blunt fringe, shockingly calm. Her iPhone wallpaper was a cartoon llama, pink bow in its springy hair.

He won't meet my eyes, stares at his shoes instead, plucking at a lace. "It came outta nowhere," he says dully.

"Chris."

Slowly, he looks up. His eyes are unsteady, nervous. Embarrassed.

"It never comes out of nowhere."

He exhales in a huff. "And here I thought you were going to say something nice."

"How long were you together?"

"Three years."

I sink the shovel into the dirt. "What changed?"

"She did."

"Why?"

He snorts. "I'm used to asking all the questions."

Maybe that's why she left you.

I dig silently, deeper and deeper.

"She's dating the PE teacher." He looks down at his shoes again, frowning. "I always hated that guy."

The soil is hard and rocky, and the walls begin to collapse and cave in, forcing me to bend and half squat. I use my entire body to push the shovel into the ground. The repetitive motions of lifting and moving the soil strain my arms, back, and legs. Still, I dig. What is it about this that makes it so confessional? That makes even a man like Chris Cooper let go and unload?

"I call her sometimes," he says plainly. "She won't answer."

"Why not?"

"I dunno."

"Yeah, you do."

"For heaven's sake," he finally groans. "Let *me* dig."

"I'm fine—"

"No," he says so abruptly that I stop and look up. "I just . . ." He looks away. "I need to do something."

I throw him the shovel, and he heaves it into the dirt, grunting.

"I feel like shit about it," I finally say. "The Oliver thing . . . it got ugly."

"Fine line between love and hate," he agrees.

"Yeah," I say, looking up at the tea trees. "But sometimes it feels like there's too much ugliness. Like it always wins out."

He sighs heavily. "I know." He stops to wipe his forehead with his sleeve. "I've been an investigative journalist for seventeen years now . . ." His voice trails off. "You wouldn't believe what I've heard. And seen."

He starts digging again. "But then one day I thought, well, maybe we need the ugliness. Maybe it's there so we don't take the good things for granted. When I used to get all angry and depressed, Linda would say, 'Look harder. Look for the good. It's still there.'"

"She's a keeper," I tell him.

"It's over. She's made that clear," he says grimly before hesitating. ". . . She said I cared more about my work than her."

"Oh," I say, finally understanding. "Do you think that's true?"

"No," he mumbles. ". . . Yes."

I nod, waiting.

"I'm an idiot, I know..." He throws all his weight into digging, like he wants to bury himself down there. "I love my dad, but... he was a journo, too, you know? He broke the Lawyer F story. Made his career. And I..." He frowns, digging harder, sweat breaking out on his brow. "Well, I'm still making mine."

"If it helps," I offer, "I have no idea what the Lawyer F story is."

"Police corruption, Sydney-wide." He raises an eyebrow. "You haven't heard of it?"

I shake my head.

"Lucky you," he says, grunting as he digs deeper. "Sometimes when I talk to my dad, he doesn't *quite* seem to be listening. Like every time I speak, he's hearing something else from far away. Something more important than me." He hesitates. "Sometimes when I finish talking, he gives me a distracted nod, like, *Oh, you've stopped talking then? Good.*"

"I do that with you, too."

He cracks a small smile.

"You've still got time, Chris. We both do."

"You sure about that?" He stares down at the dirt, grim-faced and silent, like something's been taken from him and he doesn't know how to get it back. I squint and see him, the real Chris Cooper, wondering why it's taken me this long. He's haunted by past failures, still trying, desperately, to prove he's worth something. Why do I get the feeling that he just needs someone, *anyone*, to say, "You did good. You matter."

"Yeah," I lie, "I am."

CHAPTER 11

I've spent whole summers on Dad's boat, hacking up slimy pilchards for tourists who couldn't stand getting their hands dirty. I liked it.

By midafternoon, your forearms ached, your back burned, and the sun pressed down like a weight. Heath and I would hit a point where we were so tired, everything felt hilarious. We used to call it the Tired Crazies.

One time, after hacking the heads off a dozen pilchards, I turned around, and Heath was slow dancing with an angry squid who kept inking him. I laughed so hard and for so long that Dad stormed over and screamed at me.

The Tired Crazies. I dig and dig until finally I'm on my knees, peering down into a black hole. "He's not *fucking here.*"

Donny Granger. Where are you? I know I saw my father lead you into these woods. I watched him slit your throat right at the base of this blackwood tree. I saw the blood spill from your neck and splash onto the earth.

You were buried here, Donny. *I watched it all and I did nothing to stop it.*

Now where the hell are you?

I lower my shovel into the earth, too tired even to scoop it off to the side.

"I'm hungry," Chris mutters. "Don't s'pose you brought anything to eat?"

"No, Chris, I didn't exactly think about packing a lunch."

"Maybe it's time to call it a day, then," he says flatly. He's sprawled on his back at a weird angle, staring up at the sky. It's funny to see him lying in the dirt. *Everything* is funny when you're bone-tired, hungry, and digging up some dead guy's grave.

"No," I tell him soberly, "I'm going to *dig* my way out of this mess."

He misses the joke. Damn, it was a good one. He shrugs, stretches out his legs, rubbing at his knee. "Do you really think we'll find him?"

"No," I say, "I think we've *lost the plot.*"

He stares blankly at me, but I'm not finished. "Do you know what you call a man who's finished digging?"

He raises an eyebrow.

"Doug."

He closes his eyes tight, shoulders heaving.

"Is that a *ghost* of a smile on your lips?"

"Oh my God," he says. "Please stop."

I drop the shovel, stretch my back. "You come up with something better, then."

I tilt my head, looking up through the brambles to the scraps of sky. I don't want to be stuck here at night in the darkness. Not in this place of nightmares.

"I can't," he says soberly. "I think we've made a *grave* mistake."

I laugh, "Nice one."

Chris sits up on his elbows, "Melanie," he says, "this has been the strangest day of my entire life."

"You're welcome. We'll come back tomorrow morning, same time. I'll pack lunch—"

But Chris isn't looking at me. His eyes are drawn to something ahead, farther up the trail. I follow his gaze. "What?"

"What the hell is *that*?" He stalks forward and I follow nervously behind. The ground seems to shift with each step, the crunch of leaves and twigs loud in the silence.

"Chris?"

I turn to see what he's staring at. I almost miss it at first, something pale breaking the surface, half hidden beneath a blanket of dead leaves and tangled roots. It's out of place, doesn't belong there.

Something white.

Something with teeth.
A human skull.

WE HOVER OVER THE MAKESHIFT GRAVE, looking down.

"Well," Chris finally says, "I guess we found Donny." He stands with his hands on his hips, eyes firmly fixed on the skull. More to himself he mumbles, "Geez . . . this changes everything."

He hesitates, unsure of himself for once. His breath catches mid-inhale, eyes going wide. He blinks once, twice, as if it's hit him all at once. He keeps looking over his shoulder as if someone's peering through the tea trees watching him. But I can't calm him down. I can't comfort him. Something's wrong with this. Something about it makes me want to run and run and run.

"This is a crime scene now. We need to tell the police," he finally says, snapping out of it. "The integrity of the scene needs to be maintained. The police will cordon off the area."

I don't answer. I crouch down to the makeshift grave, my skin prickling. This isn't right.

"Melanie?"

I crouch closer, inspecting the skull. At first, it looks intact. Weathered, yellowed. But then I see it. The fracture. A deep, concave depression on the side of the skull, like someone slammed it with a brick.

"Don't touch it," Chris warns.

A clump of hair is still visible at the back of the skull, filthy with dirt. But the color is still visible.

Blond.

I lean back, chest tight and aching.

"What's wrong?"

From somewhere far away, I hear myself say, "Donny had black hair."

And then I'm clawing at the ground, scratching my nails at the surface, tearing up chunks of earth.

"What the hell are you doing?" Chris reaches for my shoulder, but I throw his hand off. "Melanie!"

I reach down deeper and deeper, clawing at the dirt like an animal. The ground seems to fight me, but I'm pulled by a force greater than my own will, driven by dread and desperation. I carefully scrape away the remaining soil, pausing when my fingers brush the collarbone. The bones are bleached white and delicate, and the tattered remains of a shirt clings to the rib cage. It's stiff to the touch, brittle, the edges ragged where the seams have pulled loose. But it's the collarbones I can't stop staring at.

Because nestled between them, something sparkles.

I reach forward, fingers trembling over the collarbone where a necklace is coiled. I undo the silver clasp, now oxidized to pea green, and scoop it into my palm.

Hanging from the chain is a Christian fish pendant. Trance-like, I turn it over, reading the inscription. I read it once, twice, time slowing down to nothing. Chris kneels beside me, both hands gripping my shoulders. I can't hear what he's saying. All I can hear is the blood pumping in my ears. My fist closes around the necklace and the five words inscribed on it.

MERRY CHRISTMAS, MUM!

LOVE, MINNOW

Human remains found in Kangaroo Bay identified as woman who went missing 25 years ago

The Daily
by Chris Cooper

Skeletal remains found in bushland on the East Coast of Victoria have been identified as a Kangaroo Bay local. A bushwalker found the remains and a forensic examination identified them as Danielle Greenwood. The cause of death has been determined as blunt-force trauma to the head.

Greenwood, 37, a mother of two, disappeared in early August 1998. She was last seen around 6 P.M. leaving the general store where she worked. She was spotted walking down Echo Street toward her house on April Avenue but never arrived home.

Danielle's husband, Peter Greenwood, went missing two years later and has not been seen since February 2000. Greenwood had been threatened a week before his disappearance. His case remains unsolved.

Peter Greenwood is considered a suspect in his wife's murder. If you have information on his whereabouts, please call Crime Stoppers on 1800 333 000.

CHAPTER 12

In my family, when everything goes to shit, we fish. We can't seem to heal unless we're knee-deep in salt water. And I feel it tonight, the need to be cleansed. But as I peer down to beach 1, I can't see Heath anywhere.

I get back in the car, drive the three minutes to beach 2. But he's not there, either. Instinctively, I drive past beach 3. Heath doesn't go there. It's like a family rule. We don't speak of the beach my father nearly drowned in. But now I turn around and slowly climb the hill to beach 3, somehow knowing he's in the forbidden place.

I let Jessie out of the back seat, slam my car door shut, duck my head from the wind. I pull my beanie lower until it completely covers my ears, but nothing could drown that roar of the waves. Jess bounds just ahead of me, stopping every ten feet to turn around and make sure I'm still there. I smile a little. If there's one positive thing to come from the last few days it's watching her confidence grow. She's like a different dog, head and tail up, a little uneasy with strangers, but she's getting better. More sure of herself.

I can't say the same for me.

I stroll down the sand dunes, hands stuffed in my pockets, but I can still feel the sting of cold at my fingertips. The sky is gray and spitting. Storm's coming.

Jess launches herself into the water, chasing a seagull that lifts off into the last of the setting sun, squawking in annoyance. I stop and watch for a moment. *God*, I think. *It's beautiful.*

And then . . .

Mum.

The memory of her lying in that shallow grave hits so hard, it makes me double over. My body is still raw and weak like I'm recovering from an illness. I wait there, bent over and unsure if I'm ready to venture this far from my bed. I haven't left the house since I found her.

A handful of tourists are packing up, wringing their beach towels, stuffing their belongings into oversized bags. They're hurrying now, eyes on the darkening sky. Silly. This is the best time to be on the beach, watching a storm come rolling in. Seeing the water whip up. Sometimes you'll even see the fish come soaring out of the deep, frenzied and afraid. It's actually a great time to fish because they gorge themselves when the pressure drops like this. They'll instinctively seek to consume more food before the storm arrives.

And there he is. Heath. Waist-deep in the water, back to me. I can't see the rod in his hands. He looks like he's standing frozen in the middle of the ocean, waves angry and rising, ready to swallow him whole. He looks like a man lost.

I stumble forward, uneasy. There are sharks out there in the deep and in the shallows.

I watch as a wave rises, swelling higher and higher, pulling him in. He's shoulder-deep now, just the top of his black head showing. The wave towers above him, poised to crash. We've all been hit by one of these waves before. It's like getting slammed by a car.

I yell, "Heath!" But my voice is lost in the roar. What the hell is he doing? I run now, sprinting down the sand, feeling it grow wet between my toes. "Heath!"

Jessie raises her head, sees me running. She races up the beach until she's at my heels, and together we stand at the edge of the freezing water, calling.

"Heath?" My voice tears out of me, raw with fear. "*Move!*"

But he doesn't. He stands there, shoulder-deep in the surf, eyes locked on something only he can see. The wave's already coming, too fast, too hard, and he just stands there like he's waiting for it.

I don't think. I shove off the sand and plunge into the water.

It closes over my head, black and biting. It's so cold it burns. My muscles cry out with every movement, but I keep going. Stroke after stroke. Jessie swims beside me, nose pointed straight at Heath.

The wave crashes over him and he disappears beneath the surge, swallowed whole.

"Heath!" I gasp, choking on salt and panic.

The surface churns with white water and foam. I can't see him.

And then, suddenly, he breaks through.

He emerges with a gasp, dragging air into his lungs like someone who wasn't sure he wanted it.

Jessie reaches him first. She paddles up to his chest and he instinctively scoops her into his arms, holding her close. Water streams down his face. He doesn't even wipe it away.

I stop swimming, bobbing in place as the ocean moves around me. Heath doesn't say a word. Doesn't blink. His eyes lock onto mine, blank and hollow, like everything inside him has been gutted. Like part of him is still underwater.

I know that look.

I've seen it once before, on the face of someone who did not make it back.

Someone who turned into a ghost long before their time.

And now I'm seeing it again.

This time, in my brother.

You're not supposed to light fires on the beach. Heath does it anyway. Always has. He makes his own rules. Jessie licks at the salt on her paws, watching me and Heath drag broken tea tree branches across the sand. He places seven rocks in a circle, then scrunches old newspaper into a ball while I hunt in the shrubs for more kindling. By the time I return to the beach, the fire is golden and glowing. I dump my armload of kindling to the side, and Heath and I sit quietly around the fire, watching it burn.

It's stopped raining, but it's still cold as hell. My jeans are soaked through, burning my legs with cold; the cuffs of my sleeves dripping wet. But the dark clouds are clearing, the stars are coming out. I keep looking over at Heath, not knowing what to say. We've been silent since I plunged into the water. Silent since he finally turned around and gave me that hunted look that reminded me of our mother.

I call for Jess, opening my arms. She drops into my lap, tucks her golden head under my chin. We stare at the waves and time slows down. There's a rhythm to the water, the steady pull and crash, like the ocean is breathing. And I wonder if it's remembering my father. It was Heath who told me about Dad nearly drowning here as a child. Heath who said, *Minnow, I think when that wave took him under . . . not all of him resurfaced.*

Heath was right. A few times a month, Dad would wake up screaming. Heath would disappear down the dark hallway, footsteps hurried and frantic. One night, I crept to the door, peered in. The room smelled of vomit and, faintly, of seawater. Dad was sitting up in bed, hands wrapped around his knees, rocking like a little child. Heath sat beside him, arm slung helplessly around his shoulders.

The wave took the best of him. The worst of him remained.

I think of Dad sitting quietly at the dining table, an undercurrent of violence swimming through him.

Heath keeps his eyes on the water, but I can see the agony on his face. Can see him grappling with the enormity of this week. I wonder if he sees Mum, cross-legged on the sand, shielding her eyes from the sun. Wonder if he sees himself, reeling in a fish, dragging it out of the shallows, straining with effort, while Mum shouts encouragement: *He's a big one, Heath! What a beauty!*

"Did you know she was . . . dead?" I finally ask.

He takes a shallow breath, trying to steady himself, but his eyes never leave the horizon. His shoulders are heavy, as if the weight of the world has settled on them again.

"I didn't wanna believe it . . ." He wipes at his face. "But she always came back after a few days. Always."

Yes, she did. She'd emerge silently like a shadow, adopting her old routines until she disappeared again. We never said a word about it. We should have. Silence had a hold on our house. On all of us.

"When she didn't come back . . ." He swallows hard. "She wouldn't have left us, Minnow. Not for good. Not like that."

I lower my head, suddenly weak and bone-tired. I'm glad Jessie is in my arms. I'm that little girl again, staring at the front door. Waiting, always waiting, for my mum to come back. To come home.

"Do you think he killed her?" I choke out.

Dad.

Yes, he did.

No, he didn't.

What will hurt worse?

Because if Dad didn't do it . . . who did?

He grabs my shoulder, and I cling to it. His nod falls heavy, final. "Yes," Heath breathes. "I do."

I exhale loudly, blowing all the air out of my lungs.

"And you think someone killed *him* for it?"

Heath swipes his eyes. "Either that or he fled after. I honestly don't know."

"Did you ask Terry if he did it?"

"He says he didn't."

"Do you believe him?"

Heath leans back on his elbows, and we watch the sky darken, watch the seagulls bob upon the whitecaps. A boat skims hard over the waves, picking up speed as it races to shore. A raindrop hits my collarbone. My eyebrow.

"You *do* think Terry killed Dad." The wind picks up, pushes my hair into my mouth. "You think he did us a favor."

"Didn't he?"

The boat rushes past. The whitecaps look sharp enough to slice through its hull.

"Min." Heath pauses. "Were you the one who found Mum?"

I've been dreading this. After Chris and I found her body, he was the one who called the police. I told him to keep my name out of it, and he agreed.

I think of Donny Granger and his young son. My throat closes up, my hands shake. I've never told a soul about what happened on Soldiers' Road. I've danced around it with Chris, but I wouldn't admit the whole truth. Couldn't.

"Yeah . . . I found her," I confess. "But it wasn't Mum I was looking for . . ."

I dig my phone out of my pocket, bring up the photo of Donny Granger. "Did you ever see this man?"

Heath takes the phone from my hand, peering hard at the screen. "No . . . who is it?"

"He went missing around the same time as Mum. Supposedly he was last seen in Warrnambool, but that's not true." Heath passes my phone back. "I saw him here. With Dad."

Heath's mouth is a grim line, and for a moment I feel my body stiffen. In this town, silence is their first language. Us. Them.

Whose side is he on? Whose side am *I* on?

"Dad took him to the Wicked Woods?"

"Yeah."

". . . And?"

The woods loom in my mind. I'm deep in the shadows of the ghost gum, heart hammering. My hands are trembling, but I force them to stay still. The underbrush rustles again, closer this time. I wonder if Heath is seeing them, too, the Wicked Woods, our childhood playground. Wonder if he's remembering the other thing that happened there to Amy Anderson. The thing he never asked me about.

I don't answer, can't answer. He already knows what Dad did.

Heath grabs my hand like he's drowning, fingers digging in. "I'm so sorry," he chokes out, voice cracking with fury. "God, where was I?"

"It was my fault," I say, the words dull, lifeless. "I followed him."

I stare out at the water, trying to make sense of something long broken. "I don't even know why."

He shakes his head, his voice low but fierce. "No. You weren't the problem. *He* was. Something in him wasn't right, Min."

"You know," I say slowly, "I've carried this secret with me all my life. Every step I took, I brought that dead man with me."

I don't say it, but we're both thinking it.

And now you will, too.

Heath sighs heavily, shoulders slumping.

"I'm going back to the woods," I tell him. "I need to find Donny."

He gives me a look. "It's done, Min. Let the dead bury the dead. No good will come from digging it up." He pauses, lowering his voice. "And I still have to make a living here."

I find myself watching him closely, reading between the lines of what he's really saying.

I still have to make a living here.

"Heath . . . is there anything you're involved in that I should know about?"

There's that look again. The *don't ask too many questions* look. He turns, staring at the sea, and it's like watching a door quietly close in front of me.

"You don't have to make a living here, you know?" I tell him. "You can leave."

"I don't want to," he says plainly before nodding at the sea. "You know what that is, out there?"

"What?"

He smiles. "That's my son's legacy."

I watch the sea, listening to the waves crash and the whistling wind. We take it in, separately and together. I see Jonah, grown, skipper of the *Deep Sea*, reeling in fish after fish while my brother watches from the bow, beaming.

I open my mouth to speak, but he beats me to it. "How long are you staying for, Min?"

I half smile. "Sick of me already?"

"Never," he says sincerely. "I wish you'd work with me on the boat. I wish . . ." He hesitates before continuing, "You're not a city girl, Min. I don't understand why you won't come home."

He's right. I hate the city.

"I had my job," I offer weakly.

I don't add that I left because I was losing pieces of myself to this town, little by little. I thought that by leaving I could claim them back, but I never did. I kept emptying myself, pouring myself into

Oliver's mold, Joy's mold, becoming what *they* needed. I swam to new waters, but I was still the same fish.

"And now?" he asks gently. "Do you want to come home for good?"

When I think of home, I think of this. Heath and I, heads tipped all the way back, watching the stars. Absolute galaxies of them. A fire burning at our feet, cups of cheap noodles in our hands, plumes of steam rising to the stars, the sea, the fire, and the dark.

Home was me, diving into the water, not even feeling the cold, pulling a gummy shark out by the tail while my mother laughed.

And later, home was Heath and me, starving and empty, kneeling in the wet sand over a dying fish, watching its life ebb away as the waves broke and climbed and broke again. The glorious endlessness of it all. We ate it over a beach fire, and it tasted like salt and salvation. My brother offering me the biggest pieces, because his love for me made him forget his own hunger.

It's only at night, on a beach, watching the rods and looking out into all that darkness, that I feel at home. Fishing holds life and death. Breakdowns and breakthroughs. Hope and loss. Struggle and surrender. Life and death and life again.

The rest is just noise.

And I think of Trav, steady and silent, seeing me for who I really was and never once asking me to change. Trav, who recognized something in me that no one else ever noticed, except Heath. But unlike my brother, Trav didn't flinch, or scold, or try to fix me when I showed him my shadows. He loved me in spite of them . . . or *for* them.

Yes, I think, surprising myself. *I want to come home.* But first, I want to finish this. I want to find Donny Granger. I want to know what happened to my mum and why. I want answers to the questions that have haunted me all my life.

Jessie sits up, yawning. She climbs out of my lap and flops beside the fire, staring at the flames.

We're silent for a moment until Heath says, "Come on." He pulls me gently to my feet, and I'm so weak that my right knee buckles.

I reach out instinctively, gripping my brother's arm until my knee steadies.

I remain there for a long time. Half of me wants to fall back onto the sand and stare moodily at the water for the rest of my life. The other half wants to burn the whole town down.

My chest feels hollow, my pulse sluggish.

Sometimes it feels like there's too much ugliness. Like it always wins out.

Wordlessly, Heath pushes a fishing rod into my hands. I wrap my fist around it, watch him walk down to the water. Jessie lifts her head. "Stay," I tell her. "Stay."

I follow Heath's footsteps on the wet sand. My bare feet brush the water. It's freezing cold but I barely feel it. I wade into the shallows until I'm standing at my brother's side.

He casts in silence, and I stare into the water, thinking of my father. Of all the times he roamed this darkened beach where he nearly drowned. What was he thinking as it held him under? I see his black hair disappearing under the surface, see his outstretched hands held up like a plea. I shake my head, eyeing the water with anger. For shit's sake. Why didn't you just take him? How could you not know what he would become? And now we're carrying his sins as if they were our own.

I wait, and the water answers.

Look deeper.

The wind whistles softly through the fishing line. A seagull cries out in the darkening sky. The waves break on the shore like a cymbal crashing. A symphony of ocean sounds. It's beautiful. All of it. The waves. The water. You'd swear it listens. You'd swear it could heal.

And I ask it silently,

Free us from the past.

Please.

I cast my line, and I think I understand finally why my father kept coming back to the water. It's the same reason I'm pulled back to the woods in my dreams. It ends where it begins.

"Hey," Heath says, calling across the wind. "I love you so much."

I look at him, really look, and for a moment, it's like staring into a warped mirror. Same eyes, same nose, same lips, even. But it's more than just features. We share a too-quiet stillness, the kind that doesn't come naturally. The kind you learn. This stillness isn't peaceful. It's tight and tense, all rigid shoulders and clenched jaws. I am the quiet, smaller echo of my brother. It's painful and beautiful in a way, when you look at your brother and realize he's broken in all the same places you are.

"I love you, too," I tell him. "So much."

We stand side by side in the water. The stars are out, providing little pinpricks of light. Jessie is half asleep by the fire. Our eyes meet and she wags her tail before softly closing them again.

Sometimes it feels like there's too much ugliness. Like it always wins out.

But not tonight.

Tonight it's beautiful.

Tonight we fish.

CHAPTER 13

When I leave for home, there's someone waiting at my car.

I squint in the dark at the silent figure leaning against the bonnet. I reach for Jessie's collar, and she surprises me. She steps in front and growls at the figure. Heath is still in the water, his back to me. Even if I called out, my voice would be lost in the crashing waves.

"Minnow?"

I peer through the dark. "Colleen?"

She takes a small step forward, bundles her hands deep into her coat like she's trying to disappear inside herself. "Can you call her off?"

Colleen nods nervously at Jessie, and I realize that she hasn't stopped growling. Dazed, I reach for Jess, tucking my fingers under her white collar. "It's okay," I tell her. "It's all right."

I think.

I hang on to her collar, and the cold burns my knuckles. There are no other cars in the parking lot. No people. Just us. Colleen stands nervously in front of my car, silvery hair tucked into a black beanie, the wind brushing wisps of loose hair into her face. Jessie's hot breath steams in the darkness.

"Cold night for a walk," I say flatly.

"I heard the news . . ." she finally says. "About your poor mum. I'm so sorry, Min."

My poor mum. God, is that what she's reduced to now? My poor dead, murdered mum.

"I worked with her, remember?"

"Yeah, I remember."

She continues as if I hadn't spoken. "At the general store, on the weekends," she says more to herself. "I was the one reported her missing. It's funny but . . ." She tilts her head up, a faraway look in her eyes. "For years after, I thought she'd come walking back in."

"So did I."

"I'm so sorry, love."

I don't know what to say. Instinctively I look over my shoulder to where my brother stands knee-deep in the waves.

"Were you the one who found her?" Colleen's voice pulls me back to the present.

"What makes you ask that?"

"Just strange that the week you're back in town is the week she's finally found."

The article did not mention who discovered the body. Chris wasn't happy about it, but then, it wasn't *his* mother.

The storm's coming again. I'm so glad Mum doesn't have to spend another night outside in the cold.

Colleen shuffles closer. "They said it was blunt-force trauma to the . . . skull?"

I wince. *Blunt-force trauma.* Such a clinical way to say that someone out there struck my mum with enough force to cave in the left side of her head. My mum with her soft hands and smiles who never hurt anybody.

"Did they find the . . ." She hesitates. "The murder weapon?"

I wince again, holding a palm up as if to fend her off. "The police said they didn't."

And it's true, because we looked for it. Found nothing.

"I didn't know she was . . . dead. Didn't wanna believe that. She'd left before . . ." She lowers her head. "Lots of women 'round here do."

I see my young self, snot-nosed at the door. Waiting for Mum to come home again. "Yeah," I mutter. "I remember."

"She was with me," Colleen says. "You know that, right?"

". . . What?"

"She stayed with me, when . . ." She hesitates again, mouth grim. My chest tightens. "When he hit her?"

"That's where she went, to my house." She bites her lip. "Most of the time, anyway." I turn away, shielding my face. She reaches for me, placing a gentle hand on my shoulder, and I throw it off. "She didn't want you and Heath to see her like that."

I hold up a hand, warding her off. My throat is tight and painful. "Someone should have told us."

"Minnow." She digs in her jacket for tissues, dabs clumsily at my chin. The jacket is far too big for her small body; it swallows her. She stuffs the tissue back in her pocket and holds me by my shoulders. "She was always watching over you, you know that? Sometimes she'd walk to your school during lunchtime. Make sure you and Heath were safe."

She releases me, arms hanging loose at her sides.

That's where she went, most of the time . . .

"Where did she go the other times?"

Colleen stares at the waves with a slack expression, eyes distant and empty. "Violence does something to women. Makes them . . . not them anymore. Turns 'em into somethin' else."

"Ghosts."

She rubs the heel of her palm against her chest. "Yes."

We fall silent, watching the waves roll in, dissolving into foam on the sand. "She made it to Pine Bay a few times," she says. "Don't even know how she got there, to be honest. Local cops found her wandering the street, brought her home."

My mum didn't have a car. She walked to work, and to pick us up from school. Though, in those last few months, she'd skip days dropping us off. Heath would walk me to school while Mum retreated further and further into someone small and silent and . . .

Ghosts.

A seagull circles above, soaring on an updraft, hunting. One swoops down, lands on my car bonnet, looks in my direction, cawing.

I hold the phone up to her face, showing her the photo of Donny Granger. "Have you seen this man before?"

She squints. "I don't think so? Who is he?"

"He's also well acquainted with the woods . . ."

"Dead?"

"Murdered."

Her mouth is grim. "Your dad?"

I don't answer.

"When did he go missing?"

"Not long before Mum." I click my phone off, bury it in my pocket. "You sure you didn't see him in town?"

"No, I'm not sure. This was nearly thirty years ago, Min."

The seagull on my car bonnet inches closer.

"After Mum went missing . . ." I can't keep the sharpness out of my voice. "Why didn't you go to the police?"

"I did."

I press my palm to my heart. "Thank God, and?"

"They filed the missing person report. But she had a history of leaving, Minnow. Lots of women shoot through in towns like ours."

"But most of the times she'd left before, she went to *your* house," I argue. "And she always came back."

"And I told them that. They dragged your dad in, questioned him a few times, put the pressure on him, but he insisted he didn't know where she was."

"Heath thinks Dad killed her."

"So did Terry in the end," she admits, scraping at the dirt with her heel. "We all did." Her spine straightens, her smile cold. "But your dad got what he deserved in the end. They usually don't."

"Do you think he's still alive? Or do you think Terry killed him?"

"I think Terry killed him," she says flatly. "Wish I could take credit for it, though."

"Me too." The seagull lifts off, wings outstretched, moon glinting off its feathers. "Some people think he's still alive, you know? That he's out there somewhere . . . that he'll come back one day."

"Even if he's still alive, Min," Colleen says softly, "he won't come back."

The tide recedes and I see a shape, low and shifting, where the water meets the sand. At first, I'm not sure if I'm really seeing it. But I blink and it's still there.

"And if he does," she says heatedly, "I'll kill him myself."

The thing is moving now. Slinking, shoulders low, limbs fluid, like it learned to walk from the water itself.

Dad.

I blink again and it's gone.

"I'm sorry I didn't do more, Min." Her voice cracks. "For you . . . for Heath . . ."

I force myself to look away from the shore. "For your mum," she says softly. And it breaks something in me.

"You did what you could," I tell her.

"I didn't do enough. None of us did. And I know it's no excuse, but I had my own issues I was dealin' with at the time."

"Trav."

She nods sadly. "He was startin' to . . . act up. I'd seen it before. Felt like I was losing him."

"To what?"

I know what. But I need to hear someone else say it.

"The darkness in this town."

I stare at the vast black waves, stretching endlessly, the night wind brushing my face.

"There aren't a lot of resources for battered women and kids. They say there are, but they're lying," Colleen says hotly, and I know she's thinking of her own marriage. Trav's dad passed away when we were in second or third grade. Cancer, I think. Before that, Trav showed up to school with bruises blooming across his cheek.

"The coppers thought your dad did it. But there was no body, nothing. They couldn't keep dragging him down to the station with no new evidence." She clears her throat. "Plus, at the time, they were more interested in Hannah's attack."

Hannah Striker, the tourist attacked at beach 4. They found chunks of her flesh, bits of her torn wet suit. One piece had a tooth still wedged in it. Great white shark.

I straighten up. "When was the attack?"

"Early July, I think, 1998."

"Did you ever meet Hannah?"

"No, never heard of her before that."

". . . Donny was killed around that time."

"When?"

I try to remember. "Late July, I think. Same year."

"And your mum went missing in August . . ."

"Not missing," I say. "She was *murdered* in August."

"But nobody knew that at the time," she protests. "And nobody knows about Donny, either."

". . . And let's keep it that way."

"If you're going to look into this, you need to be careful, Minnow." She steps forward urgently. "You hear me?" She nods at the water. "That Heath down there?"

"Yeah," I say unwillingly. "Why?"

But she's already backing away, breath bursting in and out. I think that's all she's going to say, but her eyes flicker to mine. They're eerily bright in the dark as she issues a final warning.

"Be careful."

CHAPTER 14

Chris lights a cigarette and only inhales once. He holds it loosely between his index and middle fingers, and I lean back in the passenger seat, watching it burn all the way down to the filter.

"When we get to Hannah's mum's place, I'll introduce us." He taps the butt with his index finger, and ash flies out the window.

I stare down at my phone at Hannah Striker's photo. She's knee-deep in the ocean in a purple wet suit, pale-eyed, fists on her hips, long wet hair falling over her shoulder.

He pauses, gives me a sidelong look. "Maybe I'll tell her you're my assistant."

"Piss off."

"My *vulgar* assistant."

I drain the last of my coffee and wedge it into his cupholder; he stares at it bug-eyed. I pluck it out again, dump it into the waste bin neatly tucked behind my seat. He visibly relaxes.

I offered to take my car. He recoiled at the clumps of sand pooled into the grooves, the dog hair sticking to the headrests, and backed away, pretending to shudder. "We'll take mine."

His car smells of ash and pine, the seats pillowy and cool. Polished rosewood lines the door panels and the dashboard, framing a touch-screen display. The caramel seats are fully reclinable, the roof lining soft and suede.

I hate it. All of it.

I wish we'd taken my car. Wish I was tucked into its snug front seat, smelling Jessie's hair and cheese-smeared burger wrappers. Not lost in this casual opulence, giving Chris shit about the massaging seats to hide how uncomfortable I feel. How out of place. How unworthy.

"We should have just called her instead."

He shakes his head. "Whenever you can, don't call. Meet them face-to-face. Let them see you." He takes a quick puff. "You're empathetic, you're interested, and you want to hear their story."

Then he says something that leaves me sad and silent. "We're all just one person away from having no one to talk to."

"Gotta be honest." I rub my neck. "If you showed up on my doorstep, I'd slam your fingers in the door."

"May I remind you that you're the one who showed up on *my* doorstep?"

I ignore this and he reaches across my knees for the glove box. When I flinch, he draws his hand back, black Maserati watch winking in the sun. He flicks the cigarette out the window, clamps both hands on the walnut wheel.

"Sorry," he says, aghast. "I was reaching for the notepad."

The silence that follows is so awkward, it's painful.

For him.

He grips the wheel tight enough that his left knuckle goes pale. I look out my window, seeing nothing, hiding a smile, debating on whether to make the silence sting even more. This is what I want to tell Chris:

I could count on one hand the number of times Oliver and I had sex.

I imagine him side-eyeing me, hesitant and silent, until I make it even worse.

See . . . I wanted him to do things he wasn't comfortable with. That most boys aren't comfortable with.

I know this because I've asked.

"I made a list on my notes app," I tell him instead. "And there's only one question I really wanna know . . ."

He nods, grateful, loosening his grip. "Why was her daughter swimming in Kangaroo Bay, alone, in the dead of winter? A town three hours from hers. And is there any connection between Hannah and your mum?"

"No," I say, turning to face him. "There's something else . . . something far more important to ask."

"What?"

"What do sea monsters eat?"

His body deflates. "Oh, it's time for your awful puns, is it? Good to know." He nods. "I'll throw myself into oncoming traffic."

"Fish and ships."

He sighs. "How many hours until we arrive?"

I glance at Google Maps. "Two."

I place my phone face down on my lap. "Wanna play I-spy?"

"No."

"I spy with my little eye. Something beginning with *P*."

"It's not 'phone,' is it?" he asks testily.

"How'd you know?"

He exhales loudly. "I shouldn't have given you caffeine."

"I spy with my little eye . . ."

"For heaven's sake, Melanie—"

"Something beginning with *P*."

"If it's 'phone' again, I'm going to slam this car into a tree," he says, before adding, " 'Passenger seat.' "

"No."

" 'Pedal'?"

"Nope."

He leans back, frowning.

"Okay, I lied. It *was* 'phone.' "

He laughs and I feel like I've won something. Satisfied, I rest my elbow on the windowsill. "Chris?"

He gives me a wary look. "Yes?"

"If you wanna hear another fish joke—" I pause for effect. "—just let Minnow."

He sighs, reaches across for the door handle, pretends to open it. "Get the hell out."

HER NAME IS KAT, AND her house is sad as hell. Single-story, crammed into a block so small, its roof nudges the neighbors'. Two concrete pelican statues stand sadly at the front doors like forgotten sentries. One is missing half its beak, the other mottled with mold. Their eyes are beady black and desperately sad.

"Ready?" Chris asks, popping a marble-like mint into his mouth before offering one to me. I shake my head. He smooths his brick-colored hair with the flat of his palm. He's clean-shaven, skin rubbed raw, and despite this three-hour drive to Bendigo, his work shirt looks like it was ironed five minutes ago. When he raises his fist to knock, he rustles like a bag of chips.

I glance down at my navy jeans and the black cotton sleeves loose around my wrists, the angler fish tattoo just peeking through. I pull the cuff down, try to stuff it under, but it makes things worse. Now all you can see are fanglike teeth. Not a good look when you're interviewing the grieving relative of a shark mauling victim.

I blow-dried my hair before I left. When I stared at myself in the bathroom mirror, Minnow stared back. I flicked the light off, feeling like a big part of me that had been stolen had finally been returned.

The woman who opens the door has thinly plucked eyebrows and a cardigan that smells like wet cat food. She's mid-seventies with a vacant look on her face, and she holds the screen door open with her shoulder. "Yes?"

Chris inches in front of me. "Hi there, I'm Chris Cooper from the *Daily*." She stares blankly, and he adds, "The newspaper. We're working on a story about Hannah," he continues calmly. "Are you—"

"Has there been an update?"

I'm wiping the heel of my sneaker on her welcome mat when I realize what an odd question that is.

How could there be an update? Hannah was mauled to death twenty-five years ago. They found chunks of her flesh, her torn wet suit with a tooth stuck in it. Great white shark. Big one, too. Case closed.

Has there been an update?

She glances over her shoulder. "The house is a mess," she mumbles, shuffling sideways to let us in. I thank her, stepping over the welcome mat. DOGS WELCOME, PEOPLE TOLERATED, paw prints where the O's should be.

I like her already.

"I need one of those." I gesture to the mat, and she gives me a distracted smile, flattening herself against the foyer wall to let Chris in.

It's dark in here. It also smells. Chris pales at the dishes piled up in the sink and benches, slides his hands into his pockets, rustling as he does it. We step around four dog bowls overflowing with kibble and what looks like vomity water. A slate-gray cat chews silently, ignoring us. Dishcloths hang limply from a clothes drying rack in the corner. Perched atop is a long-haired white cat with magnificent green eyes. It flicks its tail as Chris hurries past.

I nod at it. "What's its name?"

She gives it an absent glance, shrugs. "Doesn't have one."

We vanish down a dark hallway, as if swallowed by a Nothingland. I know houses like this. All Nothinglands are the same. Soulless. Silent. Maddeningly so. Where cats don't have names and pelican statues are left to rot in the sun. Where the grieved sit limply on their sagging couches, waiting for nothing. I lived here, too, after my mum left. Died.

A sting of sympathy pierces my rib cage.

An elderly Jack Russell snores on an L-shaped couch in the lounge room. Crossword magazines are dumped on the coffee table next to half-empty mugs bubbling with blue mold.

But it's the knickknacks I can't stop staring at. There's a shitload of them. Hundreds even, lining the windowsills, crammed into two display cabinets. They don't look like collectibles. They look like the kind that cost fifty cents at the op shop. And yet, someone has taken great care to display them.

Kat catches me staring. "Hannah's," she mumbles, picking up a royal-blue robin and cradling it gently in her palm. "Never could stand them meself."

I nod at the windowsill where a pelican sits, mouth open wide like he's waiting for a fish to be thrown in. "Reminds me of the ones at the door."

The soulless ones guarding their Nothingland.

She walks stiffly to the rocking chair under the window, groaning when she sits down. "She always had a thing for pelicans."

Chris picks up a porcelain cat with a chipped ear. "She was living with you at the time of the attack?"

"Yeah, I used to tell Hannah that as soon as her back was turned, they were all going in the bin." She shakes her head, half smile on her lips. "She went outta her way to pick the ugliest ones," she says more to herself. "Think she felt bad for 'em."

I nod at the sagging couch. "Do you mind?"

Chris trips over a pair of kicked-off slippers and the dog bolts awake, staring blankly at him like it's never seen a visitor before.

"You like dogs?" Kat asks.

I sit down, holding out the back of my hand to the dog, who blinks at me. "Love them. I have a goldie at home. Jessie."

Chris hovers at the display cabinet while the dog whale-eyes him. "Does he bite?"

"Yeah," she says, unconcerned. "Heard there was another attack in Kangaroo Bay. Have they identified the victim yet?"

"No."

She stares out a grimy blind, sucking her teeth. "Their poor family."

Has there been an update?

I pull out my phone. "Can you tell us about Hannah?"

She flicks an eyebrow up, exhaling, like she hasn't been asked that for a very long time. The ceiling fan whirs while we wait for her response. When I'm sure she's not looking, I jerk my head at Chris, give him a *sit down on the bloody couch* motion. He grimaces at the dog, sidling past it, and sits so close to me that his knee touches mine.

"She was always up for adventure," Kat finally says. "Bit of a handful, to be honest. A rule breaker. She loved the water, swimming, kayaking, diving. Full of life, she was." She pauses, eyes darkening. "Nobody deserves to die like that."

I spent last night reading about Hannah's attack. The word that kept coming up was *horror*.

The beaches across Kangaroo Bay will be closed this week after a swimmer died from "catastrophic injuries" in a horror shark attack.

Remains of the swimmer were later found, including half a wet suit, in what police describe as a horrifying scene . . .

No one witnessed the attack. Her car was found abandoned at beach 4 on July 4, 1998. My mum went missing a month later.

"What brought her to Kangaroo Bay?" Chris asks. "It's not exactly the nicest area."

"Why's that?"

Chris nudges me.

"It's a fishing town," I explain. "Insular. Lots of grizzled old men, drunken brawls on a Friday night. The streets aren't safe. But the beaches . . . the beaches are worse. In areas where there's a lot of fishing activity, there tend to be higher rates of shark sightings and attacks. Because when the fish get caught on lines, the vibrations bring the sharks in."

Her eyes are absent, mouth grim. She says something low under her breath; I don't catch it.

"There's a lot of beautiful beaches between here and Kangaroo Bay." I lean forward and try to say the next part as tactfully as I can. "It's a strange place to swim alone and at night."

Chris pipes in, "Hannah was traveling by herself, wasn't she?"

"On that trip, yes," she says. "She'd made a bunch of new friends through her diving club. I called them her Water Mates. They were always surfing or diving up and down the coast. Lakes Entrance, the Mornington Peninsula, Phillip Island," she lists. "Warrnambool."

Donny left his home in Warrnambool in a white Mitsubishi Sigma in mid-July . . .

I bolt to my feet, and the dog lifts its head. I crouch over Kat, thrusting Donny's picture in front of her face. "Do you recognize this man?"

She squints at the photo, leaning closer and closer until her nose actually bumps the screen.

"I need my glasses," she mutters, fumbling for the side table. Her elbow juts out and a dusty candle goes flying, an empty vase wobbling like a bowling pin. I could scream.

She slips her reading glasses on and snatches my phone, bringing it to her chest. I dart a glance at Chris, who sits rigid on the couch, sweating.

"Yes. I recognize him."

Slow motion. I see myself turning back to Kat, my mouth falling open.

"I mighta met him once or twice," she mumbles, chin dipping low to her chest, still staring. "A friend of Hannah's."

"A friend since when? Had they known each other long? When was the last time you saw him?"

I hit her with questions as hot blood rushes in my ears. *Hannah knew Donny Granger. Hannah was killed in a horrific attack. My father killed Donny. Mum was murdered.*

My father is missing.

Kat passes my phone back, lowering her glasses to the bridge of her nose. "He was one of her Water Mates, I think. One of the new crowd."

"Was he meeting her in Kangaroo Bay on that trip?"

She frowns, sucks her teeth again. "I don't think so."

Chris speaks slowly, but I can feel he's as frantic as I am. "Are you sure? You said they met up with each other along the coast . . . and Kangaroo Bay isn't the sort of place a girl would travel to alone."

She's already shaking her head. "You didn't know Hannah. She often traveled alone. Even camped in her car by herself. We—" She breaks off, looks down. "We had a few tiffs about it."

The Jack Russell scoots closer to Chris, panting, showing nubs of yellowing teeth.

"This guy," I finally say, gesturing to my phone. "Do you know that he went missing, too?"

"I heard," she murmurs. "Few months after Han. I'm not that surprised."

It wasn't a few months after. They went missing at almost at the same time. Chris gives me an urgent look that I ignore.

I'm not that surprised.

I look up. "Why weren't you surprised he went missing?"

"Some of these Water Mates of hers . . ." She tucks her glasses back into their case. "They were a bit, I dunno. Dodgy?"

"How?"

She shrugs. "Just a feeling, you know? The *check your purse after they leave* sort of feeling. I didn't like them coming 'round here. I wish I'd spoken up more. Wish she'd listened."

Has there been an update?

"Can't stop accidents from happening," I murmur, eyes boring into hers.

She stares at me levelly. "It was no accident."

"They . . . found her, though?" Chris says, uncomfortably. "Injuries consistent with a shark attack."

What was left of her anyway.

"It wasn't an accident."

"I think—"

"I know what everyone *thinks*." She hisses the last word. "But something came for her before she died. Dropped off on the bloody doorstep."

Chris and I exchange looks. "What?"

"Follow me."

CHAPTER 15

When the garage door thuds closed, I think to myself, *We've made a huge mistake.* My eyes adjust to the shadowy dark, and the first thing I see is the nautical ship wheel hanging on the back of the door. A clock is nestled inside the circle, showing the wrong time. A blowfly bumps against a soiled window, buzzing weakly. A white-tailed spider lazes above it, sucking on a wasp corpse.

She's trapped us in the heart of Nothingland. She is going to leave us whining and begging in the dark.

I reach for a light switch, flicking it up with my palm. Fluorescent light beams overhead, so bright it burns. But, God, it's cold in here, a low, lingering chill that makes me pull my sleeves down further. The concrete floor is cold and hard, seeping up through my soles and not letting go.

And something else. It stinks in here. A thick sour smell that's settled into the walls, the floor. Chris wrinkles his nose, and I try not to breathe too deeply. The room is too small for a smell like this. There are no open windows, just stagnant air and that lingering funk. Whatever's causing the smell, it's been here awhile.

I step forward as the smell of decay transports me back to Kangaroo Bay. A metallic, fishy smell that makes the tourists cover their noses. But this is even worse. It's a meaty smell, rancid and oily. Rotting.

"It wasn't delivered by post," Kat says, digging around under a workbench. "It was dropped off on the doorstep at night. I don't know by who."

Chris inspects the brick wall before gingerly leaning against it. Kat straightens up, puts her hands on her hips, huffing. "Where the hell is it?"

"We can help you look?" Chris offers but makes no attempt to move. "Just let us know what we're looking for."

I stare at the white-tailed spider still munching away on a wasp husk. "That's why you asked if there'd been an update. You want to know who sent it."

"I called the police," she confesses, peeking into a cardboard box. "Local copper showed up, took a few photos, wrote a report. I never heard anything after that."

"How long did it arrive before her attack? And did Hannah see it?"

"Few weeks, I think, and yeah, she saw it." She crouches in front of a plastic tub. "She kept it hidden in her bedroom closet. Stunk the whole house out. That's how I found them . . . after." She wrinkles her nose, staring grimly inside the tub. "I've preserved them best as I could."

Chris straightens up like he's been shot, blurts out, "Holy shit . . ."

I'm so stunned to hear him swear that my attention is pulled to him. My head snaps in his direction, but out of the corner of my eye, I see it. I see her straining to lift something from the box, something massive. She staggers under its weight, and when I realize what it is, I forget everything else.

We don't move to help her. We can't.

She's holding the jaws of a great white shark. The tips of the front row of teeth poke the top of her head; the bottom teeth scrape her belly button. Even in their lifeless state, they carry an unnerving presence. You're not meant to see this. This *hunter*. This brutal masterpiece, evidence of the evil deep. It's awe inspiring, *horrifying*.

God, I think. *Hannah. She saw this for real.* She saw the top jaw, the color of sour milk, curved in a terrifying arc of teeth. She saw them coming for her, felt their serrated blades saw into her flesh. Saw that lower jaw jut forward, opening and snapping shut on her legs, arms . . . head.

I lift the jaws from Kat's hands, holding the cartilage tight in my palms, staring inside the gaping mouth, thinking of Hannah. Of the woman I saw on the first night back in Kangaroo Bay.

Not women anymore.

Just scraps.

"Why would she keep these?"

"Knowing Han, she probably thought they were cool. For a long time, I wondered if she'd bought them through her dodgy mates or something. She was into things like that. But after her attack, when I found them . . ." She shakes her head. "I called the police, but they were useless."

"I covered the Tommy Cortney case," Chris says. "Four-year-old kid. Went missing from his backyard in Tassie. The public thinks the mum's hiding something, and some asshole threw a pig's head on her porch. They found the boy three days later in the woods, alive. He'd wandered off. Maybe some sicko heard about Hannah, thought it'd be funny to leave a fake set of jaws on her doorstep," Chris finishes.

I press the pad of my index finger into the tip of a back tooth, feel the sting. They don't feel fake.

Kat shakes her head. "These were sent *before* her attack."

He hesitates. "Are you certain?"

"I am," she says. "And they were in her room. She put them there herself."

"It was no prank," I tell Chris. Kat breathes in, giving me a hopeful look that says, *You believe me, don't you?*

I do.

"Something came for Chris, too," I tell Kat. "A shark tooth, tucked under his car windshield wiper."

Chris goes still, eyes locking on mine. *You shouldn't have told her that,* his eyes say.

I draw the jaws closer until my nose bumps a bottom tooth. The smell is terrible. The tissues and cartilage have broken down, releasing putrescine and cadaverine, by-products of decay. And something else, sharp and acrid. Ammonia.

I press the pad of my index finger down harder, then draw my throbbing finger away, inspecting the blood trickling down the tip.

Everything goes silent, that sharp, *something's wrong* kind of silence. The air is thick with it. My skin prickles, my stomach sinks.

I think of the shark tooth under Chris's windshield wiper. And then the thought comes in, landing heavy and final.

I stare at the jaws, at the rows of teeth arched like a cruel smile. At the serrated edges shining in the dark, each one razor-sharp and monstrous.

"These aren't pranks," I say. "These are *warnings.*"

CHAPTER 16

Shark attack victim identified as tourist Rachel Sutherland

The Daily
by Chris Cooper

Human remains found at a Kangaroo Bay beach earlier this month have been identified as belonging to a Bethanga resident. Rachel Sutherland, 47, suffered catastrophic injuries after being attacked by a great white shark while swimming.

I hover behind Chris, reading over his shoulder and staring at the grainy photo of Rachel Sutherland. She's sitting alone at a picnic table, blond and bare-faced, smiling drowsily in the sun. I blink and she's missing limbs, blink again and she's bloodied chunks of meat bobbing in the seawater.

"They identified her this afternoon," he says, clacking away on his keyboard, eyes on the screen. "You don't want to see the photos."

"Don't need to," I tell him. "I was there."

He freezes, hands floating over the keyboard. "You were *there*? And you didn't think to tell me?"

"I'm telling you now."

"... What was it like?"

"Meaty."

He winces, holding my gaze for a moment before looking away. He grabs at a half-empty water bottle, takes a tiny sip. I watch him screw the cap back on, watch his mouth flatten into a grim line. It's quiet now, tense. The ceiling fan whirs, blowing stale air; otherwise the room is as still as a painting.

"Melanie..." Chris finally says, "I'm starting to wonder..."

I raise an eyebrow he doesn't see.

He twists at the bottle cap, lets it roll between his fingers. "You always seem to be in the right place at the right time..."

"It was a fatal shark attack, Chris. I wouldn't call witnessing it the right time."

"What were you doing there?"

"I was on the *Deep Sea*," I say, "Heath's fishing charter. Used to be my dad's."

"I spoke to one of the charter tourists." Chris frowns. "Alan Wright, I think? I tried to speak with Heath but he wouldn't comment."

I say nothing.

"Alan said she was on a night swim?"

I nod. "Near the pier."

"Did you see anything else?"

"No, it was too dark." I gesture to his screen. "When's your deadline?"

"Eleven," he finally answers. He nods at my laptop, eyes narrowing. "What are *you* working on?"

I angle the screen in his direction, displaying it, hatefully.

AFL star Tim Botkin tied the knot with influencer Lucy Graham in an extravagant ceremony at the stunning Three Bees Villa in Tuscany on Monday. The newlyweds gave fans a glimpse inside their lavish celebration on social media.

"Riveting," Chris mumbles petulantly. "Make sure to use the spellchecker."

"Piss off." I flick through the photos of the forty-two-thousand-dollar-a-night villa. "I hope they choke on their wedding cake."

"We all do."

I smile gratefully. "Are we mates again?"

For a long moment, he doesn't answer. Outside, a shutter bangs against a doorframe. I find myself leaning forward, my left knee brushing his. "Or do you think I'm gill-ty of something?"

He rolls his eyes at the pun, but I notice him softening. Relieved, I glance around his Airbnb study in Pine Bay, nodding approvingly at the glass desk and the carpet, soft and salmon pink. "Nice room."

"I write it off on tax," he mumbles, before standing up, stretching. "Dinner, too." Grudgingly, he asks, "You hungry?"

Rachel's meaty body drifts through my head, floating in a bloody current.

"... Yeah."

I BALANCE A PIZZA SLICE on my knee while proofreading my latest bullshit article, BABY JOY FOR *HOME AND AWAY* STAR!

I lean back, sighing. I've written four articles tonight. Enough for the next few weeks' rent, food, and emergency fund in case Joy sues me. But I doubt she will be considering the recent *Daily* article.

Morning, Sunshine! host Joy Marriot investigated for scamming cancer charity

> *In 2019, Logie-winning TV presenter Joy Marriot was praised after publicly vowing to donate 15 percent of her cookbook proceeds to Kids with Cancer. But as of January 2024, there is no record of any payments directly on her behalf.*

Chris made a few phone calls, confirmed what I already knew. Then he leaned back in his chair, stunned, pinching the bridge of his nose. "How the hell did she get away with it for so long?"

I was thinking of Kangaroo Bay when I answered, "The only thing necessary for the triumph of evil..."

"Is for good men to do nothing," he said brightly, nudging me with his elbow. "Well, we did something. Something good."

We did. How fantastic it was seeing that woman finally exposed. How delightful her guilty eyes looked above the condemning headline,

Joy Marriot pulled from Morning, Sunshine! Host investigated for charity fraud.

I saved the article to my home screen, re-read it constantly. All my life, I've watched people break the rules. And now, *finally*, they're answering for them.

Sometimes I re-read the texts from my lunch friends, too:

HAHA! Take that Joy, you nasty bitch!

They're saying you "attacked" her because of her charity fraud. People love you, Mel!

Are you coming back from exile now? We miss you.

I glance at Chris, who's carefully picking off the olives from his slice, placing them in an obliging ashtray. It's late now, ten-ish, quiet except for the muffled sounds of a baby crying next door.

I proofread the celebrity wedding article again, eyes sticking from hours of screen time. *AFL star Tim Botkin tied the knot with influencer...*

Chris flicks an olive at my face. It misses, sticking wetly to my shoulder before rolling into my lap. "Did you and Oliver have your wedding planned out?"

"No," I say, nodding at the villa. "But he would have loved something like that."

"And you?"

I shake my head. "I'd like something quiet. Elope on a beach."

"While the sharks watch."

"That would be jaw-some."

"Where do you get all these awful jokes? The back of a toilet door?"

I smile, remembering. "My brother. We used to know hundreds."

I nudge him with my foot. "Guess what food we'd serve at the wedding?"

He scrunches his face up before announcing triumphantly, "A shark-uterie board!"

"Excellent." I smile. "And the wedding song?"

"... 'No-Fin Compares to You.' "

"Not bad, but I've got a better one."

He raises an eyebrow, waits.

"Journey's smash hit 'Don't Stop Bleeding.' "

"Oh my God." He nods at his laptop. "Reminds me of Rachel's attack photos." I lean forward, interested, but he waves me away. "I hope her family don't see them."

"Are they all in Bethanga?"

He nods. "For the last year, Rachel had been living on the family property there."

"Why?"

"Her marriage broke up. She was staying with her parents to get back on her feet."

"And now she *has* no feet."

"Melanie..." Chris grimaces, gives me a disapproving look.

"Sorry." I lean back. "Do you know why she was in Kangaroo Bay?"

"Her mum wasn't very forthcoming about that." He sighs, rubbing his neck. "I called earlier."

"When are you going up there?"

"I asked to see her on Tuesday afternoon," he says, frowning. "Whether she opens the door or not is another story."

"And then you squeeze her for answers like a big, juicy puffer fish?"

His lips twitch. "*We* squeeze her for answers, yes. Or you could pepper her with your fish puns until she confesses."

"I'm not coming with you."

"... What?"

I press my hands flat on my thighs. "You go without me. It's better this way."

His eyes narrow. "Why?"

Silence.

"Chris, I'd like to speak with her myself."

He rests both arms behind his head, leaning back so far on his chair that it squeaks in protest. "I don't understand."

"You don't have to."

"What do you know that I don't?"

I shake my head, keep my voice light. "I'm doing you a favor. Bethanga is five hours from Kangaroo Bay. Do you know how many fish puns I could cram into a five-hour drive?" I nudge him with my knee. "You'd assassinate me."

He shifts his knee, angling it away from mine. Gently, I reach forward, pushing it back. "You know what they say. Keep your friends close and your anemones closer."

The tips of my fingers still rest on his knee. His hands are behind his head, cuffs rolled up to his elbow, revealing spidery veins running down his pale wrists. The boys at home are sunburned from infancy. It's odd to see a man so pale—fascinating, to be honest. His eyes are fixed on my fingertips brushing his knee. His breath hitches, and it's as if he's trying to keep himself very still.

I pull back.

He gives me a sidelong glance as I get to my feet and swig from his water bottle, just to give my hands something to do. I hear him sigh, hear the creak of his chair as he finally shifts in place, muttering wearily, "Fine, go by yourself, then. You're my nemo-sis now."

"You're krilling me."

"You have much to be *schooled* on."

"Makes sense. I didn't go to school."

He pauses. "What?"

"I was homeschooled from grade six to year twelve."

He gives me a puzzled look. "Who taught you? Your dad?"

"No one taught me. It was different back then. It used to be called distance education," I tell him. "They'd mail you a semester's worth of work, leave you to it. If you fell behind, they'd give you a ring. That was about it."

"There's a school in Kangaroo Bay, though," he says, frowning.

"I drove past it. One of those primary and high schools in one. Prep to year twelve."

Stupid. I should've kept my mouth shut. "Yeah, I went there."

He pauses. "Until?"

I shrug. "Until I decided I'd rather learn at home." I pointedly add, "No annoying boys asking me questions."

I turn back to my laptop, uneasy, hoping he'll drop the subject. Of course, he doesn't. I hear him shift his weight. I can almost see him crossing his arms, eyes locked on me.

"Did anything happen that made you change schools all of a sudden?" His words hang in the air, heavy with suspicion. "*And* change your name . . ."

Shit. I open my mouth, feeling caught out. I throw him a quick smile, too quick. I keep my laugh light, casual, like everything's fine. Like I didn't notice the shift in the room. "Yes, I know the rumors about homeschooled kids."

For a moment, he doesn't respond. My heart stutters. I watch his face, hoping for even the flicker of a smile, anything at all that will break this tension. His eyes are unblinking, steady, like he's trying to look past my skin and into something deeper. Then he uncrosses his arms, snorts, and the air finally loosens. "That you're a bunch of weirdos?"

"Let me guess, you went to a private school. Your socks were pulled all the way up. You cried if you didn't get homework."

"You were there?"

"It was an all-boys school, wasn't it?"

"I'm not talking to you anymore," he groans, leaning forward. "And my deadline's tonight."

"I understand," I reply, staring hatefully at my laptop.

"Got to get this story *hot off the gill*," he automatically replies, before adding, "I hate myself."

CHAPTER 17

There's a monster in this book. You just haven't spotted them yet.

I sit at the edge of my bed, leafing through the soft pages of a picture book. Mum read it to me as a child. Just once. It's one of those "monsters aren't real, it's just your imagination" lessons.

But they were wrong, I knew it even then. I look at the picture again. There, under the child's bed, something is hiding. Waiting and watching like a shark under the surface. Sometimes, you have to squint to see it.

The monster.

Mum started to turn the page, but I reached out, pointed at the monster and said, "Daddy."

I still remember the look on her face.

I close the book and place it gently on my pillow. Outside my bedroom window, Jessie sniffs at the garden beds. Heath's on life-saving duties, so he won't be home for another few hours.

I lie flat on my back, sling my forearm over my eyes. My head hurts. There are so many strange pieces to this puzzle, and I don't know how to put them all together. Are there any connections among my mum, Donny, and Hannah? If so, what? And what is it about the story that makes me feel like I'm missing something completely? Like there's something in the back of my brain that I can't quite reach?

I rise slowly, not quite admitting to myself where I'm going. Head down, I walk past the silent kitchen and stop outside my father's room. My muscles tighten. My body is physically telling me to turn around.

Even as a child, I never entered his room. Never wanted to. He kept the curtains and windows drawn, all day, all night. His life was ruled by the tides, and because of this, his sleeping hours shifted with the moon. When he was sleeping, we learned to tiptoe around the house, jaws clenched so hard it hurt. Not that our silence mattered. He was always groggy and furious no matter how quiet we were.

If his life was dominated by the tides, then our lives were dominated by his moods. If you greeted him with a polite and cautious, "Hello," he'd either ignore you or reel back and show his teeth like a twitchy wolf.

If you *didn't* greet him, he'd throw up his hands and bark, "Aren't I even *good enough* for a hello?"

He left me reeling and stupid. Made my mouth a jail, and all my words prisoners. The longer I was under his roof, the smaller my voice became.

I'm doing it again. Tiptoeing, clenching my jaw.

He's gone, I tell my body. *He's not coming back.*

Are you sure? it asks. *Are you sure are you sure are you sure?*

I open the door and step inside before I change my mind. My father's room smells like the sea. The sharp bite of salt, a heavy brine that clings to my nose. There's a dampness here, an ancient stillness. It feels like I'm underwater.

I hold my sleeve to my nose. The navy sheets on his double bed are scrunched at the end of the bed like old toilet paper. Crusty plaid shirts are still slung over the bedpost, like they're waiting for him to come back.

So dark, so filthy, so *Dad.*

I kneel beside his bed, peek under. But there's only a pair of dirt-caked boots. I reach for them, inspecting the insides, not even sure what I'm looking for. Nothing. I lift the scrunched sheets and sweep my arm under: empty. I sit stiffly on the end of my father's bed, looking around the small, filthy room. My eyes fix on his hideous wardrobe. It's taller than me, nearly as wide as his double bed. For the first time, I wonder why he needed such a huge wardrobe. It's not like he owned many clothes, and God knows he never hung them up.

I walk slowly to the wardrobe, reach for the brass handle, and pull it open. Only darkness and a pair of green waders, half spilling out of a drawer. I stare at the waders, feeling sick. Dad owned two pairs. He was wearing the others when he went missing. They were never recovered.

Leave, my body insists. *Please.*

I don't. I reach for the top drawer, just above my head, and slide it out. Inside is one of those old Peters Ice Cream tubs, filled with nails, screws, a pair of binoculars, and two dead moths.

In the next drawer is a bottle of cough medicine, half empty.

The final drawer. With the heavy waders half stuffed in, it's a struggle to pull it open. I reach inside instead, shoving my hand under the waders, feeling for anything else in the drawer. But I find nothing.

I kneel down. It's so dark that I reach for my phone and flick on the torchlight. I shine it at the base of the wardrobe. I peer inside the other two pairs of boots, even lifting them up and shaking them to see if anything falls loose. But nothing does.

I sit back on my heels, hands on my knees, frustrated. And that child part of my brain urges me to finish up and leave the monster's lair.

Leave, leave, leave.

No.

I stare at the waders, thinking. I yank the drawer open, and the hinges yell in protest. I tug and tug until the drawer comes tumbling out. It falls at my feet, and I pull the waders onto my lap, inspecting them. I reach my hand inside the left pocket: nothing. I try the other pocket, and my fingers finally touch something. It's palm-sized, the edges sharp. Heart thumping, I pull it out.

A diving club membership.

I shine my torch on it, staring at the small photo on the front. Black hair, dark eyes slightly narrowed. I pull the license closer to my face. Yes, that's my father's photo.

But that's not his name.

Michael Hunt.

I read the name over and over. Michael Hunt. Down Under Diving, Doncaster, Victoria. Doncaster is two hours away. Fifteen kilometers east of Melbourne.

She'd made a bunch of new friends through her diving club...

Dazed, I place the license on my knee and google Down Under Diving. The homepage is a wide, vivid shot of open water, sunlight streaming down into deep blue. Photos are scattered across the site: wrecks draped in shadow, close-ups of masked faces grinning through mouthpieces.

I call Kat and she picks up on the fifth ring. "Hello?"

I lick my lips, suddenly breathless. "Hi, Kat. This is Melanie Greenwood." My voice is too high, strained. "I came to interview you the other day."

Eagerly, she asks, "Have you got an update?"

I pause, picking up the license, rolling it in my fingers. "Do you remember the name of Hannah's diving club?"

She pauses for a long time, and I add, "The one where she met her Water Mates."

She clicks her tongue, and I hold my breath.

"It's been twenty-plus years," she finally murmurs. I can almost see her shaking her head. "I don't remember the exact name. It was in Melbourne, though."

"Doncaster?"

"I'm not sure. I'll search her room. See if I can find something?"

"That would be great, thanks." I stare at Dad's license. "It wasn't Down Under Diving Club, was it?"

Silence. I press my lips together.

"I'm not sure," she says. "Maybe." A chair squeaks and Kat groans. "I'm going to look now. Why do you need to know? Has there been an update?"

"I don't know yet," I tell her. "Let me know if you find the name."

She agrees, and I end the call, staring at my dad's license and the fake name on it.

What were you up to, Dad?

What have you done?

CHAPTER 18

Beach 1 is burning. Even with my cap pulled low over my forehead, I'm still squinting. The water is so bright, it hurts to look at it. It's late afternoon, when the sun's at its hottest, and there are no clouds, no breeze, nothing but the huge sun reflecting off the water, burning the sand. The heat nips at my ankles. I didn't want to come down, but Heath called and told me to meet him here. He didn't sound happy.

The beach is packed with people shielded under colorful umbrellas, talking lazily in the sun. Children bob in the shallows, parents hovering beside them. Teenagers jump over waves, knees lifted high, racing one another into the water. Groups of surfers lie flat on their boards, floating in the deep, arms dangling at their sides.

I think of Rachel Sutherland, Hannah Striker. Swimming lazy laps in the water, flat on their backs, chins tilted to the burning sky. I bet they thought they were safe, too. Hannah's mum finally got back to me this morning. She found one of Hannah's old caps with the diving club logo embroidered on the brim.

DOWN UNDER DIVING.

The same club Dad belonged to.

I called them before I came here, but the disinterested man who answered had only been working there a year. He'd never heard of Hannah Striker or Michael Hunt.

I inch around a woman lying face down on her towel, shoulders red with sunburn. They closed the beaches for twenty-four hours after Rachel's attack. But it's the summer holidays, and kids aren't back at school yet. They're hot and bored, and their parents are willing to take the risk.

I'm not going in that water.

I shield my eyes from the sun, scanning the beach.

And I find them.

Colleen is on garbage patrol, dragging her bag across the sand. Heath stands at the edge of the sentry chair, arms crossed, alert and still, eyes fixed on the water. He's not just *looking* at the ocean, he's reading it. His lifesaving shift is over, but he's still on guard. Always on guard. Scanning for the split second when everything changes. Every shift in the tide, every glint on the surface, every call, he's waiting, watching, acting before it's too late.

I hate it for him. That fear, that constant watchfulness. We learned it from Dad. Learned to be ready, vigilant, always waiting for the worst to happen.

Heath pivots a little, eyes fixed on the surfers scattered out across the break.

One of them is Trav.

My stomach tightens and I reach instinctively for my car keys. I could leave. I could go home to Jessie and pretend I didn't see the flash of anger in my brother's eyes as he looked Trav over. But I don't. I press forward, head down.

Colleen hovers behind a young couple packing up for the day, wringing out their towels, bending over to loop beach bags over their shoulders. She waits impatiently for them to leave, like a waiter itching to clear a table.

"Find anything good?" I ask her.

She looks up with dull surprise. "Just trying to clean up the mess." There's something hopeless about the way she says it. She adjusts her tennis visor with a free hand, yanking it lower, glowering at the sun.

I stand in front of her, blocking it out. "And how's that going for you?"

"Not great." She flicks her wrist and dumps the bag on the sand, a can of Sprite tumbling out. "And you?"

We share a smile.

"It's a funny thing about this town, isn't it? No matter how much you tidy up, it'll never be clean."

"Maybe," she admits, reaching for the Sprite can. "But I'm going to try just the same."

We say goodbye and I head to the sentry chair, sand clinging to my ankles.

A toddler waddles past, pink water wings attached to her wrists. Her mother follows behind, patient and smiling.

"Hey, Min." My brother turns before I even call out, a stormy expression on his face. His jaw's tight, and there's that stillness in his shoulders like something's rubbed him the wrong way.

"What's wrong?"

He glances at the surfers paddling lazily on the sparkling sea. Since I've been home, I've only spoken to Trav once. Even then, Heath had called me away. After that, we didn't bring him up again.

Truth is, we haven't really talked about Trav since he was sent away as a child. Maybe it's time we did.

"That Trav out there?" I finally ask, not waiting for an answer. "When did he come back to town?"

His face twitches. "Few years ago. I've been keeping an eye on him since then."

"Has he gotten into any trouble since he came home?"

"No," he admits.

"And he won't, either."

Unless I ask him to.

Heath scans my face. "You sure about that?"

"Yes, I am."

"I'm not, Minnow." He closes his eyes, summons a deep breath. Holds it.

Four teen girls sprint past, long hair swishing down their suntanned backs. They charge the water, shrieking.

We're still dancing around the obvious, but it's there under the surface. Heavy. Loud.

"I remember . . ." I begin, faltering for a moment. "I remember the day they told us Trav wouldn't be coming back to school," I finally continue. "Nobody knew why." I pause. "But I did."

"Police sealed the file," he says quietly.

"Lucky for him."

"And you."

I feel Heath fix his eyes on me, and I wait for him to speak. Wait for him to ask about Amy. He hesitates, the question caught behind his teeth. I take a breath, shallow and tight, as his words come slower than I expected. Careful. "Can I ask you something?"

Everything feels louder, the crash of the waves, the cries of the seagulls, my heartbeat.

"Do you know why Trav . . ." He pauses, staring at him like he wants to blow his lifeguard whistle. "Why he hurt Amy like that?"

"No."

He looks at me, eyebrows lowering like he doesn't believe me but wants to. He might think he needs the truth, but I'm not sure he's ready to carry it. So I lie again. "I don't know why. I wasn't there, Heath."

A jogger rushes past, steady and focused, headphones on. We watch until his footsteps are swallowed by the tide. I wait, silently hopeful that my brother has nothing else to say.

But he does.

"That journalist." He clears his throat. "The one that was asking around here last week . . ."

"What about him?"

"You know him?"

I shrug. "Mighta run into him in Melbourne. Why?"

There it is again. The squaring of his shoulders, the stillness, the tightening of his jaw. "Miss McKenzie . . . remember her? Your fifth-grade teacher, yours and Trav's?"

I remember her. I see her paused at the blackboard as the cop comes charging in. The cop's voice was flat, gruff. We couldn't hear what he said, but I knew.

There's been an accident. One of your students.

She scans the empty seat, the one between Trav and me. It was where Amy Anderson sat, happily sandwiched between us for most of the year. Until she wasn't happy at all. A week before the stabbing, she'd asked to be moved to the front row. As far away from us as she could get. Today that seat was empty, too.

Amy. Is she okay?

Stabbed. Left for dead in the woods.

I see my teacher's eyelids shut, chalk falling from her fingertips. The cop leans in, voice taut. *I need to speak to Travis.*

And Minnow.

"Yeah, I remember her."

"I see her in town every now and then," Heath says. "She lives 'round the corner. Retired now."

That's not quite true. She retired that year. That month. One lazy afternoon, Trav and I passed a pineapple juice box back and forth, taking small sips to make it last. Amy sat stiffly between us, elbows tucked in, trying to read. Trav slurped the rest, juice dripping from his chin. He blew up the paper carton until it was bloated and whistling. Then he crushed it between his hands, and it exploded like a gunshot. Amy bolted from her seat, white-faced, sweating. Miss McKenzie looked up from her yogurt, said nothing.

And a month later, all of us were gone. I don't remember what month it was. I should.

"What about her?" I finally ask, digging my toes into the sand.

"That journalist went to see her."

Slowly, I lift my head. "When?"

"Yesterday."

Yesterday I was poking around Dad's room until Heath came home. We took Jessie to beach 2, spent the afternoon fishing for mullet.

I fix my eyes on Trav. He's sitting up on his board, looking at the sky.

"The journo's been following these shark attacks. He covered Mum's . . . death, too. He's probably looking into Hannah's attack, trying to get a quote. Miss McKenzie is a long-term resident," I tell him, tell myself. "It's good to get quotes from the locals. For the story, I mean."

Heath's eyes settle on me, steady, quiet, and too still. "No. He's not investigating Hannah," he says. "He's investigating *you.*"

THEN

The silent girl sits on a plastic chair in the principal's office, both hands wrapped around a Coke can. The uneasy policeman sits opposite, forearms resting on the desk. "I know it's been a bit hard at home lately, Minnow."

She blinks at him like an insect, wordless.

He clears his throat, reaches self-consciously forward to pat her arm. Police can question children without parental consent, but he feels guilty just the same.

Her skin is smooth and cold. He draws his hand back. "Tell me about your mum."

"She's gone."

"She's been gone before," he says. "I'm sure she'll come back."

Danielle Greenwood always comes back. Still, they've spoken to her shithead husband, Peter. Hauled him in for questioning, twice. Listened to him swear and snarl, wounded for himself and not at all for his missing wife. "Always the bloody husband, isn't it? She's shot through, and it's not the first time, either."

And dammit, he's right. Colleen Holloway admitted as much. Danielle usually fled to her house after her bastard husband hit her. But not always.

The afternoon Danielle went missing, Peter was snapper fishing off the Deep Sea. Eyewitness saw the boat at beach 1. They're fairly confident Peter was skippering it. Fairly.

"Charge me with somethin' or get farked," Peter Greenwood had snarled.

But they have nothing to charge him with. And they can't keep bringing him in here with no new evidence. There's no body. No crime scene. Just a woman with a DV history who'd finally had a gutful and left.

And good on her.

They're keeping an eye on Peter. Dragging his dodgy mates in for questioning, and they're getting a bit bloody sick of it. Especially Terry Hargrave. Terry's a good sort, and he's not happy at all about this Danielle business. Bit soft on her, he was. And now she's gone, dead or fled, and either way, her husband's to blame. If I were Peter Greenwood, I'd be really bloody worried about Terry Hargrave.

The cop isn't too worried about Danielle. But he's sweating bullets about her daughter.

"You're mad she's gone," he says, raising a brow. "Aren't you?"

She blinks again.

A knock at the door.

The police sergeant steps in, impassive and unreadable. "Mind if I take over?" She has a soft way of speaking, like a sigh. The uneasy policeman goes to squeeze Minnow's arm on his way out, stuffs his hands in his pockets instead.

The door closes softly. The sergeant sits down, crosses her legs at the knee. Silence. Too much of it. Most of the kids have gone home for the day. The school principal waits for them in the teachers' lounge, picking nervously at a biscuit tray.

"Minnow," the sergeant finally says, leaning forward. "I want to talk about Trav. He's your friend, isn't he?"

The girl considers this. She's not sure what they are. Three years ago, Trav was slow and annoying, stuttering over the simplest words during reading-out-loud time in the library.

Two years ago, she'd nod as she passed him, cannonballing off the pier.

Last week, she stood over him as he knelt shirtless in the creek, his wrist stuffed in her mouth. She bit down deep, left baby teeth marks in his skin. After, he'd worn his school jumper all week—on purpose. Never took it off, not even after muddy, sweat-soaked games of football. Kept it on to hide the marks. For her.

That meant something. It meant that he would keep her secrets. That he understood what she needed even if she couldn't explain why.

She'd started biting her palms that summer. Wasn't sure why. Knew only that it helped dull the anger fizzling in her skull.

She'd trail Trav to the woods most afternoons. Find him lying flat in the bubbling current, held up by his fists. Slowly, she'd wade in, pulling her school skirt up, too high, making sure he was watching as she did it. He always was. Animal-dumb, that's what he looked like. But he'd roll over like a dog and raise his wrist to her mouth, offering it wordlessly. After, there were no dramatic words, just a shared look, a casual nod, like it was nothing. But it wasn't nothing.

It was loyalty.

And it was trust.

"He's done something very bad, Minnow."

The girl tilts her head to the side, maddeningly silent. Indifferent. The sergeant shifts in the seat. She's a pretty kid, but there's something off about her. Feral. Dirty-blond hair to her waist, matted. Earthy brown eyes vacant, void.

She thinks of Amy Anderson, the holes in her abdomen. She shifts again, unnerved.

"Amy sat between you and Trav, didn't she? She told me you were friends."

Were.

She gets to her feet, crouches over Minnow, chin level with her forehead. "Amy didn't want to sit next to you in class anymore. A week ago, before the incident with Trav, she asked to be moved. Do you know why?"

The girl raises her chin, shakes her head no.

She's lying.

"Minnow." She crouches lower, eye to eye with her now. "Amy said you tried to drown her."

CHAPTER 19

"What?" Chris half yells and I wince, pulling the phone away from my ear. The line is awful, loud and crackly as traffic whooshes by.

"Are you in town?"

"Out driving," he says flatly. I picture him, arm hanging out the window of his hubcap-less Audi, smoking moodily. Pop music drifts through the phone as I wait for Chris to tell me where he is.

He doesn't.

"I kept wondering why you changed your name," he finally says, and the radio dims like he's reached over to turn it all the way down. "Now I know."

I get slowly to my feet. "Come talk to me."

". . . I don't think so."

Silence again. I pluck my keys from the kitchen bench. "I'm going to drive to your Airbnb. I'll wait outside until you let me in."

Breathing. A short blast of a car horn.

I lean against the bench. It digs uncomfortably into the small of my back. "We'll talk, okay?"

"About what?"

Whatever it is you've found out about me.

"You tell *me*, Chris."

"Okay," he says, and I think he's going to end the call, but a moment later the noise completely clears. It sounds like he's pulled over to the side of the road, wound the windows up, shut the engine off.

"You know what I want to talk about, Melanie? The woods on Soldiers' Road."

I close my eyes. "I told you everything I know about Donny."

"I'm not talking about Donny." He snorts. "I want to talk about the other thing that happened there."

I've been waiting for it, but my spine stiffens when he says,
"I want to talk about Amy Anderson."

I DRIVE DOWN A WINDING lane the color of toast, past a community book library, crammed with paperbacks. A teenage girl with weedy hair pulls it open, plucks a book out, inspects it before giving me a short, perfunctory wave. I wave back, attempt a smile. It's a family street: Bicycles lean against porches, clotheslines droop with school uniforms and sheets with dinosaurs on them. A panting St. Bernard lumbers past on a lead so long, it drags on the ground. Three tweens trail behind it, giving me the same distracted wave.

The driveway of Chris's Airbnb is on a slope. I pull in, the nose of my car pointing at the afternoon sun. I'm sweating, jittery. The cicadas don't help. They're screaming in the landscaped bushes like they hate the whole world, and they really want you to know it.

I raise my fist to knock at his door, then reach for the handle instead, twisting it. It opens without a noise.

It's cold in here. An air conditioner blasts my face as I step past the empty study and into the open-plan kitchen and living room. Oak flooring, stone benchtops, signed jerseys lining the brick walls. Two reclining chairs are aimed at a TV screen the size of my car. Empty.

"Chris?"

I step past a poker table, a stack of green chips balanced on the back of an unopened deck of cards. I reach for a chip, rub the ribbed edge over my thumb. I stuff it into my pocket, and I don't know why.

"Here," he mutters. "The bedroom."

I peek around the corner of the master bedroom, and there he is, flat on his back on the king bed. It's odd to see him in shorts and a T-shirt. His brick hair is damp and dripping, his arms and legs smooth and milky. He's sulky and sipping on a Corona, three-quarters full, wedge of lime choked in its neck.

He catches me staring at it, lifts it from his lips, voice sardonic, baiting. "Want one?" He yanks open the bar fridge next to the bed. It hisses out icy air, and I notice the six-pack is five full.

"I don't drink."

He jerks the fridge shut, and the redwood doors of the wardrobe rattle softly. I hover in the doorway, staring at the shirts and slacks piled stiffly at the foot of the bed. I turn my face away, hiding a smile. Even when he loses control, he doesn't.

"I'm driving to Bethanga tomorrow morning, eight-ish," I say. "I'll be back in the late afternoon. What time are you going?"

He studies me silently. "I'm getting there earlier." He takes a pull of the Corona, lime wedge nudging his bottom lip. "I take it we're still not going together?"

"Yes, that's right."

"Why not, Minnow?"

It's the first time he's ever called me by my real name. It's so quiet, I can't even hear the cicadas. I wish I could. Wish I could throw my head back, howling, and join their chorus.

Chris runs his palm through his damp hair then sits up, legs splayed out like breadsticks. His T-shirt is white cotton, sleeveless, revealing splotchy freckles on the tops of his arms. He's gym-thin, lean. Narrow in the chest. The boys at home would say he "needs a good feed." They'd grab him up in their stodgy hands, stuff him full of fatty meats, fried chips, and yeasty beer until his chest and waist bloated like theirs.

I can't imagine Chris growing up in Kangaroo Bay. Can't imagine him with a beefy dad or yanking open a fish stomach like a packet of chips. Silky guts slide out, and Chris stumbles away, pale and appalled.

"I spoke to your fifth-grade teacher, Miss McKenzie." He pauses before adding in a low voice, "She remembers you."

"Why were you talking to her about me?"

Why were you talking to her at all?

He picks at the Corona label, peeling it off in slow, wet strips. "She told me about the girl in your grade . . . the girl who sat next to you that year." He looks up, eyes cloudy like an ancient fish. "Amy Anderson?"

I stuff my fists in my pockets, wait.

"Something bad happened to her." Another slow, soggy tear.

"And if you don't mind me saying . . . something bad seems to happen to a lot of people in your life, Minnow."

I shift in the doorway, staring blindly at the ceiling. "If you spoke with Miss McKenzie," I begin, "then you know it wasn't me who stabbed Amy."

"No," he agrees. "But you were questioned about it."

"Amy lived." My gaze snaps to his. "She admitted it was Trav who did it."

"Yeah." He pauses. "But that wasn't the first time someone tried to kill the poor girl, was it?"

"Yes, it was."

He studies me with piercing scrutiny. "Then why did she beg your teacher to move seats? Why did she beg to get away from you?"

"We had a falling-out. Ten-year-old girls argue."

"But most ten-year-old girls don't try to drown each other. Do they?"

Silence.

"That's what Amy told your teacher." He half grimaces, like he's got a stomach cramp. "And that's why she asked to be moved away from you. Even stranger," he continues, "that creek you tried to drown her in is on Soldiers' Road. The same place you took me to."

He scoots forward. "The place Donny Granger was killed." After a pause, he continues, muttering, "Allegedly. And where your mother just happened to be found."

I shake my head, looking at the pile of shirts on the bed, then letting my gaze drift up to his taut face. "Yes, Chris," I begin, "I've been meaning to tell you . . ."

I slink to the bed, drop to my knees, crawling across the navy cover. I cross my legs, eyelids fluttering shut as I whisper, "When I was ten years old, I killed Donny Granger. I dragged him out to the woods and slit his throat. Later, for the hell of it, I killed my mother. Then just for something new and different, I tried to drown Amy. Two years later, I also somehow managed to murder my father." My eyes snap open. "You know, my drunk, violent, paranoid father." I gesture to my five-foot-four frame. "I overpowered them all, you see."

He gives me a withering look that says, *All right, all right. I get it.*

"For the record," I say, "my father could still be alive."

"Heath could have killed him," Chris protests.

I shake my head. "He didn't."

"How do you know that?"

"Because the night my father went missing, Heath was at home with me," I tell him truthfully. "You don't forget where you were the night your dad went missing."

"Heath could have snuck out."

"Maybe. But the word is that Terry Hargrave got to Dad first."

"The guy who owns the pub?" He frowns, putting the pieces together. ". . . So he was the one questioned over your dad's disappearance?"

"He showed up on our doorstep a week before Dad disappeared, shoved him through the screen door."

"Why?"

"The police had been questioning Dad's mates, seeing if they thought he had anything to do with Mum's disappearance . . . I think Terry started to believe he did."

"And this Terry," he says, "he knew your dad . . . got physical with your mum?"

"He hit her, yes. Everyone knew. Nobody did anything about it."

For the first time, he falters. His professionalism cracks, and for a moment, the man beneath it shows.

"I'm sorry to hear that, Min," he says softly, looking away.

"DV is pretty common 'round these areas." I shrug before adding, "You wouldn't understand."

I don't know why I said that last part. Why I sneered it. But there's a piece of me that needs him to know, we're not the same. We never will be. That some wounds don't heal, they just harden.

Us. Them.

Me. Chris.

He stares at the wedge of lime, studying it. "So Amy was lying? About what you did to her?" He hesitates. "What you *tried* to do?"

My shoulders drop. I lean back on both elbows, sighing, thinking about things I haven't thought of in years. I tilt my chin to the ceiling, speaking to it. "The town kids used to meet up at the creek in the woods after school. It was safer than..." I shrug. "... than home, I guess. We'd pelt each other with creek pebbles, get someone in a headlock, hold 'em under, that sort of thing. Amy was... well, she didn't live here, you know what I mean? She was different from us."

We were bruised and grimy, shifty and slack-eyed. Amy was sparkly nail polish and striped swimsuits with matching caps. She looked ridiculously out of place in that piss-colored creek, waddling in like a baby duck. I didn't want her there, in our territory, *my* territory, but she was oblivious. I didn't want her sitting next to me at school, either. But there she was, chatty and painfully nice, stealing glances at Trav when he wasn't looking.

"We played rough," I admit, remembering. "*I* played rough. That's just how it was. How we were raised. Maybe I went too far one day..." My voice trails off. "Maybe it scared her. I didn't mean to."

I lift myself up on my elbows. Chris rubs the back of his neck, beer forgotten in his lap, still half full. I reach for the bottle, the heel of my palm grazing his thigh. He freezes, tight-lipped, as I shift the bottle to my knee. Without thinking, I stick my finger down the neck, poking at the lime wedge. I pluck it out, chomp into its tangy flesh, and it reminds me of something. Someone.

Trav.

We're passing the pineapple juice box between us, taking turns, each sip slower than the last. It's citrusy bright, tastes like summer afternoons and lazy violence.

I spit the lime wedge into my palm. My skin's hot, my mouth burns. When I look up, Chris is watching. His eyes drop to my hand, the half-chewed lime glistening in my open palm.

He grimaces, pretends to shudder. "Need a bin for that?"

I close my fist slowly. Juice slips through the cracks in my knuckles, runs warm down my wrist. I let the silence stretch. Then I open my palm again, pulp glistening, fingers wet. "Got something for you," I say, softer now.

"That's disgusting."

I half close my eyes, smiling. I'm not here anymore. I'm motionless and silent at the creek, staring at the boy kneeling in the amber water. He reaches up wordlessly, offering me something. I take it, quickly, hungrily. Starving for something only he can give me.

"I need to go," I mumble. "Leavin' in the morning."

We don't look at each other, and I think his interrogation is finally over. But it's not.

"Wait."

He lifts his head, and says, "Tell me about the fire."

CHAPTER 20

You comin' to the Wicked Woods after school?
Bring matches.
And a knife.

I crouch at the beer-colored creek, pressing a hot sharp stone into my palm. We used them as bottle openers, sticking the sharp ends under stolen beers, grunting with effort. Sometimes, if we couldn't get it open, we'd smash the rock into the bottle neck, press our lips to the broken glass, and drink, long and deep. Luke chugged an entire beer like that before vomiting blood and splintered glass.

The local kids used to swim here after school, tearing off our school uniforms, splashing in T-shirts and cotton underwear until Heath told me not to. Later, the year-ten boys arrived, roaming the woods in their feral packs, hot with hunger. They found me on my knees, water pooling the tops of my thighs, stuffing slimy palmfuls of creek mud in my fists, squishing it through the cracks in my knuckles.

Then one of them called my name.

Mangled hair down to the shoulder blades, he stared hard at my T-shirt and the mud in my fists, and his eyes were like a shark, starved. A Bell Miner bird chimed, once, twice, sounding like a dinner bell. My skin stung. My mouth burned hot. I prayed he would look away.

Prayed he wouldn't.

You're either the shark or the food.

For the first time in my life, I was both.

Yeah, I liked it.

I squeezed my fist tighter, letting the mud splatter on my thigh like hot chocolate.

Heath charged the water then, grabbed my elbow, pulled me roughly to my feet. He stuffed my wet legs into my skirt, marched through the creek, and split his knuckle to the bone on the boy's teeth.

That was the first summer without my mum.

She's shot through, Dad said. *Can ya blame 'er?*

In our town, mums often shot through, never to be spoken of or heard from again.

Can ya blame 'er?

Yes. I could. And did. My hometown hummed with anger, and after my mother left, I joined its chorus. I had no idea what to do with all that pain. Heath and I were expected to simply *Get on with it. You got nothin' to complain about. Why are you crying? Little bitch.*

Sometimes I slumped at the foot of my bed, out of breath even while sitting still. Sometimes I cut my palms with fishing hooks, let the blood drip onto my tongue, tasting like salt and rage.

I get to my feet, peel my jeans and T-shirt off, think of the hungry boy as I wade in. Think of him again as I drop to my knees, grabbing at mud, squeezing it through my fists. I glance at the creek bank, remembering. I wonder if the boy left town, but he probably didn't. Blood boys don't leave blood towns.

I lie on my back and drift in the filthy current, thinking about Amy Anderson. Amy was different. From us, I mean. We were mud-crusted fingernails, bare-chested and underfed. Feral. Amy was nice. Amy had bulky teeth, a limp ponytail, and a mum who dropped her off at our filthy creek on summer afternoons because she wanted to hang out with Trav and me. She didn't technically live in Kangaroo Bay, and I guess that was the first line drawn between us.

Us. Them.

Her house in Pine Bay had soaring ceilings, air-conditioning, and private access winding down to the sea.

She also had a mum.

Trav and I were the only ones invited to her tenth birthday party. I was surprised, because Amy and I weren't really friends. We just sat next to each other at school, and when she found out that Trav and I met up at the creek, she got her mum to drop her off. She never asked if she was invited. She wasn't.

Trav and I wandered into her home, slack-eyed and silent, the filthy cuffs of our jeans dragging on her slate floor. We watched a movie on her sugary pink bed, piled high with heart-shaped pillows. It started out fine, until it wasn't.

I was digging into the popcorn bowl when I saw something. Amy's pink-polished fingers inching toward Trav's hand. Her hand grew closer, grazing his. I felt myself grow very, very still. My jaw locked. My chest burned with anger.

Trav drew his hand away and tucked it into his pocket, keeping his eyes locked on the movie. Amy's hand hovered in the space his used to be, and the silence stretched and stretched. I hid my rage away, but the heat kept building.

Later that week, I invited Amy to the creek, alone.

And I tried to drown her.

I watched her floating in her striped swimsuit, eyes half closed and restful. And I crouched on the bank, hungry like a shark. I don't remember crossing the water, don't remember if she cried out when I grasped the back of her skull, shoved my knee atop the small of her back, and held her under. But I do remember her clawing at my arm, breaking the skin. I remember the pink glitter in her nail polish sparkling in the sun. I remember the fight fading as her limbs stopped thrashing. I remember the stillness, the strange calm.

In the silence, I thought of my brother. Saw his face in my mind. Surf Lifesaver of the Year. I felt guilty. Watched.

I let her go and she struggled toward the creek bank, flailing like a dying fish.

Sometime later, she quietly emptied her desk and asked Miss McKenzie if she could sit at the front of the class, away from me, please. But she didn't tell her the reason why, not until later.

Amy spent the next week in the front row and averted her eyes whenever she saw me. And I spent that time staring hard at the back of her head, remembering.

That week, I spent every afternoon in this creek with Trav, spitting water into his open mouth. He'd let me hold him under, hand cupping his skull, mouth on the back of his neck. We took turns drowning each other, over and over again. Drowning and kissing. Kissing and drowning.

Until it felt like the same thing.

I SLIP MY CLOTHES BACK ON, follow the creek's muddy mouth. In some areas, the grass is yellowing and brittle, crunching under my shoes. A moment later it's thigh-high, tickling my kneecaps. The blackbirds pause on branches as dry and bare as bones.

I pause under a ghost gum, spitting on the red dirt and scraping it in with the heel of my shoe until the ground looks like a bloodstain.

When we were children, Trav and I would stand in this spot and spit ourselves dry. We dipped our fingers into the red earth, smearing the paste all over our arms and cheeks. Shivering with energy in the fading sunset, we shook up heavy cans of gasoline, pouring them onto old clothing and setting it alight with stolen matches; then we threw our heads back, howling for the dark. We sprinted through the woods, lighting it up with fire and our madness, blackbirds falling silent as we barreled through, screaming childish warnings they needn't have listened to.

We're coming! We're coming! Watch out!

On Friday nights, our dads staggered home from the pub, a universe of rage boiling inside them. On those nights, you'd find stray kids hungry and scattered around town like dogs. Too afraid to go home.

Nobody really spoke about the violence. It's not something you speak of. It changes you, though. I watched smooth-cheeked boys turn cruel and canine. Even Trav grew sullen and aggressive, lost to his mum. Lost to everyone. All pain is the same, but what we do with it isn't.

Heath became our guardian. He built the cabin here, gave us a safe place to run to, until it wasn't safe anymore.

Something shrieks through the woods, and I glance over my shoulder, peering into the semi-dark. Skin prickling, I wait there, squinting through the woods. The birds stop chirping mid-song, the cicadas burrow, and the woods are so quiet that all I hear is the thumping of my heart.

I press ahead, squeezing past charred tree trunks, low-hanging branches that scratch at my cheeks, chin, and neck. I hold a hand in front of my face to protect it, tripping over the twisted carpet of roots, walking deeper and deeper into the woods.

Tucked away like a crouching cat is a cabin shaped like a capital A. It's half buried in broken branches and autumn leaves, as if the Wicked Woods were trying to swallow it whole.

The A-frame stretches up to the bloodied sky, and a hot wind weaves through its wooden rib cage, whistling unpleasantly. It smells gory, fresh mud and sour meat. Despite the warmth, there's a weird chill in the air. I flatten my back against a charred blackwood, unwilling to step inside.

Our real education began here.

I spent my younger years in this cabin, surrounded by boys who learned more with pocketknives than they ever did in school. Local kids who went to my school, twitchy and restless with nowhere else to go. In the beginning, I was ignored or tolerated by them because I was Heath's sister, but as we grew, I felt something shift. The weight of their stares, heavy, uninvited. Greedy. I realized finally that I needed to vanish or grow teeth. Be the shark, or be the food.

Heath and Luke showed us how to rig up fishing line, how to scale and fillet a fresh snapper. Heath was patient and encouraging, a surgeon. Luke, restless and bloody, a butcher. Heath stepped up for us, but Luke stepped back. He grew bored of us, looked at the weight of the responsibility and decided we weren't worth the cost. Sometimes we wouldn't see him for months.

Nobody asked my brother to do it, to carry the weight of these forgotten kids, but it settled on his shoulders anyway. He picked it up because no one else would and he bore it quietly. Dutifully.

But over time, the weight pressed deeper. I saw it on his face, the way he moved through the world a little slower. And even when his back ached from the burden, even when no one thanked him, he kept carrying us. It was because of Heath that none of us went hungry again. Because of him, we learned how to rip gills out with two fingers, peel skin from sinewy muscle, and pluck a liver from a rib cage, popping it into our mouths, all juicy and plump.

Some of us flinched.

Most of us didn't.

And some of us liked the violence a bit too much.

In fourth grade, I found the blood boys bent over shattered rabbit skulls, bloodied rocks in their hot, tight grips. I saw the chalky bones of a bellbird's wing dangling from the cabin windowsill like a gruesome wind chime. And I ran my tongue over my teeth while I chopped kangaroo meat into bloodied strips.

As we grew, so did the violence. A growing, pulsing rage. The cabin simmered with feral tension, and fights broke out like fires. Heath barked warnings no one listened to. And Luke stood too close, talked too smooth, encouraged our inner war. He didn't push exactly. He didn't have to.

"You're not seriously chickening out, are you?" he'd say, voice dropping low, conspiratorial. "Go on, do it . . . no one's gonna know."

Blood boys grew into blood men, aggressive and insatiable. Heath's steady influence could not reach the part of them that had already decided.

It ended abruptly.

And it ended with me.

I tried to drown Amy, couldn't, and Trav stepped in, stepped up. Punctured her belly with a fillet knife, and proved his devotion. His bloody loyalty. Trav was a minor, so he was lucky. Amy not so much. Her family moved away, out of state, I heard. Trav was sent away, and police sealed the file.

Then Heath burned the cabin down. Luke was pissed about that. Their friendship didn't survive the fire. As the cabin turned into embers, so did the last pieces of what they were to each other.

My mind drifts back to the conversation with Chris. *Tell me about the fire.*

I was there when Heath burned the cabin down, but I didn't tell Chris that. Didn't tell him how flames licked up the wooden walls and smoke poured out the window, thick and dark, curling into the sky with the smell of pine. How the roof groaned as it caught and beams snapped with loud cracks.

I only told Chris that a local saw the smoke and called the police. I didn't tell him that Heath, Trav, and I were questioned, along with the blood boys. And I didn't tell him that six years later, I left Kangaroo Bay and changed my name in an attempt to sever the ties to all that had happened there.

I pause in the woods, remembering the fire. Ash floated up like gray snowflakes, and Heath watched it all, bloodless and defeated. I hugged him and noticed how his shoulders slumped with that invisible weight he carried everywhere. I wondered if he felt guilty about what happened, and I should have told him it wasn't his fault. None of it was. The violence in the blood boys was rooted too deep, simmering too long. Heath stood in front of them, trying to hold it back, but their instinctual rage took over. Not even Heath could hold back tidal wives of violence with his bare hands.

The town kids stopped meeting at the creek after school. Many dropped out in grade nine, traded their high school education for a fishing rod or their dad's concreting business.

We never went there again.

But someone has.

I creep forward, pausing at the charred entrance. A snake skull hangs from a rusted nail, bones shining in the blood light.

A heavy animal smell makes my eyes water as I step inside. The sun is sinking low and fast, and the red-gold rays funnel down through five holes in the roof. The first thing I notice is that the wood-plank floor is splattered with blood.

Fresh.

Cobwebs hang loose from the roof, rusty spanners dangle from decaying hooks, looking like they'll fall at any moment. A roll of orange extension cord is nestled on the workbench, and around me there's a scurrying sound, like a family of mice trying to hide.

Under the blackened windowsill are four femur bones, thick with flesh, moist and pink, dangling like Christmas stockings.

The animal smell grows stronger. I survey the back of the room, pausing. A shower curtain is strung limply across the center, partitioning the room off, swishing in the warm wind. The curtain would have been pretty, once. A winding row of butterflies in a field of buttercups and leafy vines. Now it's an abomination. The colors are dull, peeling and discolored. Spots of mold dotting the buttery field.

And worse.

I creep closer, pinching the curtain between my fingers. It's stiff and crunchy; splattered across it are fat droplets of blood.

I pull it up, ducking my head as I step under. The smell is everywhere, heavy, eye-watering, like the back of a butcher's shop. Something feathery brushes my cheek. I tilt my head back, looking up.

Hanging from the ceiling, strung up by their bloodied tails, are four kangaroos.

Decapitated.

CHAPTER 21

The sky is the ocean. Blue-black and roaring, whitecaps hurtling past like clouds. There's a bitter taste in my mouth, a rattle in my teeth. I'm stretched so tight that if I don't bend, I'll break. I'm waiting for something. Someone.

My father dives out of the ocean-sky. His voice slides wetly down my ear canals: *You can hear it, too. Can't you, Min? The ocean? Calling and calling?*

Because it's a dream, it makes sense. Of course the sky is the ocean. Of course Dad is sharpening his knife in the cabin, inspecting the blade. Pointing its black tip at me.

Hungry?

He thrusts a kangaroo leg into my mouth, and I tear off meaty strips, hungry as a shark, letting them dangle down my lips like noodles before slurping them up.

Chris grimaces at the cabin door. *What are you eating?*

I turn my face away, chewing frantically. *Nothing. It's nothing.*

I ROLL OVER, MOUTH PRESSED into the seatbelt. I wake slowly, my lips tasting like plastic. Outside my back-seat window, the sun burns through, the seatbelt buckle iron-hot. The back of my neck drips with sweat as I snatch my phone up. I scan the screen, holding my breath. No missed calls from Chris. From anyone. My last two texts to him have gone unanswered.

On my way to Bethanga. We could meet up after?
Chris?

Nothing. I drove past his Airbnb this morning; his car was gone. I haven't heard from him since I stumbled out of his bedroom.

I throw my phone onto the passenger seat, climb into the front, and start the engine, stewing. I pull out of the rest stop, swiping at the sweat on my cheeks. The steering wheel's so hot, I have to hold it with the pads of my fingertips.

Bethanga is on the southern border of New South Wales, sandwiched between Melbourne and Sydney.

I've been there once, years ago, a last-minute road trip with housemates. I spent most of the weekend looking out the window as the Murray River snaked past, smiling at the short-necked turtles as they poked their heads up in the coffee-colored water.

On the left side of the Hume Highway are fields of canola flowers, butter yellow and burning. On the right, thirsty stretches of sunburned fields. The famous highway is 840 kilometers long, I'm one nap and three coffees in. Just over an hour to go.

I pass the exit for Glenrowan, deep in the dark heart of Kelly Country. Thousands of sheep chew absently in stationary groups, and the bony branches of skeleton trees claw at the hazy sky. In 1880, bushranger Ned Kelly was captured here in his homemade armor at the Glenrowan Inn after that infamous, bloody shootout with police. The Kelly Gang's Last Stand. We call him a hero.

Of course we do.

Five months later they hung him in the Old Melbourne Jail. They took us on a school excursion to see his hangman's noose. We were five.

I glance at my phone again in case Chris has messaged.

He hasn't.

THE DOUBLE-BRICK HOME IS PERCHED atop an elevated block. An expansive redwood deck runs the length of it, overlooking golden-green rolling hills. The house is barely visible from the valley road beneath, and it's so quiet here, just the soft whoosh through the golden elm trees and the distant clucking of chickens.

But there's something very wrong here. I can feel it.

I shut the driver's door but can't seem to untuck my fingers from the safety of the door handle. I pull my phone out of my back pocket, and text Colleen.

I'm here.

I hesitate, wanting to add, *If something happens to me . . .*

What's going to happen to you, Minnow? You're chatting to a bereaved mum. You'll spend a probing hour with her, leave before 2 P.M. You'll be home at seven, propped up in bed, Jessie breathing softly beside you.

I'll message you when I'm done. Should be an hour.

I wait for her to message back, glancing nervously at the silent house, muttering *Come on, Colleen,* under my breath.

She texts back, *Ok. Good luck.*

My shoulders relax, but my eyes survey the porch, uneasy. I tuck my phone back in my pocket, lock the car door. I walk stiffly up the hill, feeling like I'm diving off a life raft and paddling into a stormy sea.

SHE PRESSES A SWEATING GLASS of cordial into my palm and tells me to call her Deb. She didn't ask me if I wanted the drink. Didn't ask me to remind her what newspaper I work for. I called her on the way, gave vague answers to her vague questions.

Who do you work for?

I work for Trident *mag. Before that, I worked for the* Mill.

When journos shoot their shot, I'm always surprised how few questions are asked. No one wants to look stupid. You tell them who you work for, and they just nod silently, wait for you to lead.

And I did. *I'm not far from Bethanga. I'd love to talk to you about Rachel.*

Silence.

I was raised in Kangaroo Bay. I—

You were what?

Raised there.

. . . You said you're in the area?

Deb has a small voice, a tight jaw, and she taps her foot repeatedly. Her yellow T-shirt has a stain near her belly button, her silver bob windswept. Her house has floor-to-ceiling windows. There's a ceiling fan in each room I passed, and an aboveground pool.

"Thank you for seeing me." I sip from the sweaty glass, rub the condensation on my jeans, hope she doesn't notice. "I'm so sorry for your loss."

She gives me an absent nod, eyes raking the pool. I inspect it, gripping the glass tighter, worried it'll slip.

"She was a strong swimmer, Rach," Deb mutters, hateful eyes on the pool. "The lake's just down the road, too."

Lake Hume is one of the largest in Australia. I passed it on the way through. Sunshine glittered off the surface as speedboats rocketed past, pulling inner tubes with squealing kids. Elderly couples lazed in the shade of towering ghost gums, and rowdy teens crowded the Bethanga Bridge, preparing to dive in.

"No sharks in the fucking lake."

The rage in her voice silences me. Her spine's rigid, eyes stormy. I get the feeling she's keeping so much in when she really wants to howl in pain like a wolf.

A dull-eyed man shuffles into the kitchen, barefoot and silent. Absently, he flicks the kettle on, and I look to Deb, but she ignores him. I call out a soft hello that's lost in the gurgle of the kettle boiling. He dumps a tea bag into a mug, trembles as he fills it. No milk. It steams on the counter, and he watches it silently like he's too tired to hold it. Finally, he shuffles out.

"What was she doing in Kangaroo Bay?"

"Something bad."

I blink, grip loosening. I fumble for the glass, clamping it in my hands. "What does that mean exactly?"

"You said you're from Kangaroo Bay?"

I nod.

"There's a lot of bad types down there."

"Yes, there is," I tell her. "How do you know that?"

Her breath stalls. "I don't want you printing what I'm about to tell you," she says, emphasizing each word. "Nobody's figured it out yet."

I nod quickly, lean forward.

"We used to live in Kangaroo Bay."

"When?"

"Late seventies to the late eighties. Rented a house on Jupiter Court with Rach's dad." She falls into heavy silence, lips pursed. ". . . He wasn't a good man."

"Violent?"

A door clicks closed, followed by the faint rustle of footsteps on carpet.

"Yeah." Her jaw clenches tight. "I left him. Fled, actually. Went back to my maiden name."

"I'm sorry to hear that."

"You said your name was Greenwood?"

"Yes, Minnow Greenwood."

She frowns, shakes her head. "Doesn't ring a bell. But then, we left in 1987."

"How old was Rach when you left?"

"Ten."

If Rachel was born in 1977, then she would have been in grade five when Heath was starting school. I make a note to ask him about her.

"Rach was . . ." Deb's voice drops. "Unwell. Always had been. That town made it worse."

The town made it worse.

I'm standing on the cliff edge with Colleen. Her eyes are full.

Felt like I was losing Trav.

To what?

The darkness in this town.

I fix my eyes on the pool, thinking of my father. Trav. The blood boys in town. The violence in their bellies coiled like snakes. Did the town tug it loose? Or do we cling to that excuse because it's easier?

"What do you mean by *unwell*?"

"She was a brooder, you know what I mean? I used to call them her dark moods. She was like that even as a child. It was hard to pull her out of it."

"How long would these moods last?"

"Sometimes minutes. Sometimes months."

"Depression?"

She considers this. "Yeah, and . . ." Her voice falls off. "I don't know. Something else, I think."

I wait, eyes on the pine-green carpet.

"We used to fight about the movies she'd watch . . ." She pauses, seems to brace herself. "Lot of horror movies. Gore. Just nasty stuff."

"You said she was doing something bad," I murmur, eyes flicking up to hers. "Tell me about that."

Silence.

"She got into something she shouldn't have . . ." Deb finally says. "Think it pissed a few people off down there."

"Got into what?"

She frowns like I've asked the wrong question, gets to her feet. "I searched her room . . ." She shifts her weight, considers her next words. "You need to see something."

She tips her head in the direction of a light-filled hallway.

I get to my feet and follow.

THERE'S A SIGN HANGING FROM the firmly shut door of the spare room.

TO PLANT A GARDEN

IS TO BELIEVE IN TOMORROW

Deb's face falls when she reads it. I imagine her hammering that nail in with grim determination, tugging at the sign until it hangs straight. Then she steps back, nods once, thinking, *Yes, this will help her.*

It didn't.

She straightens her spine, twists the door handle, steps inside. It's a country bedroom, a cherrywood rocking chair in the corner, a crocheted blanket folded neatly at the foot of a brass bed. It smells like dead wattle in here.

Deb reaches tenderly for a sage-green pillow with a ruffled fringe. "She moved back in after she left her husband. They were getting a divorce. It was supposed to be a new beginning for her." She smooths the pillow with her palm. "Stupid of me."

I stand in the center of the room, eyes on the single bed. "I'm sorry." A painted mason jar sits sadly on the bedside table, stuffed with drooping wattle. "What did Rachel do for work?"

"Store manager at Kmart," she says automatically. "Was, anyway. She resigned after her marriage fell apart. Though to be clear, the marriage had been falling apart for years."

"Why?"

She pauses, anchoring her attention to the rocking chair. "... I'm not making excuses for her. But she really did need help, and she never got it. And I *know* she tried. I took her myself." She shakes her head, gaze darkening. "Doctors, psychologists, psychiatrists, you name it. They put her on every drug known to man. Nothing helped."

"Helped what?"

"Her violence."

I nod, wait.

"She said she felt it . . . stirring in her blood. Her father was the same."

You can hear it, too, Min, can't you? The ocean? Calling and calling?

I rub my forehead, mumbling, "Tell me about her husband."

"He wasn't a saint, either," she adds, eyebrow slanted in disapproval. "Couldn't keep his penis in his pants. And when Rachel caught him . . ." She lowers her head. "It was just bad, you know? All of it."

"Was he from Kangaroo Bay?"

"Sydney." She places the pillow back. "After they split, she moved back in with us. She barely got out of bed for a year. But in the last few months she was getting out more. Making long-term plans." She shrugs helplessly. "We felt she was getting better."

TO PLANT A GARDEN

IS TO BELIEVE IN TOMORROW

So what made Rachel start believing in tomorrow? "What was she doing for money?"

The question hangs in the air.

Something bad.

I turn to Deb, who looks away. "Something illegal?"

"She was on government benefits," she finally mutters. "Just 'til she got on her feet."

"Divorces are expensive. All those lawyer fees," I prompt. "Was she worried about money?"

"... Little bit."

"But she had the cash to keep traveling to Kangaroo Bay."

Silence.

"What was the purpose of the trips?"

"Meeting up with old friends."

"Who?"

"She never said," she admits, raising a hand in her defense. "Yes, I should have asked. I doubt she would've told me, though."

"Did you believe her? That she was just meeting up with friends?"

"I wanted to."

Silence. The bedroom window is framed with a lace curtain, sheer as a nightgown. Golden elm leaves flutter past as the sky darkens.

I nod at the bed. "Mind if I sit down?"

She shrugs, reaches for the sage pillow again, holds it against her chest. I sit down, spine straight, hands flat on my knees. "There's something odd about Rachel's attack."

She says nothing, but I watch her clutch the pillow tighter.

"Why was she swimming at night? And alone?"

"For someone else it would've been strange, yes," Deb admits. "But like I said, she was different. She wasn't afraid of doing things like that—swimming at night."

"She wasn't just swimming."

She pauses, eyes narrowing. "Yes she was. Eyewitnesses said so."

"I know what they said, but it's not true."

"How do you know?"

"Because *I* was there. I was one of the eyewitnesses," I tell her, looking up. "And I know what she was really doing."

CHAPTER 22

The summer storm's coming. The wind bends the rosebushes and petals flicker past as the first raindrops fall.

"You were there that night?"

"I wanted to tell you in person."

She stares grimly out the window. "Was it fast, at least?"

No.

"Yes."

"Then you know what she was doing."

"I do now."

What was she doing for money?

Something bad.

In the ocean shallows are huge snails that live near rocky reefs and areas with plenty of seaweed. When cooked, they're buttery and salty, chewy like calamari. And they're worth an absolute shitton. Greenlip abalone. Diving for them is illegal in almost every state in Australia, including Victoria.

"She was diving illegally for abalone." I look up. "Wasn't she?"

She slumps a little. "Yes, she was."

Abalone poaching is dangerous, the fine is huge, and you could find yourself in the jaws of a hungry shark. It's certainly happened before, and it'll happen again.

But the demand is ridiculously high. Two to three hundred dollars for a kilogram. High risk, high rewards. Rachel was in financial trouble. She was raised in Kangaroo Bay, so she knew where to find them.

"I couldn't tell the police why she'd go there." She bites her lip. "I couldn't tell them about the other thing, either."

"What other thing?"

"She was threatened. At work."

"When?"

"Not long before the attack. Less than two weeks," she says. "Someone sent her a text message and a video."

"Her husband?" I prompt. "You said they'd had issues."

She shakes her head firmly. "No, this was different."

"Who sent it, then?"

"She didn't recognize the number. We downloaded one of those apps, a *find out who called me* thing. But we couldn't find much. We even tried entering the number into those reverse phone lookup websites."

"And?"

"Nothing. No results for that number." She pauses. "I reckon someone bought a cheap mobile just to send her the message. They probably ditched it after."

"What did the text message say?"

"This is what happens to rule breakers."

"... *What* happens to rule breakers?"

She hesitates. "I think you need to see the video."

The video is low quality. Grainy, speckled. Random dots scatter the laptop screen. The colors are muted and washed out. It looks like it was shot on an early model phone or an old camera.

"Rach took her phone with her to Kangaroo Bay. They never found it. But she transferred the video to her laptop." Deb hovers over me, grimacing. "She watched it over and over again. We fought about it. I don't know how she could watch something like that. I certainly couldn't."

I squint at it, trying to make sense of what I'm staring at. Then I realize. It's a woman, swimming in the open ocean.

She's in a wet suit, arms thrust out like she's telling someone to back off, her face flushed with fear. I fumble for the sound, turning it all the way up. The woman stammers something, shoulders raised, gesturing frantically at something off-screen. I can't hear her, but I can feel her terror. Can see her chest rising and falling, can almost hear her short, rapid gasps.

Deb staggers back. "I can't watch this . . ."

She bolts out the room, and I eye her warily, wondering what's coming.

Then it happens.

The shark's dorsal fin slices the surface, water rippling as the powerful tail propels it forward, straight at the woman. She paddles desperately, eyes darting over her shoulder as the fin grows larger and larger, cutting too easily through the water. I hear her now. Screaming.

I wonder who the hell is filming this. And why aren't they helping her?

The woman yells something as the shark goes for her head, then she's silent, face a pulpy mess, part of her jaw ripped away. She bobs in the water, dazed and bleeding from her mouth. The dorsal fin towers over her head like a witch's hat, tail viciously slapping on the water. It surfaces briefly, bites down hard on her arm, pulls her under, thrashing so violently, her bloodied legs break the surface.

Then she's gone.

Video's over. I sit heavily on Rachel's bed, replaying it again and again. Purple wet suit. Pale eyes. I pause the video, zooming in, fingers shaking.

Deb peers in, "Evil, isn't it?"

Evil is what people do to each other. All this shark knew was that it was hungry, and she was there.

I pull out my phone.

"What are you doing?"

I glance up from the screen, Deb inspects me from the doorway, tight-lipped and suspicious. Uncertain, she takes a small step forward as if she's changed her mind about having me in her house. She repeats, louder, "What are you doing?"

I'm filming the video with my phone. For a moment, the room is entirely silent except for the tinny sound of the woman's screams.

"Recording it." I gesture to my phone, avoiding her eyes. "Just in case."

We wait in strained silence as I record the entire twenty-seven-second video. I study the screen, blood rushing in my ears. When it's done, I click my phone off. "Do you know who the woman in the video was?"

"No. I told you, I haven't watched it. I can't."

"I do. I know who it is."

Purple wet suit. Pale eyes.

I raise my head. "This is Hannah Striker."

CHAPTER 23

This is what happens to rule breakers.

I know what everyone thinks, Hannah's mum hisses, *but her death wasn't an accident.*

Was Hannah an abalone poacher, too?

I hear myself saying, "Hannah Striker was taken by a great white in Kangaroo Bay in the late nineties . . ." I pause. "Something came for her, too. Shark jaws. Her mum always believed her death wasn't an accident."

"My God," Deb mutters, pressing a hand to her throat, sinking hard onto the bed. "Are you sure it's her?"

This is what happens to rule breakers.

"I think so." I stare at the screen. "Did Rachel ever mention that the girl was Hannah?"

"No," Deb says, frantic now. "If she'd known who it was, she wouldn't have gone back to that damn town . . ." She trails off, stares at the sign on the door. "Tell me about that night. You said it was an accident."

"It *was*," I say, thrown. "I saw it . . ." I add guiltily, "She was alone in the water. We were the first on scene. It truly *was* an accident."

Blood burns in my ears. I reach dully for my phone: 2:21 P.M. I need to text Colleen, need to head home. But I can't get up.

"Have you shown this to police?"

"Only you."

"You didn't show Chris?"

"Who?"

"The other journo," I mutter, looking up. "Chris Cooper. From the *Daily*."

You know. The boy with the brick hair and milky skin. Freakishly clean. Snobbish. Smiles at my fish puns and pretends not to.

She shakes her head, dazed. "I haven't heard from him."

I grip the bed. "He called you the other day . . ." I trail off, trying to remember when that was. "He told you he was coming here to talk to you. Today."

She just stares at me.

"He called you," I repeat.

"Yeah, he called me. But he never showed up."

Blood whooshes behind my temples. I stare at the drooping wattle on the nightstand, thinking.

"He hasn't messaged you since?"

"No."

I get to my feet, vision blurring. Everything is moving and shifting, and none of it makes sense. I fumble for my car keys. "If he calls you, let me know. Please."

My car is steaming hot. I sink into the seat, wincing when the belt buckle brands my hip. I swipe at the sweat trickling down my collarbone, wind the window down.

I'm heading home now.

I don't wait for Colleen to message back. I call Chris again.

Straight to voicemail.

I end the call and ring again.

And again.

And again.

THE SKY IS THE OCEAN. Blue-black and roaring.

I race down the highway, watching the sky darken. Rain falls in scattered drops. There's a stillness, an unnatural quiet. I clench my teeth and wait for my father. He's in the wind, bending the branches of the blackwood trees. He's the jagged streak of white-hot light. And he's the roar that follows.

I stare at the sky, wondering how much of my father is in me.

My mother looked at the ocean and saw the hand of God. She

was calm there in a way she never was at home. *What a savior we have, Minnow. Before we even call him, He answers.*

To my father, the ocean was violence. Death and life and death again. The dark heart of it calling and calling. *You can hear it, too, can't you, Min?*

Sometimes I hear two calls.

I still wonder who I'll follow.

The rain falls in torrents, drenching the sunburned fields. Sheep huddle together like bloated clouds as the wind howls around them. Some shelter under a lone ghost gum, heads lowered, wool dripping, bleating at the blackened horizon.

The road is flooding, and the windshield wipers struggle to keep up with the punishing downpour. I slow the car, squinting through the blurry glass, but I can barely make out the lane markings. I grip the wheel as the wind picks up, shoving the car from side to side as headlights glow faintly in the mist illuminating a road sign:

VIOLET TOWN 5 KM

REST AREA 1 KM

I pull slowly into the rest area—too slowly, apparently, because some asshole beeps me from behind. I flinch, heart thudding as I steer the car into the parking lot, tires lurching over puddled potholes. The air's cooler, drying the sweat on my skin. I shudder when the breeze slips through the window crack.

I kill the engine. I'm still four hours away from Kangaroo Bay, and I feel it badly. Flashes of lightning split the sky. Rain hammers the roof, gushing down the windows. It's so loud, you'd have to yell over it. I feel like I'm underwater.

I clench my jaw, remembering the dream.

I'm stretched so tight that if I don't bend, I'll break. I'm waiting for something. Someone. But this time, it's not Dad I'm waiting for. It's Chris. I call him again, swearing when he doesn't answer.

The wind finally calms, the rain eases. Ahead are the flickering lights of a toilet block, the harsh, bright glow illuminating the chipped concrete. I step out the car, shivering when the wind hits my skin. There's only one other car in the lot, parked at the farthest end.

The toilet door creaks when I push it open, revealing a poorly flushed toilet, graffiti on the lid:

DON'T BLINK.

I pee quickly. The soap dispenser's empty, the mirror's missing, muddied water pools in the corners.

DON'T BLINK.

Uneasy, I peer over my shoulder, tuck my hands into my pockets. Outside, the rain's stopped like it never even started. But the air's heavy, thick with that post-storm atmosphere. The sheep remain under the ghost gums, matted and dripping.

The other car is still there, silent and grave as the air itself. It's parked under a tea tree, the white bonnet covered in crescent-shaped leaves.

I stop walking.

It's an Audi. White.

And it's missing hubcaps.

I stumble forward, running. The pavement's slick, water splashes up my ankles. *Don't trip, don't trip.* I'm breathless when I reach the driver's-side door and lunge for the handle. Locked.

I peer in, terrified I'll see Chris in there. Terrified I won't.

But he's not in there. The car is empty, silent. Abandoned.

I peer desperately through the back window. How long has it been sitting here? I snatch my phone, call him again, sweeping my gaze through the car. Breathlessly, I wait, praying I'll see his phone screen illuminate.

But the car sits quietly, crescent leaves stuck fast to the bonnet, dirt spraying the roof and license plate like nature itself is trying to swallow it. If Chris saw the state of his car, he'd race to the nearest car wash and frantically scrub it.

Chris.

My eyes water, the back of my throat burns. I lean heavily against the driver's-side door.

I CHARGE INTO THE VIOLET Town petrol station. A tired-looking attendant leans on the register with a magazine in his hand. He barely glances up as I stalk forward, asking if he's seen Chris. I pull up his *Daily* photo and the attendant squints, scratching his stubbled chin. He gives me a slow shake of the head and I thank him, heart squeezing tight.

I race home on the darkening highway. The sky is the color of eggplant, and looming shadows race with me, chasing me down. My eyes fix on a charred tree trunk and a shadow crouched beside it, staring hungrily at a bleating lamb. Fox. I speed up, the hum of the engine lost in the cicadas' hateful chorus.

The sky darkens, the highway feels endless. And Chris is out there somewhere, lost in this great dark.

It's 9 P.M. when I finally make it back to Kangaroo Bay. I shouldn't have worried. Heath's car isn't in the driveway. He's not waiting for me.

But something else is.

I pull onto our front lawn, headlights cutting through the darkness.

I wish they didn't.

The beams light up our porch, the pickle-green awning and the front door. At first, it seems like a trick of the light, but my eyes focus, and it becomes too clear. There's something on my doorstep. Waiting in the dark.

I climb out my car, headlights flickering as I step around them, headed for my front door. The world falls silent as I stare at what's waiting there.

I crouch slowly, reach for the two triangular-shaped objects left on my doormat. They're bigger than my palm, and they gleam in the night, the serrated edges as sharp as a knife.

Shark teeth.

THEN

Always take a knife.

If there's one thing my father drilled into us, it was those four words.

Always take a knife.

Dad steps into his seaweed-green waders, pulling the black straps over his big shoulders. Heath and I stand silently on the wet sand, watching as he clips the straps in place.

He reaches into his fishing tackle box, rusted, bloodied, and caked with sand. He pulls out his knife. I hate it. The black handle, the black blade. The way it catches no light. I feel sick when I see it.

I turn away, staring at the crashing waves instead. It's midnight and dark as hell. Even the moon only offers up a sliver of light, as if to say, You're on your fucking own, kid.

Heath once told me that a single wave could travel for days just to crash on the shore. I used to wonder if the waves were angry about that. Traveling all that way, and for what? What did they see on their journey, and was it enough? Maybe that's why they poured all their anger into it. That one glorious moment on the beach.

Boom.

As soon as we got to the beach, Dad insisted on shutting off the torches, the headlamps. Any scrap of light, gone.

"The fuckers can see it," *he said, nodding hatefully at the water.*

He's so paranoid of the ocean and everything in it. God knows why. He's more carnivorous than everything in the sea.

I keep my eyes fixed on that sliver of moon as my father draws near. He crouches in front of us, eye level to Heath but towering over me.

"Look at me, Minnow."

But I won't.
The moon. The merciful slice of light.
And my father, the darkness.
He grabs the side of my face with a freezing hand, drags it back to look at him. Only him.

"What do I say?"

"Always take a knife," I recite.

"Why?"

His breath is cold. His hand hurts me. My eyes fill and I can't find my words. Heath's eyes never leave me. He wants to step in, to shield me, but he knows it will make it worse. Instead, he stands there, every muscle tense, every breath shallow, watching and waiting for the moment things tip over the edge, when he can finally jump in and save me.

Dad releases my cheek, cuffs me with the back of his hand.

"Dad!" Heath steps forward, pleading.

It only angers him further. His curses fill the air, making it foul. My head is ringing.

"If you stumble, you're dead. If water gets into your waders," he growls, "they'll fill up like bloody floaters. And you see that?"

He points the sharp black tip of his knife to the rolling sea.

"That ocean doesn't give a shit if you drown in it. It doesn't care that you love it. It's ancient and restless and hungry." He pauses, rubbing his thumb over the handle. "So hungry it hurts."

He straightens up, thinking. He's calmer now, some of the color returning to his ruddy face. That's how quickly he changes. It's jarring. It makes you watch him across the room for clues. Hypervigilance. That's how it starts.

"All it cares about is that you're right there in its mouth," he says. "You're not Heath or Minnow anymore then, you understand me? You're just food for the fuckin' sharks."

"And you're either the shark or the food," I recite.

He brightens a little, pleased. "Good girl."

This time, he cups the side of my face, gently, gently. My cheek still stings from where he hit me, but I know it's my fault. Not his. If

I'd only answered faster. If I hadn't been so slow, so stupid. My fault. My fault.

"So when you're out there, castin'," he says again, "always take a knife."

I can't nod fast enough, and he softens.

"Here, see?" He clips his black knife into the sheath strapped to his waist. "If you feel the water get in, you drop the fuckin' rod and you grab for your knife. Cut the straps, and make sure not to cut your damn self while you're at it. Get the waders off, quick as you can, and swim to shore. Understand?"

I nod again. But no, I didn't really understand.

It was Heath who explained later.

"The water will carry you away, Min. Fast as anything. That's the danger of casting into the water at night. It's hard to see out there, and it's so damn loud. If you stumble, or a big wave hits you, the water will funnel into your waders, filling them up. And it's so cold that the shock of it'll make you slow. By the time you realize that . . . Just take a knife, always. Okay, kiddo?"

I did not want to walk out into that water at night. But Dad insisted on it. You need toughenin' up, he said. It was years later I realized he was saying it more to himself and using us as an excuse.

"Not yet," Heath pleaded on my behalf. "She's too young for that, Dad."

But all I could think about was my father's words, and I imagined what it would be like out there alone in the dark. The shock of the cold water filling you up, carrying you off into the darkness while the waves silenced every one of your screams.

My father was not afraid of sharks. But he was afraid of that. I could see it in his face. Heath and I weren't scared of the water. Sometimes I think he hated us for that.

He made Heath do it as often as possible, step into the waders and the black water, casting as far as he could where the bigger fish waited. Snapper, whiting, harmless gummy sharks. Enough food to last for weeks.

I never understood why he insisted on fishing the beach at night.

He had the Deep Sea. There was no need to plunge into the cold ocean and battle the black waves. But the truth is, he hated the boat, too. More, I think.

And the older I grew, the more I realized these night trips were his way of proving to himself that he was still in control. That maybe, next time he entered the water, the fear would lessen. But it never did. It must have been maddening for him, relentlessly grappling with fear, trying to out-stare it in the dark. And losing each time.

For a man like my father, control is everything. How unacceptable it must have felt to him that his own children loved something he feared so deeply. Maybe that's why he dragged us down there in the dark—maybe he was trying to make us fear it, too. He didn't realize that he was my ocean. He was the cold, dark water, and all the fucking monsters in it.

I watched my father step uneasily into the water, one hand on the rod, one hand tight on the sheath. I watched until he merged with the darkness, disappearing.

I THRASH AWAKE, SWEATING. The ocean hums through my pillow. Seawater sloshes through my ears. Jessie lifts her head, gives me a look: *Are you okay?*

Chills tiptoe down my neck. The ocean calls again, urgent. Dazed, I tumble out of bed, pull open my closet, stare into the dark. The soles of my feet are dripping. My head feels like a water balloon. I tilt it to one side and half expect seawater to pour out in a salty torrent.

I dig at the back of the closet like a dog, find it. I tie the sheath flush to my ankle, pulling the strap until it cinches tight. The second strap wraps just above the curve of my calf, anchoring the knife in place. The handle is made from polished kangaroo bone, smooth and pale. Cool to the touch. I found the femur bone in the Wicked Woods when I was a kid and shaped it into a handle, clean and white.

I watch the Hannah video, turn it up as loud as it will go. Hannah screams and the ocean calls and calls, melting together into one unholy roar.

I fall asleep, sweating and shaking, until I don't know which is calling.

Fears for Daily journalist Chris Cooper: Car found abandoned near Violet Town

Herald Sun

A frantic search is underway for missing journalist Chris Cooper. He was last seen three days ago at a Benalla service station at 11 A.M. and his white Audi A5 Coupe was discovered last night, abandoned at a rest stop five kilometers from Violet Town.

Family and police hold concerns for his welfare.

"My son wouldn't just disappear. Someone knows something," his mother, Joanne Cooper, said. "As a mother, I'm begging the public—please, if you have even the slightest clue about where Chris is or what might have happened to him, please speak up now. We just want him home."

Anyone who sees him or has information about his whereabouts is urged to contact local police or Crime Stoppers on 1800 333 000.

CHAPTER 24

Let me tell you about sharks.

You know they're down there. Hunting, feasting, waiting. But you're stinging hot in the sunshine, your skin's turning pink, and the water is calling. So you go.

You're knee-deep now, waist-deep. That's when you remember the stories, isn't it? That's when they flood your mind like a wave crashing in.

Girl mauled by bull shark in knee-deep water.

Great white attacks surfer.

But God, it's bright and hot, and the water is so cool on your sunburned skin. So down you go, into the deep. Still, you feel the tug of fear. But it can't be you. It won't be you.

Until it is.

I STUMBLE DOWN THE SHORE, thinking, *Someone's going to die today.*

I step around a young family collecting shells in the shallows, past a couple strolling hand in hand, past a woman my age, sunglasses perched on her nose, magazine in a ring-heavy hand. I pause, inspecting them all. Which one of you is it?

Who's dying today?

I look out across the water. The surfers paddle and scramble, jostling for position, chasing every wave. But not Trav. He's straddling his board, calm and silent. He hasn't moved in minutes. When the right wave comes, he'll know. Until then, he'll wait for it. As long as it takes.

There's no news on Chris. Not a damn thing. But there's someone in this town who knows everything. And I'm here to find him.

The sun's going down, stretching long shadows across the shore. I look for Terry. Find him on the pier. He's hunched on a plastic fishing bucket, back slightly bent, shoulders relaxed in that quiet, patient way only years can teach.

A tattered cap shades his eyes, but he seems to know I'm coming. The weathered wood creaks beneath my shoes as I head to him, salty breeze tugging at my sleeves. His line cuts through the air with a soft swish before it splashes into the water. "Hey, Min."

I stop a few feet away, eyes flicking from his rod to the sea and then back to Terry. He's not looking at me. His eyes are focused on the water below like he knows all its secrets. There's something heavy in the air, but he doesn't acknowledge it. He just casts his line again with a smooth, practiced flick. He's squidding, and judging by the fresh ink staining his hands, he's caught a lot.

"Ask your questions," Terry finally mutters.

"I don't know where to start," I admit, taking a step closer. I fix my eyes on the surfers, seeking out Trav. He's waiting beyond the break, reading the rhythm of the water. The swell rises and he catches it, feet finding his board like it's a part of his body. The wave curls behind him, cresting over his shoulder. It reminds me of Heath's broken trophy. The golden surfer. The golden wave. Beautiful. "Trav works for you now?"

He nods, reeling in slowly. "He's a good skipper."

"And easily led."

He lifts an eyebrow, fingers still curled around the fishing line. "You can't make that boy do anything he doesn't wanna do."

That's only half true. If he loves you, there's nothing he won't do for you. But does he love Terry? This surrogate father figure. Half mentor, half shadow.

"He needed a job, I gave him one."

"Is that *all* he does for you?"

The old man doesn't answer right away.

I step closer. "Anything *I* should know about?"

"Depends who you're gonna tell, Min."

Chris. He knows I've been working with Chris.

My heart pounds in my chest as the silence between us stretches. "That journo ... someone left a shark tooth under his windshield wiper. Now he's missing."

His brow arches in quiet amusement. "A shark tooth. Did they?"

"Was it you?"

He lets the line float for a moment, then reels it in, thinking carefully before speaking. "Your mum ..." He sits there for a long moment, the sound of the lapping water filling the space between us. "I was always sorry I didn't do more."

"Sorry you didn't do more for *her*? Or for Heath and me?"

His shoulders sag. "All of you ... the kids, too."

His gaze is distant now, lost in the past. And I realize he's talking about the blood boys in town, forced out to the Wicked Woods while their dads got shitfaced and violent at his pub. Then I think of Terry's paternal hand on Heath's shoulder, how my brother leaned into it. Trav skippering Terry's beloved fishing boat.

"Maybe you thought you could make it up to Heath, to Trav," I say slowly, "by getting them involved in something they shouldn't be. Something lucrative ... illegal?"

I move closer. "And you were worried about Chris finding out, so you sent him a warning. Now he's gone. Just like Hannah Striker."

There's the briefest flicker of something on his face when I mention Hannah's name. When he speaks, it's with a certain weariness that makes his words feel like they're laden with too much history. "Drop this, Min."

"I can't."

"If you love your brother ..." His eyes flick to mine. "If you still love Trav ... you'll drop it. You'll leave it alone."

I'm about to speak when the scream rings out. Silence sweeps over the beach like invisible hands are holding our mouths shut.

Conversations cease. Children stop laughing. Even the surfers are frozen on their boards, heads lifted high, waiting.

And then someone screams out, "Shark!"

A fin strikes through the surface, only meters from the small group of surfers. They cry out in alarm, bolting up on the boards, pulling their limbs out of the water as the fin surges closer. The shark is huge, the dorsal fin towering over their heads. The surfers huddle together, gripping their boards tightly, as the fin circles them.

"Oh my God!" A woman bolts up from her towel, pointing at the shallows. "There's *two* of them!"

Emerging from the shallows is another fin, racing through the water like a nightmare. A man stands waist-deep, frozen, eyes locked on the fin. The people on the beach bolt to their feet, pointing and yelling at the two fins.

"Get out of the water!"

"Shark!"

"Get out! Get out!"

Amid the panicked screaming, Colleen lurches forward, running for the water. "Trav!"

I race after her, down the pier, jumping onto the hot sand, weaving among the screaming people. Colleen charges for the water as the swimmers come scrambling out. Panicked, they run for the sand, looking over their shoulders the whole way.

"Oh my *God*!" someone is yelling. "It's got him! It's got him!"

My heart thumps hard as I chase Colleen down, almost knocking over a woman holding a screaming toddler, and a man hauling a teenage girl out of the shallows.

Colleen reaches the water. She's ankle-deep and screaming out for her son. "Trav!"

I finally catch up to her, grabbing her around the waist, holding her back. I can feel her heart hammering under my forearm. She pushes at my chest, tries to free herself, but I hold her tighter. With a cry, she glances desperately at the water. It's empty now except for the surfers, still coiled together. Trav. Where's Trav?

Colleen struggles harder, while I frantically count the surfers.

One, two, three . . .

It's got him. It's got him!

Oh God.

"Trav!" Colleen shrieks in my ear, momentarily still from shock. "Where is he?"

A wave begins to form, rising and rising in the water. In a quick movement, the surfers paddle hard for it, and even from the beach I can feel their desperation, their terror. They scramble for the wave, riding it to the shallows, as the people gather in a loud line on the beach, yelling encouragement.

Two surfers make it back, sprinting to the shore as soon as their feet hit the sand. The third staggers like a sleepwalker, dripping blood. His knee buckles; his eyes roll back in his head. A woman rushes for him, shrieking as he collapses into a bloody heap on the sand. She throws herself beside him, placing a hand on his shoulder, shaking him. "He's in shock!" she yells out. "Someone call an ambulance!"

The other two surfers hover over him, eyes wide and vacant.

"I'll do it," a man calls back, digging into his shorts pocket, pulling out a phone.

"His arm . . ." someone calls out, voice heavy with horror. "My God, his *arm*."

The beach is tense, silent now. Mothers snatch their toddlers into their sunburned arms, slinging towels over their shoulders, ushering their older children to pack up, *quick, quick, quick. Don't look.*

A teenager huddles under a beach umbrella, knees pulled tight to her chest, speaking tearfully into her phone. "Mum . . . come get me." Her voice breaks. "*Please.*"

A bundle of school-aged kids flee to waiting parents, sand flying beneath their feet.

"You need to get here," the man hisses into the phone, staring grimly at the surfer, "and you need to get here *now*."

Only Colleen and I notice the final surfer emerging from the water. Trav. Waves crash behind him, spraying foam as his surfboard cuts through, gliding to shore. He almost looks like a part of the ocean itself. The sun glints off the water, and the black fin rises behind it like a towering shadow.

For a moment, it looks like the shark is hunting him down. But Trav glides effortlessly back to shore, and the fin hovers in the hull of a cresting wave before sinking back to the depths.

Trav watches the injured surfer from the shallows, seawater dripping from his chin. He makes no attempt to help. Instead he eyes the bleeding boy with barely concealed hunger, veins pulsing in his throat. There's a damp sheen on his skin like he's sweating out poison and failing. His eyes are dilated and darting rapidly, lips curling back like a wolf that's gone too long without a good, bloodied meal.

Or a shark.

Colleen calls his name over and over like he's a child trapped in a fever dream. He ignores her, runs his tongue under a spiky incisor, eyelids half closed.

And I stand on the shore, thinking.

I know why the sharks don't want him.

He's one of them.

CHAPTER 25

I found the note sticky-taped to the back of my bedroom window.

You've been gone so long you missed everything.
Trav.

I replaced his note with my own.

Meet me at the Wicked Woods tonight.

I squint at the sunset, and a fat bead of sweat drips onto my fist. The bats screech in the ghost gums, wings pulled tight against their teeth. I shiver under the tree shadow, watching the crows clambering up and down its powder-white branches. They call for the night, their whole bodies *hungry* for it. Their nighttime orchestra has begun, and tonight, nothing in the world could stop the dark.

My town is stirring, casting off the sunset like a shirt that doesn't fit. *Bring me the dark*, it insists. *The darkness is ours. The darkness is mine.*

The Wicked Woods shudder with the weight of the madness, and I'm stretched so fucking tight that if the bats screech any louder, my bones will burst out of my skin to tumble through the red dirt, and I will be nothing more than a feast for the crows. There's something right about that.

I spit on the red dirt and wait for Trav against the backdrop of a blood sunset. I see us as children, him with his matted blond mullet, my dirty-blond hair to my waist, sprinting through these woods, lighting it up with fire and our madness: *We're coming! We're coming! Watch out!*

We were so young, then. Hungry for everything.

Sometimes, to avoid Dad, Heath and I slept at the cabin. Luke and the older boys would wander down, drunk off stolen cans of beer, and pass out on the cabin floor. Heath remained alert enough to check on me throughout the night. Trav and I slept under the stars as they blazed above and the nights dragged and burned, like a sun refusing to set. I'd wake in the morning with his hair in my mouth, his cheek in the hollow of my throat.

The sun finally surrenders to the night, and darkness enfolds us all. I lean against the ghost gum, stomach uncoiling. I exhale shakily, blowing red dust into the dark night. I wait for Trav, and I wonder. All our lives, we played games according to my rules. Even Amy. I still believe I'm the reason he stabbed her.

A crow lands at my feet, wings folded disapprovingly behind him, talons caked in the rusty dirt. I spit on the ground, rub it between my fingertips, and smear it onto my forearms.

The crow lifts off, and I watch until he's just a speck in the night sky. Trav arrives, head down, hands in his pockets, and I whisper to no one, "He's back."

TRAV NODS ONCE, INSTANTLY LOOKS down like he's done something wrong, plunges his hands back into the deep pockets of his black board shorts. His black T-shirt is sleeveless, hooded.

You've been gone so long you missed everything.

I have. I've only seen Trav in a full-length wet suit. The man standing a foot away is covered in tattoos, from the arches of his feet to the tops of his thighs. Two sleeves end neatly at his wrists. His lower half is sea-themed, swirling waves and busty mermaids, twin anchors on both knees.

But his arms tell a different story.

Woods. These woods.

I scan his forearms, and he slowly lifts his head.

A grove of towering ghost gums reach up to his elbow. Trickling through is a bubbling creek, lit by moonlight. A crow sentry circles the sky, guarding a boy perched on a bone-white branch. The boy is bare-chested and filthy, eyes set on the creature half hidden in the creek bed. Me.

In his tattoo, I'm half fish, half girl. Not a mermaid or a siren. Something else. My scales are molar-shaped and shine wetly in the moonlight. The colors are repulsive, the red of raw meat, tobacco-stain yellow. Crammed in my mouth are rows and rows of needle teeth. My hair is mud-slicked, my hands are shark teeth, and there are two incisors where my eyes should be.

Trav spits on the dirt, scrapes it in with the heel of his reef walkers. The creek hums over my left shoulder. I slink to it, wordless, wondering if he'll follow.

He does.

A handful of stars shine weakly, spilling their reflection onto the creek. They look like they're trapped in there. My favorite spot was the shallow trench lined with sun-warmed pebbles, slick with silky mud. It's not lost on me that the fish-girl was hiding here.

I sink to my knees and plunge both fists in, grabbing at pebbles. Trav steps around me and lowers himself like he always did, propped up on his palms, the tips of his toes. I squeeze the pebbles in my fists, and my blood burns thick enough to turn me to stone.

"Did the surfer make it?" I finally ask, half opening my fist, peeking in.

"Think so."

Did you want him to? Or did you want to watch as the life drained out?

Like you did with Amy.

I inspect a pebble, rub it with the back of my thumb. It's oval-shaped, the color of a ghost gum, looks like the moon. How instinctive it is that I want to give it to him. Ten-year-old me would have reached out, fist clenched. *Guess what I got?*

He'd scramble forward, wait for my fist to open. I'd make him wait, too. Just enough to make him sweat with need. Then I'd uncurl my fist, place it into his sun-brown hand. *You can have it.*

The thing about Trav was that he could never accept a gift without giving one in return. A simple gift like a moon-shaped pebble and he'd disappear into the thorny gully where the wild blackberries grew. He'd emerge, shirtless and bloodied, T-shirt tied in a tight knot, bulging with berries.

Did I take advantage of him?

I'm not sure.

I know only that something changed the day we went to Amy's house. I don't know if Trav felt it, too. Maybe it was only me who went home to an absent mother, a rage-filled father, briny sheets, and a paper plate of bloodied kangaroo. Maybe I was the only one who burned and burned and burned.

Violent kids are overt or covert. The blood boys simmered with hot anger and obscene punch lines. Meanwhile, I was small and wordless and raging so silently.

The afternoon I tried to drown Amy, Trav was there. Watching from the low branches of the ghost gum. I never told anyone that. Only he and I knew.

I hauled Amy up, her swimming cap askew, ears burning red. Half of me ached to apologize, the other half said, *Let the fucker drown.*

Trav had that watchful, predatorial hunger. Was I surprised he finished off what I couldn't?

No.

Was I sorry about it?

Yes.

And no.

It's hard to be mad at someone who sees what you desperately want and gives it to you, no matter the consequences.

I don't know what to say and I suspect Trav feels the same. I roll the pebble in my fist and get to my feet, the creek bathwater-warm. I hover over him, and he watches me silently, raising his chin.

"Got something for you," I say, revealing the moon pebble.

He gets to his knees, reaches up, and I have a flashback that leaves me sweating. Dizzy, I drop the stone into his palm, stagger back.

"Thank you," is all he says, holding it up to the moonlight.

"Where's Chris?"

He closes a tattooed fist over the pebble.

"Trav?"

"I don't know what you want from me."

"I want to know where Chris is. Will you tell me?"

He won't answer. Cradles the pebble in his hand, opening it, closing it. *You've been gone so long you missed everything.*

"What have I missed, Trav?" I ask softly.

He gives me a doleful look; *I'm not going to answer that.*

"Do you know what happened to my mum?"

"No," he says emphatically, eye contact unwavering. "If I did, I'd tell you."

Trav never lied about what he did to Amy; he admitted it frankly when he was brought in for questioning. I've never known him to lie to me, either. I believe him, but I'm not going to let it go.

"Do you remember Hannah Striker? The first attack?"

He nods, once.

"Before her death," I begin carefully, "someone left a pair of shark jaws on her doorstep. Do you know anything about that?"

"On her doorstep?"

That's a strange question to ask. Why not, *Did you say shark jaws? Someone left a pair of fucking shark jaws for her? Why?*

"What do you know about Hannah?"

He sighs like I'm asking the wrong question. "We were, what"—he frowns, calculating—"ten when she died. She was swimmin', yeah? It happens."

"Yeah, but what doesn't happen is someone dropping off shark jaws right before the attack."

"I don't know anythin' about her," he insists.

"Something came for me, too. Teeth. Great white."

That gets his attention.

"Who left it for me?"

"Heath leaves the house most nights, yeah? 'Bout midnight?"

My spine stiffens. "Yeah. He and Luke check the nets."

"... Do they?"

I flinch, dropping my head. There's a heavy feeling in my stomach, a sudden coldness behind the back of my ribs. I didn't want to believe Heath was a part of any of this, but there were times I wondered. In a halting voice, I ask, "Where do they go?"

He glances up the winding track, past the ghost gum, like he thinks he's said too much already.

I press ahead. "Do you know there's a video of Hannah's attack?"

There it is. The hunger. That flash of heat and teeth, like his mouth is flooding with saliva, body aching with a craving that has nothing to do with choice.

"You watched it," he says quietly. "Didn't you?"

"I had to."

"Right," he murmurs. "And how many *times* have you watched it?"

Since I got home from Rachel's mum's house, I've been bolting awake from fever dreams and reaching instinctively for the video. I watch it until I'm sick and sweating and my father murmurs approvingly in my ear, *You can hear it, too, can't you, Min?*

"I had to," I mutter again, lowering my gaze. "There's something about the video . . . I can't explain it, but there's something I'm missing. Some clue. I feel it."

That's what I keep telling myself. I watch it not because I'm drawn to the violence. But because there's something in the video that holds the key to solving it all.

He says nothing. I step forward, nudge his abdomen with my knee. "Would you lie to me?"

"*For* you."

There's a hum in my skin. A heavy pulse in my neck. Everywhere I turn, there are memories of us. The cabin. The creek.

I think of Chris, smell his peach soap, hear his work shirt rustle, see his nose wrinkle when I swear.

Then I think of a boy with a matted mullet. Magpie wing cradled between his palms. He splashes silently into the creek, drops to his knees, reaches up, offers me something. Everything.

My eyes drift to his forearm. He catches me watching and nods just once. *Yes, you remember.*

He raises his arm, the one with the Wicked Woods and the fish-girl-teeth.

And I grab it up greedily like I always did, stuff it in my mouth, bite down hard while he tugs at his board shorts and runs his tongue over his teeth.

CHAPTER 26

I clutch the monster book tighter, never reading a word. Jessie naps beside me, flat on her back, paws in the air. In the lounge room, Heath's sprawled on the couch, watching TV with the sound on low. Occasionally, I hear the distant sound of a laugh track, and the noise makes my jaw clench. Makes me grip the book even tighter until my fists ache.

I glance at my phone: 11:50 P.M.

Ten minutes to go.

As time ticks down, my stomach churns, my breathing accelerates. I feel like I'm running a race, even though I'm lying in bed.

The TV finally shuts off. Footsteps on the floor, coming closer, closer. Jess rolls over, lifts her head.

Heath knocks twice. "You decent?"

"Yeah," I answer quickly, dropping the book onto the blanket. "Come in."

Heath pokes his head in. "I'm off," he says almost apologetically. "Gotta check the nets now."

Jessie wags her tail at him, and I manage a nod. Heath tilts his head to the side, concerned. "You all right?"

"Yeah!" I say. "I'm good."

With a steady, unblinking look he examines me. Uneasy. And I ask, "Did you hear about the ghost shark?"

Something in his body softens, as if a weight has slipped off his shoulders. For a moment, anyway. "Wow," he says softly, hand hanging loosely from the doorknob. "Thought you'd forgotten those stupid jokes I used to tell you."

"They weren't stupid," I insist. "I loved them."

"Really?" He gives me a smile, pleased. "I'm glad to hear that."

He hovers in the doorway a moment longer, eyes misting. I wonder if he's thinking of all the times we fished side by side as kids. Wonder if he's thinking of the long lulls of silence and me, growing bored and restless, waiting for my rod to finally go off.

Hey, he'd say, *what's a sea monster's favorite meal?*

How do shellfish get to the hospital?

"Call me if you need me," he says. "I'm only five minutes away."

"De-*fin*-itely."

"Nice one!" He grins, pulling the door closed. "Night, Min."

I sit up. "Wait!"

He whirls around, surprised. "Yeah?"

I feel stupid. "The ghost shark," I finally say. "It vanished into *fin* air."

He offers a rare laugh, but his eyes are assessing, watchful. A heavy silence settles after. "I love you, Min," he finally says. "See you in the morning." He closes my door with a soft click, and Jessie rolls over again, paws in the air, eyes closing. I wait, jaw tensed. Heath's car finally rolls past the bedroom window, towing the *Deep Sea*. And as soon as he pulls out of the driveway, I throw my blankets off and get to my feet.

I STOMP DOWN TO DAD's room and pull his door open, bracing for the fishy smell. I head to the wardrobe, breathing shallowly through my mouth as I wrench it open. I find what I'm looking for and stuff it in my overcoat pocket.

It's just past midnight when I rush out the front door, the wind relentless. My shoes slap against the pavement, the streetlights flickering overhead. The street's empty, but the shadows feel alive. I glance over my shoulder for just a second, barely slowing down, my stomach rolling in fear. But no one's out tonight. The neighbors' cars are tucked inside garages; the lounge room lights are off. Everyone's asleep. No one is going to witness what I'm about to do.

Go, I tell myself. *Go!*

I run as quietly as I can, headed for beach number 1.

The moon shines down like a weak torch as I climb the sand dunes, avoiding the roads. I step over rusty beer cans, stumbling through the sand, leg muscles cramping as the sound of the waves roars closer and closer.

By the time I reach the top, my forehead is covered in icy sweat and the stitch in my side makes me gasp in pain. I retreat to the shadows, hands on my knees, my breaths quick and shallow.

I straighten up slowly, looking over my right shoulder to the empty parking lot. Heath would've parked his car at the dock before climbing aboard the *Deep Sea*. I wonder if he's made it here already, or if I beat him to it.

I'm still scanning the lot when I hear the sharp sound of laughter behind me. I drop to the ground, crouching low, gulping down breaths to stay quiet. My ears ache with the noise of the waves and, underneath it, the crunching of footsteps on gravel.

Soft laughter, a voice calling out, half lost in the wind, "Don't go chasin' the bloody wombats!"

Shit.

My shoulders tighten when I see the dog. A black Lab, ten meters away, sniffing at the tussock grass.

Shit. Shit. Shit.

I crouch there in the dark, legs burning, frozen to the spot. If they spot me . . . how the hell am I supposed to explain to this stranger why I'm crouching in the sand dunes in the dead of night?

Unless . . . this person isn't a stranger.

I peer through the tussock grass to the parking lot, narrowing my eyes when I see the silhouette of a man. I scan his features, but it's too dark to see his face.

The dog lifts its head, sniffs once.

And looks straight at me.

"Come here!" the man yells. I flatten my hands on the ground, ducking so low that my nose touches the sand. The dog barks urgently, and my heart seizes in fear as the man climbs the side of the dune, swearing under his breath.

I stop breathing.

"Get here now!" the man commands, slipping his hand into the dog's collar, roughly pulling it away. The dog won't stop barking. It rises up on its back legs, straining hard. I flinch with each bark and wait, breathless and anxious, until the barking subsides and the footsteps retreat. When I'm sure they're gone, I raise my head and scan the parking lot.

Empty.

I get slowly to my feet. With a quick glance to my left and right, I creep to the edge of the clifftop, the boom of the waves pounding my eardrums as I get closer. Wind claws at my hair, stinging my eyes as I hide in the shadows, staring down at the dark water.

And there it is.

A blur of white cruising through the darkness. I reach into my pocket and dig out the binoculars, scanning the scrawl of words on the side of the boat. Yes, it's her.

The *Deep Sea*.

I hover there at the cliffside, standing sideways to shield my body from the wind. I scan the boat through the binoculars, not even sure what I'm looking for as it races through the water.

My pulse quickens when it starts to slow down near a marker buoy. The captain gets to his feet, hands still on the wheel as he peers over the side into the water. Heath. A man beside him is tucked into the passenger seat in a loose ball of limbs, eyes fixed on a mobile phone. Luke.

The boat comes to a stop, bobbing on the water, disappearing for a moment as a wave rolls past. And when the view clears, I stare down and freeze.

Heath is standing in the middle of the boat, staring straight at the clifftop. I swear, he's looking right at me. Instinctively, I duck, but there's no way he can see me here. I'm hidden in the darkness, dressed all in black. Even if he had binoculars, he'd struggle to spot me. So, why is he staring so intently at the clifftop?

I glance behind me, terrified the man and his dog will reappear. I brace myself to run, ready to flee at any second. But there's nothing. Just the dark and the wind blowing over the tussock grass.

I turn back, bringing the binoculars slowly up to my eyes. He's moving now, stalking up and down the boat, pointing at the water as Luke leans over the rail, looking down. Heath crowds in beside him, peering intently into the water.

Shark nets, Luke had said. *The VFA put 'em up last month. Two meters under the surface, a hundred meters long. S'posed to reduce the chance of an attack.*

I raise an eyebrow in surprise as Heath drops into the skipper's seat and Luke shines a torch on the surface. They must be looking for any tangled wildlife.

Stingrays, turtles, none of the big boys yet . . .

The *Deep Sea* cruises parallel to the shore as Luke shines his torch alongside, inspecting the nets. I lower the binoculars, feeling foolish. I don't know what the hell I expected to see, but it wasn't this.

But then.

Luke whirls around, eyes scanning the clifftop, his body frozen. From his spot at the skipper's seat, Heath glances first at the deserted beach, then slowly raises his head to the parking lot. I check it, too, pausing to glance over my right shoulder at the empty lot.

What are they looking for?

Heath turns to Luke, and it looks like he's calling out something over the idling engine. Luke walks quickly to the kill tank. He crouches down, wrenches it open, and reaches in.

The next part happens so fast that I'm reeling.

Heath guns the engine. The *Deep Sea* speeds down the length of the net like it's running a race. Luke scrambles to the rail, and I look down at his hands. He's holding something. Whatever it is, he's struggling with it. It's tucked under his chin, spans the entire length of his chest. A barrel. Silver.

I watch as Luke sets it on the ledge, opening the top with a quick twist and spewing its contents into the water. Heath glances at Luke, and just as quickly turns his focus back to cruising alongside the net. There's an urgency now to their work. *Quick. Get it done. Get it done.*

Get what done?

Luke's at the kill tank again, hauling up another barrel. He drags it to the side of the boat, opens it. I hold the binoculars tight against my face, breathless. I squint hard, staring at the contents of the barrel as it spews into the water.

Blood. He's dumping gallons of blood into the ocean. He empties it, throws it back into the kill tank. Reaches in with both hands, pulls something out.

Oh my God...

Luke throws kangaroo hunks into the water, hind legs and tails like he's throwing a ball to a dog.

The cabin in the woods... the decapitated kangaroos. I stagger back, the binoculars slipping from my hand as the realization hits me.

They're not keeping the sharks away at all.

They never were.

They're bringing them in.

CHAPTER 27

The next night, they come for him.

And my brother goes. Willingly.

The black utility truck pulls silently onto our shitty lawn. Headlights off. Waiting. There's something predatorial about it, a shark on the hunt.

Heath pulls the front door closed behind him, stalking past the lounge room window, just another shadow in the night. I've seen this so many times before. Hushed voices walking off into the darkness. Only it was always Dad and Terry. I crouch at my bedroom window, calves tight, squinting through the dark.

My nose pokes the windowsill as I stare at the blond driver, heart tight.

It's Luke.

Heath slinks into the passenger seat, head down. Luke half turns, arm hanging lazily from the wheel, watching Heath buckle himself in. Quietly, he pulls the car out, and I duck lower, race to the kitchen, and snatch up my car keys. When I'm sure the truck has pulled away, I peek through the blinds and make a break for the door. My jaw clenches when I slink into my car, shut the door, and start the engine. Headlights off, I follow.

It's a warm, clear night, cloudless, but I can barely see Luke's car. He speeds down the main street, merging with the darkness, and I trail carefully behind. This is going to be a long, tense ride.

But it's not.

Less than ten minutes later, I raise my chin in surprise when the truck turns sharply. I drive past, noting the sign: NEPTUNE ROAD. I count to sixty and when I can't see his taillights, I turn the wheel, looping back.

Neptune Road is a wide-open country strip stretching into a humid horizon. Cows munch behind barbed-wire fences, and a stray napkin flutters past bits of shredded tire and crushed beer cans. The road is lit only by a crescent moon and the flickering headlights of a flurry of cars pulling into a shack of a house.

I squint ahead, searching for Luke's car, but I don't find it. I pull slowly into a winding driveway, gasping when a red Holden swerves in front, cutting me off. I go to slam my palm into the horn, but stop just in time, glaring instead at its taillights.

The yard is the size of a football field. It's sunbaked and potholed, crammed with cars. They've parked everywhere, blocking the driveway, nudging the mailbox, front bumpers so close the noses kiss. I parallel-park on the shoulder, facing the road, then kill the engine and wait. Watch.

Men lurch out their cars, red-faced and sloshing beer. They greet one another loudly, slapping backs, embracing drunkenly. There's an *everyone's shitfaced at the pub* energy thrumming in the air. That weighted atmosphere where beefy men start to get spitty and shovey, and women and children feel the need to tiptoe around them. Like me.

Uneasy, I count over forty cars, most of them utility trucks with enough Aussie pride stickers to start a shop: A frowning koala waving an Aussie flag that reads, FUCK OFF WE'RE FULL. Yellow-and-green maps of Australia and nestled inside, the Southern Cross and a kangaroo mid-hop. Victorian license plates, mainly. I jot down their numbers and the handful of out-of-state plates. NSW. QUEENSLAND—

People stomp in and out of the squat house, past a kelpie dog tied to the porch, panting in the heat. Men carry icy coolers stuffed snugly with beer. Solemn women slump in deck chairs, balancing toddlers and swatting at mosquitoes.

But mostly . . . I lean forward, squinting. Mostly they ignore the house like they don't even see it. Like that's not what they came for.

My eyes follow a pack of staggering men, five of them, so drunk they're holding one another up. They stumble past the barking kelpie tied to the porch, swearing aggressively at it before disappearing around the corner.

I tap my index finger on the steering wheel, scanning for Luke's black vehicle, but I can't find it anywhere. Still, the cars keep pulling in with rowdy men in groups of two or three. All of them bypassing the house, stomping impatiently to the backyard. I watch with interest as a purple Holden glides in, pop music echoing out the car window. A pink-and-white decal on the bumper reads CUTE BUT CRAZY. And taking up nearly the entire back window are two stick figures, a woman kneeling in front of a man, mouth in his lap, declaring, NICE GIRLS SUCK!

What is it with these people and their car stickers? I watch five women spill out, late twenties, bubble skirts, rose tattoos. One of them carries a box of cask wine, and from the way they're all walking, it's clear they've been sampling it.

I cram a cap on and follow. We sidle past a drunken teen sitting cross-legged on a car bonnet, chomping hard on an ear of corn. Past the panting kelpie. One of the girls coos at it, thrusts the back of her hand up to its muzzle. It licks the back of her palm, and I hover behind them and freeze. This is the pub dog. The ancient kelpie that hangs around the courtyard. The one that rolled in the magpie carcass when I first arrived in town. I know whose dog this is.

Pulled up to a shattered back window is a black truck. Luke's. Empty. I keep walking, following their drunken steps, breathing in the peachy tang of the wine. But we don't get far. Ahead of us is a traffic jam of men, impatient and yelling over one another.

I rise up on my tiptoes, peering over the head of the girl clutching the cask wine, scorpion tattoo on her neck. There's an angry huddle waiting outside an industrial steel shed.

Someone snarls, "What's the farken holdup?"

"Hold ya horses, mate!"

I sink back to my feet, uneasy. There's a weight in the air, something cruel and carnival-like. I inch forward with the drunk girls until we're sweating outside the open mouth of the shed. A hefty man with a face like porridge waves us through, winking hard at the girl carrying the cask wine, who ignores him.

"Farken slut," he mutters.

Inside, it's cave-like and dirty, crowded as hell. There's a hundred people, at least, packed in tightly, restless and loud and waiting for something. Mostly men except for a handful of women cowering behind them, arms looped nervously through theirs, as if trying to hold them back. Calm them down.

From what?

I squirm through the feral crowd, cheeks filmy with sweat. It's windowless and humid, smells like body odor and meat. A Yamaha fishing boat is tucked in the corner, dripping. The *Titan*.

An elbow clips my shoulder, but I keep inching forward, pulling my cap lower, eyes on the floor. I squeeze through until my chin is inches from a man's shoulder. I try to step around him, but I'm smushed in. A tall man in a high-vis shirt smeared with oil stains pushes past me, shoulder bumping mine. He shoves his way through, and a beer-clogged voice snarls, "Watch where yer farken going, mate!"

The oil-smeared man gives him the finger. I stand on tiptoes, watching him settle at the far front of the shed. I blink in surprise when I see what he's standing in front of.

A stage. I narrow my eyes, staring at it. The elevated stage is scuffed plywood, the backdrop, three plastic shower curtains strung together. There's no special lighting or sound equipment, only five black steps leading up to the silent rectangular stage.

I try to step back but can't. Behind me, a fight breaks out. Two beer-soaked voices, a crash of fists, and a woman's pained cry. "He's drunk," she pleads.

I can't see her, but I bet she's desperate and exhausted, placing herself between the brawling men and her raging husband.

Leave him, I want to tell her. *It won't get better. It's in his blood.*

My ears throb with the noise that's growing louder and louder like someone turning the radio up. I want to run. Want to stay.

The men shift or sway in their spots, arms crossed or palms flat on their meaty stomachs, irritable. On edge. What are they all waiting for?

I'm stuck behind the man in front, sandwiched between sweaty limbs, the bridge of my nose brushing his black T-shirt. I'm drowning in the air, breathing through a sweaty sheet.

For a moment, I'm twelve years old, back in Heath's cabin, watching the blood boys slice kangaroo meat into marbled strips while Heath hovers behind, grim-faced and silent. As the blood boys grew, something began to shift. You could feel it. Something knocking inside their skulls, anxious to get out. A power struggle commenced, a bloody tug-of-war. I watched the blood boys battle for control, and Heath battle to keep it. Some days, I felt sandwiched between them all, guns pointed in every direction.

I feel it now. Here.

The man stumbles onto the stage, clutching a beer can in each fist. I rise up on my toes again, watch him trip up the final step, landing hard on his left knee. He raises the cans in the air, victorious and bellowing, "Didn't spill a drop!"

The blood men reward him with a football-like roar. He remains there kneeling onstage, chugging hard from one can, then the other, draining both before crunching them in his fists. "Showtime's in ten, fellas!"

The roar intensifies, a wave of sound. I sink to my feet and the crowd buzzes with anticipation. Cheers and chants and slapping backs, elbows shoving bodies forward, itching to get closer to the stage. I slink back, chin tucked to my chest, letting them push forward as I pull away. I peek at my phone, note the time:

1:50 A.M.

The porridge-faced man is gone. No one's guarding the door. No one cares anymore. The cask wine girls are sitting on the boat's smooth hull, pouring the plastic wine spout directly into their open mouths. The girl with the scorpion tattoo slides into the skipper's seat, pretends to drive it. No one tells her off. She honks the horn twice, but it's lost in the swell of noise.

I slink outside, peering up the entire length of the shed. A drunk man leans against a blackwood, using it for support as he fumbles with his belt, unzips his jeans. He mutters to himself as he pees, and I wait until he stumbles back inside, face flushed and laughing to himself.

I disappear outside, scanning the dark yard. The edges are lined with barbed wire, the grass limp and yellowing. Lawn chairs are scattered around a fish cleaning station under the shade of a ghost gum. A rusted boat is parked next to a hammock, its hull streaked with moss, weeds, and grime.

Stepping quickly, I walk the length of the shed, looking for doors. Behind me, the crowd hums with noise.

1:52 A.M.

Not long until showtime, whatever that is.

At the far back of the squat land are two sheds tucked to the right-hand side. One shed is larger, with a wide roll-up door. I turn slightly, looking behind me, but there's no one there.

I run, sprinting hard for the larger shed, weaving around broken beer bottles as it looms closer. I make it to the roller door, pausing once to look over my shoulder. A squat man carries a beer slab into the industrial shed, and I duck to the ground and wait.

1:54 A.M.

Six minutes to go.

I crouch beside the roller door, panting silently, lifting my head, watching the squat man disappear inside. Then I grip the door and yank it up as quietly as I can.

I peer into the darkness, blinking hard. High ceilings equipped with exhaust fans—that's the first thing I see. The second is the washing machines. Four of them, silver and black, stacked side by side along the left wall. On the right, four bathtubs in a vertical row. I blink when I see the five gas stoves lining the back wall, four burners each in a gridlike pattern on the cooktop. Blink again at the giant stainless-steel cooking pots discarded around the room.

I creep forward until my knee brushes the first tub rim. I look down. Then I stagger to the next, and the next.

Each bathtub is three-quarters full of something soaking in filthy, coffee-colored water. I reach in and pull one out. The shell is oval shaped, encrusted with algae, and it fits snugly into my palm. I shuck it open with my knife, the meat inside smooth and pale beige.

Abalone. A shitload of abalone. A processing facility. Illegal as hell.

I plunge my free hand in, grasping another in my fist. I rub my thumb over the slimy flesh, shaking my head. There's easily a quarter million dollars' worth here.

I peer behind me before slipping the abalone back into the water. Then I remove my phone from my pocket.

1:56 A.M.

Four minutes. Quickly, I pull the roller door down, gliding it smoothly down the tracks. I spend the next minute snapping photos, wincing each time the flash goes off. I find three Cryovac machines perched on a shelf, near the last bathtub.

I shake my head as I snap more photos. So they wash them, dry them, and then vacuum-seal them here, before exporting them. Is Heath involved? Has he always been?

... And do I want to be?

1:57 A.M.

Three minutes until showtime...

I pause, thinking of the stage. Is that what showtime is? Is this whole fucked-up night an illegal abalone ring? Do they go out under the cover of night, bagging it? Bringing it back, seeing who caught the most?

Got to go. Got to go.

I reach for the roller door, yanking it up a foot before crouching low and looking under. Nothing. I make a break for it, diving out, pulling it closed behind me. Then I stalk across the yard, shaking my head, thinking the night can't get any wilder.

I couldn't have been more wrong.

CHAPTER 28

Two a.m.

Showtime.

The shed hums with noise.

I hang back near the door, watching the drunk girls tumble off the boat, landing hard on their feet. It's tense now, charged with anticipation. The blood men are restless, sweaty with adrenaline, elbowing one another in their meaty ribs, a menacing edge to their voices.

The porridge-faced man reappears, body coiled, eyes flickering like a patient snake. He slithers behind me, guarding the door, hands twitching at his sides, breathing heavily into the back of my neck. I step forward but I'm blocked in again, sandwiched between bodies, too tight to maneuver my way forward or back.

No one moves. No one can.

2:07 a.m.

"Hurry the fark up!"

"I don't have all night, boys!"

"Wasting my *farken* time!"

The shed pulses with each shout. I sweat hard, feeling like the walls are constricting. Every curse, every shift of weight, a spark. If we wait any longer, the whole damn shed feels like it will burst into flames.

Then I see them. Standing together near the stage. Trav. Terry. The older man's hand rests on Trav's shoulder, not heavy but steady, reassuring. Reminds me of my first night back in the Roo Bay pub when Terry reached out for Heath, fatherly hand on his shoulder.

I duck lower, hoping they don't see me, as an ironic cheer erupts, so loud I feel the echo in my ribs. I peek over the man's shoulder, eyes on the stage, watching a struggling man ascend the steps. He's hunched over, waddling like a duck, straining under the weight of what he's carrying. His face is contorted with effort, veins in his neck bulging, shoes squeaking as he inches forward.

Two red-faced men at the side of the stage urge him on, raising beers, eyes glazed. "Good on ya, Dave-O!"

"You got this, matey!"

The man onstage grunts with effort, pouring sweat under the shed lights, reminding me of a weight lifter. He pauses, shifting his grip, and his drunk mates urge him on, slapping their knees, yelling encouragement. The blood men raise up a cheer like a cresting wave, and it's so loud, the walls rattle.

Urged on, the man grunts again, heaving and struggling to the end of the stage where Luke awaits, microphone loose in his left hand. I tug my cap down, but nothing could pull Luke's eyes from the man. Luke's laughing his *holy shit* laugh, slapping his stomach, delighted. Finally, the man staggers to the finishing line—the weigh-in platform.

He heaves the catch down and the thunderous cheer crashes into the air, erupting all at once, as if the blood men had been waiting and waiting to let it loose. The man straightens up, rubbing the small of his back, his smile huge. But my eyes are on his mako shark.

Showtime.

The shark has small black eyes, a sharp nose, long, narrow teeth protruding from the mouth. Looks like absolute hell. A shortfin mako is a speed-swimming shark, the fastest on earth. Three to four meters in length, weighing anywhere from 60 kilograms to 150, and capable of leaping clear of the water when hooked. They can even land in the boat if you're not careful. Sometimes one will play dead when hooked on a longline, only to spring to life once you've got the bastard in the boat. They're highly sought after as a game species, if you can get them. The fillets are pale pink, like flake. A good eating shark.

And the thing is, it's not illegal to catch them.

So why the hell are we here?

Public weigh-ins take place on the boat ramps. We have two in

Kangaroo Bay, both with fish cleaning tables and a fish weighing station. News travels fast when someone's caught a big mako. You gather your mates up, stop at the bottle shop, then head down to the boat ramp. You offer the fishermen a Carlton Draught each, then watch the weigh-in, half drunk and envious.

Then you stand on the sidelines like pelicans, watching them slice the fillets into thick steaks of pearly meat.

Maybe they offer you a few fillets, maybe they don't.

After, everyone gets shitfaced and violent at the Roo Bay pub.

I look around the shed, willing my heart rate to slow down, but it keeps speeding up. Why are they holding the public weigh-in here? Away from the town? Away from everything?

I inch back, sweat dripping down my knees as the man ties a rope around the mako's crescent-shaped tail and Luke winches it up. As the digital scale tallies up the weight, shouts call out.

"Seventy-five kilos!"

"Sixty-four!"

"Hundred kilo, just like ya mum!"

Beery laughter rings out, and I look desperately for another exit. I scan the faces at the front of the stage for Heath, but I don't see him.

"Sixty-eight kilograms!" Luke calls when the scale numbers stop flickering. "Nice one! Dinner's on Dave-O!"

Dave-O gives two thumbs-up to the crowd. He saunters off, slapping high-fives to the front row, and Luke brings the microphone to his mouth, eyes alight, announcing, "Bring on the next!"

I STARE AT THE FINAL MAKO, strung up by its tail, bleeding from its mouth. There were three of them. The biggest, seventy-four kilograms, caught by a shitfaced trio of fishermen spoiling for a fight.

Dave-O's crushed. His mates are steel-jawed and edgy and trading harsh words with the sneering trio. There's a fight in the air; everyone feels it. Luke doesn't seem to notice or give a shit. He's crouched at the front of the stage, smiling, talking easily to the girl with the scorpion tattoo. Behind him, the trio size up Dave-O's mates, faces etched with aggression.

Watch out, Luke, I want to yell. *For once, take something seriously.*

The head of the trio is being held back by his friends, spittle forming in the corners of his mouth. The shitfaced duo yell back, accusing him of cheating. Luke shoots them a glance, but that's it. He doesn't say, *Easy now!* Or, *Come on, boys, calm down.* Like Heath would.

Luke just watches with interest as they yell insults. Looks like he wants to say, *Ooh, keep going! I dare ya.*

Heated seconds tick by. The head of the trio strains hard against his mates, who are struggling to pull him back. The crowd comes alive again, sound bouncing off the walls, swirling around the room. Someone is about to get hurt and I want to get out of here before that happens. But no one's leaving, and I don't know why.

2:48 A.M.

Do something, Luke.

He doesn't.

Someone else does.

The girl with the scorpion tattoo climbs the stage. The room quiets for a moment, and she curls her lips into a subtle smile, aware of the effect she's having on the male-heavy crowd. Their bodies seem to stretch forward, gazes fixed on her. Even the trio behind her falter, murmuring appreciatively, skirmish forgotten as they stare at her tanned thighs. She blows the crowd a kiss, and Luke holds the microphone up to her lips. She reaches for it, but at the last moment, he lowers it until it's level with his crotch. The drunk front row thinks it's hilarious, slapping each other's backs, whistling and hollering. Smiling, she bends down and grasps the microphone firmly in her fist. Egged on by Luke, she brushes her lips over the microphone head, whispers seductively, "Get ready for the real show, boys!"

It happens fast. Behind me, the porridge man screams, "No photos! You hear me? Keep your phones in your farken pockets!"

Luke quickly ushers the men offstage, and the scorpion girl hurries next to the weigh-in, body vibrating with anticipation.

What the hell. What the hell.

I dart a glance behind me, inching my body sideways, stomach plummeting. The crowd shifts, murmuring restlessly. Even the temperature seems to rise. They know what's coming. I don't.

I take another step back, trying to weave through the press of bodies, but every movement is a battle. I nudge my heel back, shifting my shoulders as I try to push through. But the crowd doesn't part, and the harder I push, the tighter the space becomes. A knot forms in my chest. I'm stuck.

A call rings out: "Here she is, boys!"

I wait for the crowd to erupt in noise. Whatever they were waiting for is finally here. But it's deathly silent. The hum of conversation fades; shoulders straighten as a charged silence settles over the room. Time seems to stretch, and there's no sound at all now, just the steady pulse of waiting.

Then I see it.

What they were all waiting for.

I see it. But I can't believe it.

My mouth falls open. The man in front of me holds his breath, shaking his head over and over.

Eleven men stagger up the stage, buckling under the weight of a massive, slick shark. Its death-gray tail swings wildly as they struggle to maintain their footing. Their voices are terse, communicating in sharp, quick words, hunching under its massive weight; every step forward is a battle. They grunt in exertion, heaving and hauling, trying to hold on. The crowd finally responds, cheering them on, shouting encouragement.

But I just stand there, frozen, pulled back to my first night in Kangaroo Bay. The night Rachel Sutherland was attacked.

Another great white spotted in Kangaroo Bay.

Beasts from the deep.

The exhausted fishermen reach the scale to thunderous cheers. Dazed, I watch them tie the rope to the tail, the winch groaning under the massive weight. The roar of the crowd is deafening as the numbers on the scale shoot up, and Luke screams out, "Six hundred twenty-four kilograms!"

But it's not a mako.

It's a great white shark. Protected. Illegal.

"No photos!" the porridge man keeps screaming. "No photos!"

They're not keeping the sharks away at all. They're bringing them in.

So many sightings. So many attacks. And now I know why.

Because here in Kangaroo Bay, they've been hunting them all along.

CHAPTER 29

I stand in our front doorway, dazed. The lights are all off. Jessie emerges from my bedroom, tail wagging lazily, still half asleep. I pat her absentmindedly, and she leans against my knees, yawning. She trots back to my bedroom, looking over her shoulder, waiting for me.

I don't follow.

Instead I shuffle to the dining room table, thinking of all the times my father sat here, sharpening his fishing knife.

I never really sat at this table. I preferred the floor, the couch, anywhere that felt safer. Some days, I just hid in my room, curled up and hoping not to be noticed. But the nights were worse. If Dad was in one of his dangerous moods, Mum would bundle us into Heath's room instead. Heath always gave Mum and me his bed, curling up on the floor in a nest of spare blankets. After she was gone, Heath continued this. He'd quietly shepherd me to his room, letting me sleep in his bed whenever Dad was in one of his silent rages, while he took the floor without a word. Later, we slept in the cabin to get away from him.

Even after Dad was gone, I never sat at his table. Like the boat, the table was *his*. I press my fist into the wood, and I swear I can still feel his rage rumbling through it. I'm sure I see the outline of him, sitting there, oblivious to everything but his anger. Sharpening his knife, over and over. I'm sure he thought that the more he sharpened it, the safer he'd be.

He was wrong.

They never recovered the knife. Or him.

I think of Terry Hargrave, and the afternoon he shoved my dad through the screen door. How Dad went missing a week later. I'm glad Terry did what he did. Thankful.

I lower myself into my father's chair, resting my forearms on the table. I stay that way until the car pulls into the driveway, its headlights blasting light through the house. Jessie barks twice, emerges from my bedroom, listening.

I close my eyes. I empty all the air from my lungs, lower my head, and wait. An image comes to mind: my grandfather as a young man, fishing the back beaches of Kangaroo Bay, wanting more. And here it began, our long legacy of violence.

Their filthy blood.

Heath's blood.

My blood.

My eyes snap open. I push back from the table, my head hot and spinning as keys rattle in the door and Heath steps inside.

"Min?" He flicks the lounge room light on. "What's wrong?"

I don't answer. His footsteps quicken until he's kneeling at my side. "Are you hurt? What is it?"

I shake my head. He pulls out a chair, sits down, peering at me anxiously. Jessie hops on the couch, sighing before she closes her eyes.

I place my palm on the wood. "I know what you're doing. At night."

He blinks slowly, waits.

"I followed you. First to the beach . . . then to . . ."—my voice drops—"the weigh-in on Neptune Road."

Nothing.

Then he leans back in his chair, scratching his jaw.

"You're bringing the sharks in," I say. "Aren't you?"

When he doesn't answer, I look away, watching Jessie sleep. "It's illegal to hunt a great white. They're protected, but you know that."

Jessie sleeps peacefully on her side, golden chest rising and falling with each gentle breath. "You know what's also protected?" I turn back to Heath. "Abalone."

"The house there and that back shed . . . I know who it belongs to," I continue, thinking of that squat house with the kelpie tied up on the porch. "Terry Hargrave. It's his place."

Silence. "So you use the family boats as a front for the real businesses? The *Deep Sea*, the *Reel Easy*, and the *Titan*," I prod, losing patience now. "Illegal shark fishing. Abalone poaching. Terry, you, Luke . . . Trav."

"Dad."

I lift my head.

Heath rubs his beard. "Dad and Terry started it, back in the day. Luke's dad, too. Hell . . ." He pauses, frowning. "Lot of the boys around here were involved. Still are."

"That's why you hate the tourists. Don't want them sniffing around." I pause, stomach churning, thinking of Chris, then Rachel. "Don't want them taking your abalone . . ." I lean forward. "Tell me about Rachel Sutherland."

"She was a poacher."

"So are you."

He sniffs, "It's different with us."

"Is it?"

"It runs in our blood, Minnow."

". . . Maybe it's time it runs out."

His eyes flick to mine. "I know you," he says simply. "And I know you don't mean that."

"Tell me about Rachel," I repeat. "She grew up here, did you know that?"

He nods. "I don't remember her back then. But she knew the right spots around here." He hesitates. "It wasn't the first time we'd seen her."

"But it was certainly the last." I stare at the table. "Had you spoken to her before?"

He nods reluctantly. "Yeah. Luke and I had some words with her. Same with Trav and Terry."

She pissed off a few people in town.

"You were pissed off she was poaching abalone." I can't help but smile. "From you."

"Hey." Heath leans in, gently tapping my knee. "Abalone poaching is dangerous. We all know it. We all take risks." He sighs. "She was just in the wrong place at the wrong time. It happens."

"What do you know about Hannah Striker?"

He hesitates.

"Heath?"

"She was a courier."

The words ricochet off the table. *She was a courier. She was a courier.*

I'm transported back to the abalone facility. I'm staring at the Cryovac bags and wondering, *How the hell do they export all this?*

I see Hannah's mum, sitting in her rocking chair, explaining, *She traveled a lot. Up and down the coast.*

"How did she do it?"

"We sell it domestically. Interstate. Never overseas."

"How?"

"We vacuum-seal it. Transport it by car to wholesalers, food markets, duty-free shops in Sydney and Surfers Paradise," he confesses, before pausing. "In Melbourne, though, we sell direct to one source."

"Down Under Diving."

He arches a brow. "Yes. The owner has a network of buyers."

I pinch the bridge of my nose, taking it in. "Hannah was an abalone courier."

"Not just abalone," Heath admits. "With the sharks, we sell the jaws and fins. And the teeth. You can charge thousands for the jaws, especially."

The jaws.

I sink in my chair. The jaws in Hannah's room. What if no one sent them? What if Hannah simply kept them for herself? But then I think of the shining teeth left for Chris, left for me. And the video sent to Rachel.

"I spoke to Hannah's mum," I finally admit. "Hannah was friends with Donny Granger. The guy you don't remember," I add pointedly. "Was he a courier, too?"

"I never knew him," Heath insists. "I never met Hannah, either. But I did ask Terry about it."

"And?"

"Yeah," he says shortly. "He admitted that Hannah worked for Luke's dad . . . and Donny worked for ours."

I lean back, relieved, piecing it together. "So Donny and Hannah were members of Down Under Diving in Melbourne. They met Dad there. Maybe they found out he was selling the abalone. And maybe they offered to courier." I pause. "That's why no one saw Donny here. He would have been in and out. And anyone who did see him here . . ."

Wouldn't have told the police, because they knew what he was doing.

"Then why would Dad kill him?" I ask.

"I honestly don't know," Heath says. "I woulda been sixteen, seventeen at the time. I never knew Donny. I never knew Hannah, either. Yeah, I told Rachel off a few times, but that's it." He pauses. "I'm sorry she died."

I bite the inside of my lip, dig into my pocket for my phone, pulling it out. "Heath. There's a video of Hannah's attack."

"What?"

Wordlessly, I aim the screen at him. He frowns. "Do I wanna see this?"

"No, but you're going to."

I press PLAY, watch it with him. Looking from him to the screen, the screen to him. That feeling rises again: *I'm missing something. There's a clue in the video. I know it. But what?*

I frown at the screen, taking in the gory details. Hannah raises an arm to fend off the shark. It takes her under.

"If Hannah was just a courier . . ." I say, "then why was she in the water?"

But Heath's not listening, he's staring at the screen, eyes glassy with that hollow look that comes from staring too long at something you wish you hadn't. His mouth falls open, face pale as he inches back. "Bloody hell."

I watch him carefully. I think of Trav eyeing the bloodied surfer.

Of Luke chopping hunks of roo meat in the cabin, whistling as he did it. Of Terry punching my dad on our doorstep, watching his head rattle on the floor with a satisfied and righteous nod. Of the men in the shark shed, clutching stubbies and boiling with violence. All the blood boys in the woods.

I'm not that surprised Heath is hunting sharks or poaching abalone. Some would see it as an offense. He sees it as his birthright.

Isn't that what he said about Jonah on the beach?

That's my son's legacy.

Our family has been fishing these waters for three generations, soon to be four. It's ours, and if Heath bends and breaks the rules... are they truly broken? They were never our rules, anyway. It's a lawless sea. For us.

I'm not sure if he's right or wrong.

I watch him pale at the video, and I know he's never seen it before.

"What do you know about Chris?"

He frowns. "The journalist? He called me after Rachel's attack. Asked for a comment. I said no." He shrugs. "That was it."

"He went missing."

"I heard."

"And?"

"And nothing, Min," he insists, voice final. "Wasn't his car found up north, anyway? In *Violet Town*?" He stretches the words. "There's some bad sorts up there."

"And here."

"We're not bad people. These beaches belonged to our grandfathers, our dads... now they're *ours*," he pauses, before adding, "Mine."

Silence.

I wait, watching his face harden as he stares at the table. And I wonder if he, like me, can feel the echo of Dad's violence—rumbling through the wood like a current. Is Heath remembering himself as a child, losing the daily war against Dad's rage, and the battle to protect us from it?

"One day, they'll be Jonah's, just like they should be," my brother continues softly. "God knows I fought for them."

It's the first time I've ever heard him acknowledge the weight of everything he fought for—the hardship, and the cost.

God knows I fought for them.

I fall into silence, lost in thoughts. All those years with Dad, enduring his moods, his silences, his *abuse*. Because that's what it was. Abuse. Heath fought to keep the house after Mum and Dad were gone. Fought to keep food on the table. Fought to keep the *Deep Sea*. And he did. Heath was just a teenager competing against grown men when he took over the boat. He fought and fought and fought. For me, for him, for Jonah.

Do I blame him for what he's done?

No, I realize. I really don't. Maybe *my* legacy is letting Heath keep his.

Don't I owe him that?

I sigh heavily, exhausted. Heath hesitates before reaching for my hand, squeezing it.

"Maybe this journo *did* find out about this business down here," he finally says. "But so what? You think we're gonna kill him for it?"

"Yes."

Wounded, he mutters, "I'm not a murderer, Min."

"Someone is."

"Dad was. Dad's gone."

"They'll take your fishing license," I finally say. "You'll be banned throughout Australia. And the fines . . ." I look up. "What do you reckon the fines are for illegal shark hunting and abalone poaching? You'd lose it all," I say, looking around the house. "All of it."

"Who says they need to know?"

It runs in our blood, Minnow.

Maybe it's time it runs out.

I know you. And I know you don't mean that.

"How much do you earn?" he asks carefully. "As a journo?"

"Why?"

". . . You can make more."

We stare each other down. I think of the Wicked Woods. Of Trav.

The ocean roars in my ears. I place my palm against it, stuffing it down.

"Do you miss it?" he prods. "Fishing?"

When I don't answer, he looks down at his hands, examines them. "You belong here, Min. You always did."

He's right. But I left Kangaroo Bay because I didn't want to be another ghost of a woman.

Then it happened anyway.

Didn't it?

I rest my elbows on the table, place my head in my hands. I feel like everything I ever fought for turned out not to be worth much in the end. I left town to escape the violence. I left so I wouldn't become another ghost floating around, silent and agreeable and scared. I had hopes I'd expose the liars and bullies and abusers, and gain my voice. But I lost it anyway. To Joy, to Oliver.

And I still haven't found out what happened to Mum. Or Chris. I'm still wordless and broke, and the ocean keeps calling.

Heath wraps his arm around me and for a long time, we're quiet. Then I mumble two words into his shoulder. ". . . How much?"

"Enough to buy your own place," he says. "Enough to buy anything you want. Or need."

"I need to find out what happened to Mum and Chris and why."

"And we'll do that," he says. "Together. But stay."

I want to. I do.

But for now, I get heavily to my feet, staring at the table, dazed and exhausted. I squeeze Heath's hand as I step past, heading for my bedroom, and mutter good night under my breath.

I sit on my bed, waiting for Jessie to come trotting in. She dives on and tucks her chin on my knee. I stroke her head, thinking.

THE OCEAN IS SCREAMING. IT'S angry, thunderous, hungry. The water presses in around me, squeezing the air from my lungs. Drowning me. I'm lost in the depths, pulled deeper and deeper into an abyss that feels alive and hungry.

The water around me shifts. I sense it before I see it.

The shark.

Its silhouette slices through the black, cutting through the water like a blade. It's coming for me, eyes locked on mine with unblinking hunger.

I thrust my hand out, thrash away, but it keeps coming, closer, closer.

The ocean roars again. But beneath it, something drifts up from the depths. A distant sound, just beyond my reach.

Laughter.

I thrash awake in the dark, sweating. I sit up, eyes darting around my bedroom.

How many times *have you watched it?*

I'm missing something . . . There's a clue in the video. I know it.

And in the quiet dark of my room, I finally know what it is. I snatch up my phone, but my hands are sweating so badly, I drop it on my knee.

Swearing, I wipe my palms on the sheet before grasping the phone tight, turning the volume all the way up, and replaying the video.

I watch Hannah Striker lash out, thrusting her arms to fend off the attack. I watch the horror in her eyes as the black fin rises high above her head, teeth reaching for her jaw.

It's only a moment. It happens so fast that it's not surprising I missed it. It's during the attack when the shark goes for her head. There's an eerie lull as she bobs in the water, part of her jaw ripped off.

I hold the phone to my ear.

And listen as hard I can.

And there it is.

The missing clue. I rewind it, breathless, pausing the attack just after her jaw is ripped away. Underneath the rush of water and the white muffled noise, something clear rings out.

Laughter.

The person filming the video is laughing.

And I know that laugh.

I know who's filming.

Shaking, I pull the phone away from my ear and place it on my knee. I stare stupidly at the video, shaking my head over and over. I know who it is. And I can't believe I didn't realize sooner.

For a long moment, I pause in the dark, shocked. There's a heaviness in my stomach. A sudden coldness that breaks out over my skin.

But this time, it's not the video. It's something else. Something's wrong. My body goes rigid when I realize what it is.

Jessie.

She's not on my bed.

I stare blankly at the empty space where my dog sleeps. Jessie never gets up during the night. It's like a warning repeating over and over: *Jessie never gets up during the night. Jessie never gets up during the night.*

Where is she?

I throw the covers back, muscles tense, skin clammy. Jessie. I grasp my phone, flick the flashlight on, slide my feet to the floor, breath coming out in panicked gasps. Jessie!

I bolt to the door.

And I hear her.

Whining. It's coming from the backyard. I rush out my bedroom and reach the kitchen, panting. I fling myself to the back sliding door, and shine my light against the glass, praying I'll see her there.

But she's not there.

Something else is.

The sliding door rushes open, and a shadow flashes in my vision. It reaches out with two hands, dragging me outside. I swing around so fast I lose my balance. As I go down, I aim my light toward the shadow, but the person kicks my phone away, and I grunt as the phone spins free of my grip. I flounder, struggling to get myself upright, kicking and kicking. Panic flashes through me and I strike out in fear, swinging my fists. I scream, and a hand clamps around my mouth, the other hand yanking me back violently. My skull hits the ground, hard. Gasping, I flatten my palms on the dirt, try to heave myself up.

Jessie.

The blow comes from above, striking the back of my head so hard my cheek slams onto the dirt. I flip over to my back.

And I watch a heavy fist come raining down.

THEN

Blood drips down the black tip of his fishing knife, and the ocean roars, "More!"

The blackwood branches sprawl out like arms, casting dappled shadows across Donny's dead body. The last of the sunlight flickers on his face through the leaves. His hands are still, one leg bent, dirt smudged along his forearms. Blood gushing from the slit in his throat.

Everything around him is quiet. But it's too heavy, like the Wicked Woods themselves are waiting to see what he'll do next.

The ocean rings in his ears, calling again, "More!"

Blackbirds clamber up and down the sweaty branches of a ghost gum as the light thins, a haze of gold catching on the leaves.

"More, more, more!"

He shakes his head as if to clear it and the sea sloshes around at the base of his skull.

He turns to leave when he hears it.

A breath.

Not wind. Not an animal. A human breath, low and close.

He freezes. Eyes flicking to a ghost gum. There, under its shadow, is someone. Watching.

His fishing knife seems to vibrate in his hand.

"More," roars the ocean.

CHAPTER 30

My name is coming from far away.

"Minnow. Min," someone is calling over and over. It's my mum. She's sitting in the lounge chair, holding her necklace up to the light.

Minnow, it's so beautiful.

She clasps her hand around it, eyes filling with tears. *I just wish I deserved it.*

You do, I try to tell her, but my mouth won't work. *You did.*

This isn't right, my brain whispers. *This is wrong . . .*

I blink hard, my vision spotty. I can't orient myself, but I know someone is standing over me. A man in a black hoodie, track pants, and a gray beanie pulled low over his ears.

"Luke?" I mutter, tongue thick in my mouth.

"Look who's awake," he calls back.

I blink hard, trying to clear my vision. But it's him. For a moment, I think it must be Saturday morning at my house. Luke's stayed over after playing videogames all night with Heath. I'm stumbling out of my room in pajamas, rubbing my eyes. Even at that early hour, Luke would already be up, bright-eyed on the couch. "Look who's awake!"

And then he laughs. That guffawing *holy shit!* laugh from the first night back when Rachel Sutherland was attacked.

The same laugh from Hannah Striker's video.

Because Luke was the one filming it.

My senses sharpen. I blink twice and my vision begins to focus. The back of my skull aches, a pounding throb that makes me nauseated. I shut my eyes tight as my vision spins.

"Minnow," he calls again. "Min."

But underneath his voice, there's another sound. A steady hum, soft at first.

An engine.

It's dark and I'm lying on my side, the wind stinging cold on my neck. I try to sit up, but my reflexes are too slow, my head sluggish and sore. I can't remember how I got here. Or why the sleeves of my arms are damp and why the world is rocking beneath me, sending waves of nausea rolling through my stomach.

All I can think about is Jessie.

Luke calls out again, but his voice is still too far away. I'm light-headed and desperately thirsty, confusion giving way to panic as I start to understand the facts: I'm on the *Reel Easy*. My muscles ache. My arms feel like they're made of wet sand. I try to move, to sit up, but I can't.

His calloused hand cups the side of my face. "Wake up, Min."

"Jessie," I croak out. "Where's Jess?"

His grip loosens a fraction. "Tied her up in your garage. She's fine. For now."

I wrench my shoulder, yelling, trying desperately to get to my feet.

He climbs into the skipper's seat, reverses the boat, makes a sharp right turn. Luke guns the motor, and the boat powers over the waves, freezing spray splattering over the bow and hitting me full in the face. I gasp, shaking my head as the salt water stings my eyes, drips down my cheeks. The wind thunders through my ears as Luke guns the engine.

When we were kids, Heath and I used to take turns lying on the trampoline while the other bounced as high as they could. It sent your body flying in the air for a few moments. Sometimes the force would send you ricocheting off the trampoline, over the hot metal prongs before landing hard on the ground.

This is worse. We speed over a wave, and my entire body lifts off the floor. I'm completely weightless, flying. Then a moment later, we drop so low and so fast that my body falls like a rock, slamming down so hard it makes my teeth rattle. I groan in pain, my shoulder aching, teeth feeling like they're about to shatter.

The engine roars faster, the bow bouncing higher and higher, slapping the waves, spray flying everywhere. My body tumbles back, rolling over and over as we crest a huge wave. I can't even throw my arms out to stop myself as my head hits the back of the stern with a sickening crack. Black spots fill my vision. I'm dazed, the roar of the engine silenced by the screaming pain in my head.

We climb higher, higher, my back pushed against the stern of the boat, like someone's holding me down. I can't move. Can't get free. We reach the wave crest. I brace for my impact as the boat lifts into the air, taking my body with it. My stomach drops. For a moment, I'm terrified I'll fly off the edge, over the side, plunging into the water. I shut my eyes, clench my jaw. We plunge back down, my ribs taking the full impact of the fall. I groan in pain, breathing low and shallow because it hurts so much to breathe.

I keep my head down, eyes closed as we soar through the water. My head throbs, my ribs burn with pain.

And still the engine roars, taking us farther and farther out to the dark water.

I SHUT MY EYES AND mouth as more icy salt water comes pouring in, funneling down the back of my jumper and the waistband of my jeans, pooling in my socks until I'm soaked to the skin. Salt water burns my eyes, leaving them itchy and stinging and flooding with tears.

I feel like I'm lying face down in a bathtub, unable to move as the water fills and fills.

I turn my cheek, jaw clenched, eyes burning. The wind softens from an angry shriek to a soft cry. The water is calmer now, the boat cruising over the waves. The engine slows. I look up. Luke's hand hangs loosely from the throttle, his back to me as he scans the water.

Get to your feet, I command myself, heart thumping fast. I roll painfully onto my side, digging my elbows into the floor, trying to heave myself to a standing position. *Quiet,* I tell myself urgently. *Quiet.* I grit my teeth as the pain roars through my ribs, and I blink rapidly to clear the salt water from my eyes. I curl my knee back, fingertips reaching for the back of my calf.

Where my knife is tucked under my jeans.

Always take a knife.

I silently thank my father as the boat comes to a stop. Luke hovers above me. My skin prickles. I know Luke. I've known him all my life. I've sat beside him on the lounge room floor, just me, Heath, and him, playing endless games of Uno.

But then I see him in the cabin, butchering kangaroo, blood splatter hitting his chest. He keeps chopping, unconcerned. Blood boys turn into blood men . . .

He's leaning over the rail, eyes alight. "You should see them, Min. They come in hard, and they come in *angry*.

"They're mindful predators, sharks," he continues, before adding, "Usually anyway. But when they smell the blood"—he licks his lips—"they eat the legs first, sometimes the head."

"Like Rachel Sutherland."

He snorts. "Heath warned her over and bloody over again to stop poaching in our area. Bitch wouldn't listen." He spits over the side. "Your brother's too soft on people, Min. Always has been."

"The night she was attacked . . ."

He shrugs, but he can't stop grinning. "She was free diving for abalone near the pier again. I gave her a nice little scare."

"You were chumming. You brought the sharks right to her."

He tilts his head, eyes gleaming as if remembering. "Hell of a show."

You didn't enjoy the show?

"You showed her Hannah's video."

"I sent it to her, yeah," he says, unconcerned. "Called up that Kmart where she worked, got her number. Bought a cheap burner phone. Sent her a little warning along with the video."

"This is what happens to rule breakers."

He grins. "Yes, I know you went to see Rachel's mum, Min. You're not gonna last long in a town like this if you don't stop looking into shit. You should know that."

I ignore this. "What rule did Hannah break?"

He frowns. "Hannah was a greedy bitch. She and Donny both."

"You knew Donny Granger?"

"Hannah was Dad's courier. Donny couriered for your dad. I used to help them load the abalone into the coolers. Packed 'em into their Camry for transport. Then our dads found out they were overcharging. Pocketing the difference."

"Then what happened?"

"We wanted to teach 'em a lesson. We took Hannah on the *Easy*, told her we were going poaching." He pauses, remembering. "I threw her in. Dad was gonna let her swim back. Except..."

"You chummed."

He grins. "They were around anyway. I mean, God knows we'd been hunting the great whites for years. Chumming to bring 'em in. I swear, when they heard the engines, they'd come roarin' in, looking for a feed."

"And they found one."

"Sure did!" He grins. "Hell of a show. My dad wasn't that upset about it."

"And Donny?"

"Your dad took him to the woods. I honestly didn't think he'd kill 'im, but..." He shakes his head admiringly. "Your dad was a fucking nutter by then. And paranoid as all hell."

I see my father, hunched over his fishing knife, dragging it across the whetstone again and again. "We're all nutters, I s'pose," Luke admits. "Lots of sick shit went down in those woods."

I know he's thinking of the cabin. Amy.

"I can't explain it," he continues. "I'm like the sharks when they smell blood. It changes 'em. Changes *me*, too."

"You're either the shark or the food."

He points his finger at me in satisfaction. "Your dad was right about that, Min. Everyone needs a bit of shark in 'em."

Can you hear it, Min? The ocean? Calling and calling?

"That's what Dad meant," I mumble. "He used to hear the ocean calling. It drove him mad."

"Do *you* hear it?"

"... Sometimes."

"There's an ugliness in you, too, you know. I've seen it. You used to rip fish guts out with your bare hands," he says, laughing. "You were a feral little thing. We all were. And Amy . . ." He smiles at me, admiration shining in his eyes. "We all know what you did to her, Min. What you *tried* to do. When I heard 'bout what you did on TV, I thought, *That's her. That's our Minnow.*" He laughs. "To be honest, I thought you'd come back to join the family biz."

"I didn't know what the family biz *was*."

"Now you do," he says flatly. "It's not too late."

"Right," I say, motioning to the boat, to me.

"I'm not gonna kill you, Min. Your brother would hunt me down." He crouches, rubbing his chin. "But I *am* gonna teach you a lesson."

This is what happens to rule breakers.

The words don't process at first. Then I know.

"Look," he exclaims, hauling me to the rail. "Watch."

I tense, waiting. He stomps to the kill tank, yanks it open, snatches out chunks of bloody meat. Grinning, he throws it overboard, even lifts his knee like a baseballer and throws a kangaroo femur into the waiting ocean. Then he positions his body behind mine, his breath warm on my neck. There's a chill in my blood. A sudden stillness in the water. Something's wrong.

And then out of the darkness,

A fin.

CHAPTER 31

They come in hard.
And they come in angry.

He's right. My body freezes as the shark fin circles the boat. There's a splash and silence. It disappears in the shadows like it's made of them.

They position themselves below you . . . then they strike.

My heart thrashes so hard in my chest, he can probably feel it. He's going to *throw me to the fucking sharks.*

I'm frozen at the rail, inhaling quick and sharp, peering down into the deep. But all I can think about is Donny Granger.

I shiver, chest rising and falling erratically, my thoughts tumbling over one another in a chaotic rush.

Your dad was a fucking nutter by then. And paranoid as all hell.

Paranoid . . .

In my mind, a door creaks open. My stomach drops, heavy, like the ground has fallen away. "What was he so paranoid about?"

My body is tense, bracing for something . . . Any second now, everything will change, and I won't be able to stop it.

"He thought he saw someone in the woods," Luke says, "the day he killed Donny."

For a moment, my brain doesn't even understand it. I hear the words but they don't make sense. Not yet.

And then I'm hiding under the ghost gum's shadow. A branch snaps in the distance, and my heart leaps into my throat. I press back harder against the trunk, hoping the shadow will swallow me whole, hoping the tree will hide me completely while my father murders a man.

It didn't. Dad saw someone hiding in the woods.

I clench my fists, my knuckles paling from the pressure. I try to steady myself but I can't. If Dad saw me in the woods, why didn't he come after me?

Then, like a puzzle piece fitting into place, the realization floods through me.

I whirl around, facing Luke. The silence stretches, sharp and painful. "Who did he think he saw in the woods?"

I breathe in sharply, the ground beneath me shifting. Everything feels muffled and distant. I stare blankly at the circling fins, time slowing down to nothing.

"Your mum," I hear Luke say, "He thought he saw your mum."

My body shuts down and I retreat into stunned silence. My lips part, but no words come out.

"She was always running away," he says. "Taking off to Pine Bay. The cops even brought her back a couple of times. He was paranoid as hell that she was going to say something to them about Donny."

I stand there staring ahead, the weight of everything pressing in on me.

"It wasn't Mum he saw in the woods," I hear myself say. "It was me."

A suffocating mass seems to collapse my chest with every breath. But my body doesn't react. It freezes like it always does. My mind's gone quiet, a dull hum repeating the words over and over again, *He thought you were her. He thought you were her . . . and that's why she's dead.*

Luke opens his mouth, his words slow and measured. "I'm sorry, Min. Truly."

A flash of movement catches my eye. The water is disturbingly calm, pale moonlight reflecting off the waves, casting eerie underwater shadows.

But then . . . a dark shape slices through the water just beneath the surface. The water ripples around the fin as it moves along the side of the boat, circling. It happens quick. There's a jarring thud against the side of the boat. It tilts sharply, and I'm knocked off-balance. I reach back for Luke, arms thrashing out, gripping his forearm to keep from falling.

They come in hard. And they come in angry.

Luke gazes at the water, his face lit with pure, wide-eyed excitement. A smile spreads over his mouth as he peers eagerly over the side of the boat, eyes sparkling like a child.

"Look at them!" he exclaims, transfixed. "Look at them!"

But I'm not looking at the sharks circling the boat. I'm looking at the hold near the skipper's chair. In the cramped storage space beneath the hull, something's moving. I squint in surprise, angling my body, staring. What is that? Past the coils of rope stiff with salt, and a cracked bucket, there's something tucked away in the far corner. It's half buried under a folded tarp, and it's moving.

Bang.

Another low echoing boom vibrates through the fiberglass, up through the deck. I feel it in the soles of my shoes, the base of my spine, and the whole boat seems to shudder. My eyes flick to the water, but I see nothing. No shape or shadow. But I feel them, waiting impatiently under the surface.

"They're here," Luke whispers, "and they're pissed!"

A flicker of light catches the edge of my vision. My heart skips as I turn from the water and scan the dark space of the hold. There! Another glint of light. Sharp, sudden, and gone just as quickly as it came. I freeze, trying to find it again.

The world feels too still. Too silent. But the air feels tighter, charged.

And then I see it. Jutting out from beneath the tarp's crumpled edge is a hand, limp and pale. And something else: a flicker, a flash of light, a watch, glinting in the moonlight. My breath catches.

Gold-plated.

Black.

Maserati.

Chris's watch.

Yes, I know you went to see Rachel's mum, Min.

The other car is still there, silent and grave as the air itself. It's parked under a tea tree, the white bonnet covered in crescent-shaped leaves.

It's an Audi. White.

And it's missing four hubcaps.

The tarp shifts, and a low groaning sound rises from underneath. The hand twitches before going still, and the groan comes again, louder this time. "Chris!" I call out. "It's me, it's Minnow."

Luke tears his gaze from the water and fixes them on the moving tarp. "You're finally awake, ya weak sack of shit?"

"You followed me to Bethanga," I hear myself saying, tearing at Luke's forearm that holds me in place. "You followed Chris."

There's no hesitation. No remorse. Just a bubbling glee in Luke's voice as he watches a sharp silhouette rise slowly above the water. "Terry told me to keep an eye on him. And you. We just wanted to scare you away from finding out the whole story, Min."

The shark tooth on my doorstep.

"You're either the shark or the food. I'm the shark," Luke says, cheek grazing mine. "What do you think Chris is?"

I stand motionless, body trembling. The tarp shifts again, fabric rising slightly with another pained groan.

What do you think Chris is?

My friend.

A dorsal fin circles methodically, watching, waiting. I can't move.

I don't fight. I don't flight. I just freeze, and yes, I hate myself for it.

I think of the last fight with Oliver where he was standing over me, screaming. And I just stood there, lips numb, and *took* it. Took everything.

The boat lurches sharply as a shark strikes again, sending a violent tremor through the boat. *Move. Move.*

But it's Luke who moves. Luke who drags me across the hull, forearm at my throat as he rips the tarp off Chris. He's crumpled on the ground, eyes wide and distant. His face is pale, streaked with blood and dirt, and his body's twisted at an odd angle. His bloodied hands curl weakly, reaching for nothing. Or maybe he's reaching for me.

"Chris!"

His eyes flutter, straining to focus. I reach for him desperately, but Luke pivots, moving me bodily to the gunwale as he loops his free arm under Chris's shoulders. With a strained grunt, he lifts him, and Chris's head lolls against his chest.

Fins cut the water, one after another, steady and deliberate. Waiting for something or someone to be thrown in.

"Minnows. They're not just little fish," Luke pants. "They're *bait*fish."

A memory comes to me. Heath and I splashing about in the shallows, eyes on the minnows darting through the water. So quick, so quick. How many times did we snatch for them only to come up empty-handed?

I don't fight. I don't flight. I just freeze.

No. Not anymore.

You'll have to catch me first.

I reel backward, smashing the back of my head into Luke's nose. His hand drops from my throat, and the one holding Chris in place falls to his side with a smack.

Chris crumples to the floor with a grunt, and pain ricochets through my skull.

Quick!

Luke is half bent over, hand cupped to his mouth, hot blood spilling down his fingers. With a roar of anger, he flings the blood over the side of the boat, straight into the water.

A splash. *They come in hard, and they come in . . .*

God, I think, *they're waiting.*

"Chris!" I scream. "Get up!"

Quick, quick, quick! Adrenaline swims through my body. I reach down to my ankle, fingers closing around the knife handle. With a roar, Luke charges forward, bloodied hands thrust out. He throws himself against me, knocking me off-balance, and I collide hard with the helm. My knee buckles, my cheek slamming into the wheel.

"Chris," I yell, blood filling my mouth. "Chris!"

Weakly, Chris lifts his head, eyes dull and unfocused. His lips part, a shallow breath catching in his chest. Even the effort of raising his head seems to cost him everything. There's a flicker of recognition as his eyes stare into mine. I keep calling, voice cracking. "Get up! Get up!"

Luke's on me again, swearing, panting, hauling me to my feet, both hands cupping my underarms. He drags me back, grunting with effort.

I spin around, strike out, and slam the knife into his shoulder. He lets out a strangled yell and I wrench the knife out, raising it again, forcing all my body weight behind the next blow.

But before I can strike, it feels like an earthquake hits the boat. There's a huge *bang* so loud, it rattles in my ears and teeth. I hear Chris call out in pain as I'm knocked off my feet. And then I'm just falling.

Desperately, I grip the knife as I fall backward, groaning in pain as I land hard on my elbows. For a moment, I'm stunned, lying on my back, staring up at the dark sky. And then, splashing all around me, spray hitting my hair, my face.

The sharks, I realize. They're bumping the boat. Frantic and angry. My vision is murky, fading in and out. I can't see Chris but I can hear Luke. Laughing.

I raise my head painfully, the back of my skull throbbing. I blink hard. Luke is standing on the rear bench seat facing the water, wind ripping through his blond hair. One hand is clamped tight on his shoulder. The other hand pumps like he's at a rave. He yells into the night air, kicking the back of the hull in a frenzy. "Get it, boys!" He releases the hand clamping his shoulder, and the blood pours out in an angry stream. He flings the blood into the water, yelling down, "Come and get it!"

Bang. I grunt as the boat is knocked hard to the starboard side.

They're gonna tip us over.

The boat rocks violently in the water, and waves of nausea roll through my stomach. I grab desperately for the rail, wrapping a fist around it, hauling myself up.

Luke smiles at me, teeth bloody, blood pouring down his neck, nose, and chin. I wrench myself up, but it's too late. With an angry roar, he surges forward, pulling Chris off his feet, dragging him across the deck. There's a struggle, brief and panicked. Chris swings his fists with the last of his strength, calls out something that's lost in the roar. I charge, racing across the deck, raising the knife over my right shoulder.

Then a shove. One push, and Chris is thrown over the side, arms flailing for something, anything. For one awful second, he hangs in the air, caught between the sky and sea. His eyes catch mine as he goes over, terrified, desperate, lost. Then the splash, sharp and final. And something else . . .

A scream, sharp and primal, cutting through the air as the sea explodes in a torrent of teeth and flesh.

Luke charges me, no words, no hesitation, just the pounding of his feet against the hull, muscles coiled, eyes locked on mine. Then, the impact. Bone against bone, shoulders smashing together. I'm slammed into the side rail, my jaw smashing into the metal.

Dazed, I look up, staring hard into the water as a black fin sinks below the surface taking Chris with it. The moment seems to last forever. I stare at the empty space where he was moments before, heart pounding against my ribs. None of it feels real. My body slackens in shock as the surface churns with violent energy. It's chaos overboard. Jaws snapping, teeth glinting.

They position themselves below you . . . then they strike.

Luke staggers to his feet near the skipper's chair, blood dripping off his teeth. He charges a final time, blood streaming out like a tap running, the heat of his fury building with every step. And I charge back, running straight at him like I have nothing left to lose.

At the same moment, we both raise our hands.

I lash out, sinking the knife into his chest.

And he raises both palms and shoves me backward.

For a second, the entire world goes blinding white. I can't see a thing. All I know is that I'm falling, falling, clawing at nothing. The wind shrieks through my ears, my hair, and the blinding white sharpens and sharpens until I feel like I'm fainting and falling at the same time.

My shoulders hit the water first, hard. The back of my skull a moment later. Then I'm under, sinking below the freezing surface, and despite the blinding white that enfolds me, all I feel is darkness.

CHAPTER 32

Bubbles brush my cheek. For a moment, I'm suspended there, watching them escape from the side of my mouth, drifting up. The back of my head throbs. All I know is that I'm under the water.

And there are sharks all around me.

Fear travels like a flood down my veins, pooling into my heart with a violent gushing surge. My panic makes it hard to think, and my throat and chest are already starting to burn.

I tilt my head up. It's so dark under the water, it's hard to even see the surface. My body begins to rise, and I scramble frantically for the surface, arms thrashing. Then I see it. Blood dripping down my wrist and elbow.

Sharks can smell a drop of blood a mile away...

I grab my wrist as I rise, clapping my free hand around it, trying desperately to stem the blood flow.

Don't splash.

My chin breaks the surface, and I gasp for breath, ignoring the searing pain in my ribs as I suck in breath after breath. I tread water painfully, hand still wrapped tight on my wrist, making my movements as small as possible. My eyes dart around the surface and my breath catches in my throat. Oh my God. Where's the boat?

I bite my lip to keep from crying out as I frantically scan the surface for the *Reel Easy*. I replay the last moment before Luke pushed me off. I didn't fall far from the boat. I couldn't have. I twist my body carefully, trying not to make any large movements.

And something brushes my left foot.

I go completely still, heart smashing against my rib cage.

Shut up, I tell my heart. *They'll hear it!*

My body is sinking, my chin dropping below the water. I reach out instinctively, pushing at the water so I don't drop below the surface.

Be still. Breathe!

My lips and chin shake so badly, it's hard to snatch a breath. My breathing is raspy, terrified, my muscles tense and tight.

Find the boat!

Find the fucking boat!

I'm looking over my shoulder, desperately scanning the surface, when the first hit comes. I don't even have time to cry out as I'm thrown off-balance, cheek hitting the water, arms and legs pirouetting. The impact knocks the wind out of me, emptying my lungs, leaving me numb with shock. I hang there, dazed, shaking my head as if to clear it.

It comes to me in fragments.

The cold. Water filling my ears. A ringing in my head. Bubbles everywhere. Blood dripping down the cuff of my wrist. The dark, the dark.

And something else. I go completely still, peering down through the water.

There's something below me. Circling.

A shadow in the water.

If a shark is in attack mode, try to fend it off with your hands. Strike at the most sensitive parts . . . the eyes or gills.

I thrust my arms out in front of me, and the blood drips onto the surface. I spin in a frantic circle. The boat. My only hope is getting back to the *Reel Easy*. I can't think about Luke. Can't think about anything else but getting out of the water.

I squint hard and see the faint outline of the boat twenty meters away, the skull and crossbones of the *Reel Easy* flag flapping softly in the wind. I surge forward, freestyling as fast as I can, terrified Luke will gun the engine and leave me here. But the boat isn't moving. It's drifting in the current, eerily silent.

Get to the boat. Get to the boat.

But what if Luke's pulled the boarding ladder up? It happened before on the *Deep Sea*. It must have been summer because the sky was bright and blue and endless. And hot. I wanted to ask if we'd be going home soon, but I wasn't dumb enough to speak when Dad was fishing. So, I lowered myself over the side and jumped in. But when I rose up to the surface, Heath's anxious face peered over the side.

Just cooling off, I called out. *I'm coming back in now.*

Dad snorted, raised an eyebrow. *How you gonna get back in?*

I treaded water, confused. I'd thought I'd haul myself up the stern of the boat, near the outboard. Wordlessly, I swam to the back and tried to pull myself up.

I couldn't.

Freeboard, Heath told me later. The term for the height of the boat in the water. *Ours is two and a half meters, Min. If you jump off, there's no way to get back on . . .*

My legs start cramping. I grab at my left calf. My hand is so numb that I can't even feel it, and it's too far to swim to shore.

I race for the boat, swimming as fast as I can. I'm halfway there when something grazes my left knee. I lash out, thrusting my fists under the water, kicking hard. My foot connects with something solid. I kick again, harder. Water rushes into my mouth. I choke on it, spitting it up, hitting and kicking the whole time.

I duck my head under, throwing punches, striking left, then right, exhaling with effort, a stream of bubbles escaping my mouth. They stir the water up, like someone's blowing smoke in my face, and I can't see a damn thing. My arms are floating up near my chin, lost in the bubbles, aching with the effort of striking through the cement-like water.

For a moment, everything goes still. My mind slows, my lungs empty. Then the water begins to clear. It happens so slow and so damn quick. My head is tilted back, watching the little bubbles float up, up, up to the surface, like vapor floating up to a dark sky.

Something tugs at my chest, like it's gripping both sides of my heart in its cold fists.

It's *here.* It's *here.*

Some things you're just not supposed to see. Some things are so horrific, your brain goes slow with the shock of trying to process it.

Like this.

Like this *thing*.

This is what my family have spent a lifetime hunting. It charges out of the deep, so fast, too fast. My mind is numb, slow with terror.

Death. It looks like death.

Flat black eyes stare through me, like it sees only my bones, flesh. And wants them. Wants them all.

The world stops. *Torpedo-shaped body.* The words are dredged from the back of my mind. It's huge, shockingly huge. Bigger than the whole sky and ocean put together. It's covered in scars, running down its pointed snout, stretching under its chin. Angry. Red. Gouge marks.

And its mouth is a conveyor belt of teeth.

Its *wide-open* mouth.

Sharks rip their prey into mouth-sized pieces . . . and swallow them whole.

I scream, the sound ricocheting through my ears and the water. I push both arms out in front of me, curl them into stupid fists, and start swinging.

Closer, closer.

Two arm lengths away.

It's not stopping. It's not stopping.

I feel like I'm paused at a pedestrian crossing, and the car in front of me won't slow down. It's hurtling forward, closer, closer. I swing my right fist as hard as I can, and it flinches away, my fingers skimming the rough surface of its cold skin. I pull back as it charges past my face, sinking lower in the water. Heart pounding so hard, my entire face is numb.

Get to the boat!

I resurface noisily, scrambling to the *Reel Easy*, my arms so heavy that it's hard to lift them. But it's closer, so close I can see the aluminum hull glinting in the dark.

I slap my fist against the side of the hull, tilting my head all the way back, trying to scan the boat for Luke. But I can't see up over the side. I can't see shit.

Where's the ladder? Where's the ladder?

I tread water beside the boat, legs and arms growing heavier as the fin cuts through the water, straight at me.

There!

I lunge for the boarding ladder, gripping the rail and hauling myself out. I scramble up the stairs, pulling my feet up, darting glances over my shoulder as the fin ducks below the surface.

I collapse in the boat, heart roaring in my ears.

The *Reel Easy* is dead silent. I peer at the skipper's chair.

Luke.

I clamp a hand to my ribs, breathing slow and shallow. Luke is slumped in the chair, my knife stuck in his chest.

CHAPTER 33

We just want him home.

I swipe at my eyes and try to swallow through the lump in my throat. We've been driving for hours, wordless and silent, eyes firmly fixed on the road ahead. But all I can think about are Chris's mum's words.

We just want him home.

My throat closes and I grip the wheel tighter. Chris isn't coming home. He's never coming home.

"Let *me* drive, Min," Heath urges from the passenger seat. "Please."

I shake my head, swiping at tears with my sleeve. "No," I say, the first word I've spoken in hours. I need to do something. Isn't that what Chris said on that crazy morning we spent digging for Donny Granger?

I need to do something with my hands.

God, Chris. All he wanted was to make his name. To be loved and forgiven. To be *enough*.

I stare out the windshield, thinking. Isn't that what any of us want? To be more than our sins. I swipe at my eyes again, my attention drawn to the cheerful sapphire-blue sign. A humpback whale breaches above the words WELCOME TO NEWCASTLE.

Heath stares intently out his passenger-side window and Jessie pokes her head out the cracked back window, golden ears flapping in the breeze. I found her in the garage, tied up, her eyes wide with panic. But as I untied her and led her into the house, she began to settle. I gave her something to drink, spoke gently. Little by little, the fear in her eyes started to fade. Luke didn't hurt her, just tied her up to lure me out. The bastard. The fucking dead bastard.

When I got home, it was early morning, and Heath was still asleep. I had a steaming shower, pulled Jessie into my lap, and sat with her on the couch, oddly calm. We stayed there for hours, watched the sun rise.

When Heath woke up, he found us still sitting there, saw the bruises on my cheek, the dried blood on my mouth, and his face went white.

I told him everything. About what Luke did to Hannah Striker and Chris. Rachel.

What Dad did to Mum.

And what I did to Luke.

By the time I'd finished, Heath's head was in his hands. I thought of the years between us. All those times he was strong for me so I could break. And now here he was, breaking, finally. Falling apart after a lifetime of holding everything together.

It started with a breath that didn't quite land, like his lungs were folding in on themselves. His shoulders, always pulled back like armor, dropped. It was like he was being crushed under the weight of everything he never let himself feel.

He tried to cover it up. A hand over his face and a rough swipe of his sleeve. But he wasn't fine. He was breaking, piece by piece. Because it turns out, you can only carry something until you just can't anymore. One day, all those things you survived by the scrape of your teeth will demand to be paid in full.

I stepped forward, arms open, and slowly, he folded. His weight shifted into me, hesitant at first, and then all at once, like he was exhausted from holding himself up for too long.

His breathing came in stutters. Not sobs yet, only sharp, shaky inhales. And I simply held on. Arms around his back, no words. Just that weight shifting from him to me.

But I felt strong enough to carry it. To carry us both.

"I'm going to the police," I said, gripping his shoulders and meeting his eyes. "You need to leave for a while. I'll pack your things. Let's go."

NEWCASTLE IS POSTCARD BEAUTIFUL. Water so clear you see every pebble on the bottom.

I pull into the beach parking lot and shut the engine off.

I watch the water lapping softly on the shore, watch the seagulls creep over to a family spread out on a beach towel, picking through a box of hot chips. The mother throws a fistful of chips high into the air and the seagulls cry in excitement, soaring up and snatching them in their beaks before they hit the ground.

Heath squeezes my left hand tight. He shifts in his seat, sighing.

Sometime later, a car pulls into the lot. Tara's grip is tight on the steering wheel as her eyes scan the row of cars. And then she sees Heath, and her whole body seems to relax as if she had been holding her breath the entire drive.

She parks quickly and rushes toward him, stopping a few feet away. She looks like she's ready to say something, but her words seem to catch in her throat. Maybe she notices the way Heath's slumped in the seat like he's smaller somehow. The way his hands are wrapped tight around the edge of his jacket like he's trying to hold on to something, anything.

He finally looks up, face softening when he sees her standing there, unsure whether to close the distance or wait for her to come to him.

She closes the space between them as he opens the passenger door, falling into his embrace like the world outside doesn't matter anymore. She still loves him, I realize.

He pulls back just enough to look at her, eyes soft but guarded, like there's something he wanted to say for a long time.

"I'm sorry," he murmurs, his voice low, rough.

She shakes her head like she's not sure what to say yet. Heath admitted that Tara knew about the abalone ring, the illegal shark fishing. She'd wanted him to stop, but he refused. He crossed lines and told himself it was temporary. Just until the bills stopped piling up, just until he could fix up the house. He told himself he was doing it for them. For their future.

But I don't think so.

He's not a blood man. Never will be. He doesn't lose his temper or lash out, but sometimes, I wonder if he feels a pull. A tug like a fishing line to let the controlled part of him slip away and become something else, if only for a little while.

Is that what the shark fishing does for him? Does his pulse surge, a strange, electric thrill rising in him as he pulls the fishing line back? Can he taste the violence on the tip of his tongue as the great whites thrash, magnetic and bloody in that great black sea?

Maybe.

But if he does, the violence stays there where it belongs. He doesn't bring it home. Which is more than I can say about Dad, Luke, the blood men in town.

And me.

Wordlessly, I grab his bags and pile them into the other car while he climbs in. I give Tara a quick hug and open the back door, where Jonah's fast asleep. I kiss him on the cheek and quietly shut his door.

Then I kneel at Heath's side and squeeze his hand. He squeezes back. We look ahead to the powdery sand and the water, sparkling in the sun while wispy clouds drift by. The horizon stretches endlessly, the sea meeting the sky forever. I crouch there, feeling like the whole world is over.

Or it's just beginning.

I open my mouth and wonder what the hell I can possibly say.

Heath beats me to it, straightening his back, attempting a smile. "Eel be back."

I laugh. "Any fin is possible."

I stand up, biting my lip when Tara starts the engine. I shut Heath's door and tuck my hands in my pockets, stepping back. But he winds the window down, smiling now. "Tanks for the ride."

"Best fishes!"

As the car pulls away, I raise my hand in a small, hesitant wave. There's a lump in my throat, a quiet ache in my stomach. My hand is heavy as I wave goodbye, wishing I could stop time. The space between us widens, and it feels like the world has quietened. I watch my brother roll down the road, getting farther and farther away. I lower my hand, fingers flat against my sides as if the last of our connection has been lost.

But he calls one final time: "Hey!"

I raise my chin, wait.

He smiles from the car window, yells out for the whole world to hear, "I'll love you for a krill-ion years!"

I laugh, raising my hand again to wave goodbye. This time, it doesn't feel heavy and final. It just feels right.

The engine fades first, the car growing smaller and smaller, merging with the horizon where the sea meets the sky.

I lean against my car, watching him until he's a speck in the distance. Time stretches for a moment, and then his car vanishes completely as if swallowed by the brilliant sea.

CHAPTER 34

The room smells like sweat and cigarettes. I sit with a painfully straight back, cross my legs at the ankles, lay my palms flat on my thighs, and wait.

God, it's silent in here. No clock. No TV. No windows. Nothing but a bare lightbulb hanging from the ceiling, two metal chairs, and a shitty foldable table bolted to the floor.

It's far too bright in here. I find myself squinting in the harsh light, listening to the distant bustle outside the closed door. Muted voices, soft laughter, doors banging shut. The longer I'm alone, waiting in the silence, the more I want to surrender to it. The words I long to spit out are beginning to retreat. They're stomping to the back of my throat, heavy and defiant.

They don't have to know.

You don't have to say a word.

You can take Jessie and go anywhere. Anywhere at all.

I exhale shakily, my knee bobbing up and down in the torturous wait. I look desperately over my shoulder to the closed door. *Hurry up,* I urge silently, *I don't know if I can do this.*

I gasp when the door bursts open.

"Sorry 'bout that," the sergeant says, but he doesn't look sorry. He looks impatient and a bit irritated. "Coke, yeah?"

I nod. He places the red Coke can on the folding table, slaps down a notebook, and eases into the metal chair opposite me, sighing heavily like he hasn't sat down all day. He's tall, thin-lipped, hairline receding to the crown. The only interesting feature is his ears. They're slightly sharp at the top, pointed even. I can't stop looking at them.

He uncaps a pen and commands, "What's your date of birth?"

"September 13, 1989."

"Spell your last name for me."

I reach for the Coke can, grasping it tight in my right palm. "Greenwood," I say, clearing my throat. "Spelled like how it sounds."

He looks up frowning. "Spell it anyway."

I do. I listen to the scratch of his pen on the paper, wondering if it's too late to flee.

They don't have to know.

You don't have to say a word...

He finishes writing and catches me staring at the door. "Can you tell me what brought you in here today?" he asks, pausing to glance at his notepad. "Minnow?"

I place the Coke can on my knee and grip it tight as my throat begins to close up. I can't get any words out. I nod instead, once. My throat is so painfully tight it hurts to breathe. I crack open the Coke can and force myself to drink.

He waits, rotating the pen in his fingers. "They said you had some information about abalone poaching and illegal shark fishing?" he prompts, leaning forward. "It's in Kangaroo Bay, you said?"

His eyes are eager, his patience thinning. Cops have always been suspicious of my town. They came in every few years, different uniforms, same questions. Always left with nothing because no one was talking.

Until now.

I drink again, struggling to swallow as my throat constricts. It feels like someone is choking me. I push the can back onto the table and clasp the base of my neck.

"Miss Greenwood," he says directly, "are you able to talk?"

"Yeah, I'll talk," I finally say, my voice a whisper. "... I don't know where to start."

"Start at the beginning."

That makes it easier. I sit silently, wondering how to begin. In telling *my* story, I'm also telling my father's. And his before him. All of our sins and stories, tangled together like fishing line.

"I came back home last month and . . ." I begin.

But no . . . I close my mouth and stare intently at the floor. It's not right to start the story there. Go back further. Where does my story begin? I wait in the hot silence, deaf to the bustle outside the door.

I see only my memories spinning slowly through my head. For the first time since I can remember, I allow myself to inspect them all. One after the other.

And then I see it.

I'm watching TV, cross-legged on the floor while Dad sharpens the knife behind me. I keep looking over my shoulder at him, terrified he'll catch me looking.

I straighten up, my eyes drifting to the police officer's. He taps his pen on the notepad, eyes narrowing.

"I can never think of my father without a knife in his hand."

The policeman scribbles furiously, nose an inch from the paper. He can't keep up with me as I pour out memory after memory.

". . . Fish can tell a storm is coming days in advance. Can sense a change in the pressure system long before there's any sign of rain. We were like that.

". . . I keep my eyes fixed on that sliver of moon as my father draws near. He crouches in front of us, eye level to Heath but towering over me. 'Look at me, Minnow,' he says . . ."

Sometimes I have to pause because my voice is shaking too badly to continue. Sometimes I stare at the floor, and it becomes the rolling black ocean. Sometimes I'm standing on the hot beach, watching my brother reel in fish after fish.

But I keep talking. Keep telling the story.

I speak until my throat aches. Until I drain the Coke can, and the cop has taken pages of notes. Finally, he glances up like he's waking from a trance. "I'll get you another drink."

He bolts out of the chair so quickly that he collides with the corner of the desk. He yanks the door open, and for a moment, there's a sea of noise. A phone ringing. Someone calling out, "McPherson? Where's McPherson?"

Then the door shuts. And it's just me and the silence.

I slump in my seat. I've been speaking a long time, and the quiet is so loud, my ears begin to ring.

But I did it. I told the whole story. I told him about Chris and Hannah and Rachel. About Luke and the family business. About the abalone facility on Neptune Road. The illegal shark fishing. About what Dad did to Mum.

But there's a few things I keep to myself. That Heath was involved in the poaching and shark fishing. What I really did to Amy Anderson.

And the other thing . . .

The one thing I will never tell anyone.

I fold my hands over my knee. I thought the story was over, but a voice is missing. And then the voice speaks. I swear I hear my father's voice echoing in the room. I lift my head and listen.

He speaks of the sea.

He says, *I hate the ocean. I hate myself for loving it once.*

He spews out his hate for it, bitterness clogging his voice. *It's violent and restless. So hungry it hurts.*

But I hear something else, a pulse behind that anger. Then I'm standing on the shore as a child sprints past, eyes full and bright as the sun. He flings his schoolbag off his shoulder and dives straight into the water. And it's so beautiful. All of it. Watching my father as a child, splashing about like a young dolphin.

Until the wave comes.

I don't see it take him. I just feel the heavy dread, something that makes my chest burn, makes me want to leap to my feet and scream and scream and scream.

Then,

Nothing. Only darkness, like the scene has been wrenched out of the film. Like it's so painful, he erased it entirely. But it's not gone. Not really. I sense that he carried it with him everywhere.

Then I'm standing in my father's bedroom doorway, watching.

He's in my brother's arms, shaking like a child. The room smells like salt water and the floor feels like the ocean. I feel disoriented, seasick, like I'm pinned underwater, not sure which way is up.

And I know without him telling me, that he spent every day like this. That for my father, there is only Before the wave. And After.

The water gives and the water takes, my father told me in a bitter voice I knew well. But hasn't it taken enough already?

Yes, it did. It took that boy with the bright eyes. The boy who loved the ocean so much, his own father had to drag him out by the ankles. That boy never came back.

But I'm wrong.

Because right here in the room, the boy speaks.

He says, *Have you ever crouched beside a rock pool on a cloud-soaked morning? Watched the raindrops fall down like feathers?*

He says, *Have you ever waited in the water and watched a summer storm come rolling in?*

Have you ever fished on a dark beach at night while a fire crackles at your feet? Chugged down a cup of noodles, salty and hot, while the waves crashed on the shore?

I have.

I hear it in his young voice. Before all the rage and fury, there was love. Oceans of it. The sea was the great love of my father's life. But the day the wave came for him, that love drowned. And in its place, hate rose up, setting off a chain of events that led us straight to this moment.

Because the ocean doesn't give a shit if you drown in it. Waves crash, tides pull, rip currents steal you away. And sharks wait in the shallows, silent and patient.

Sharks have been around as long as the dinosaurs, and there's a reason for that. You're the predator or the prey. My dad taught me this. Kill or be killed. Eat or be eaten.

He wasn't wrong. In this town, the men were sharks, the women and children, the food. We spent our lives at the mercy of their hunger until we were pushed out, hunted, or consumed.

You can feel it, can't you, Min? The ocean? Calling and calling?

Yes, I felt it. Still do.

My father sits beside me, broken.

He tells me the ocean was his greatest wound.

And I tell him he was mine.

"... Minnow?"

The sergeant slips back into his seat. "We have your statement. You're free to go. But..."

I look up, jaw tightening.

"There's something I still don't understand," he begins, leaning back. "The coroner examined Luke. His coronary artery was severed. But we can't find the knife."

"It wasn't on the boat?"

"No. We searched it thoroughly." He taps his pen once against the notepad. "Luke was a fisherman. He woulda known not to remove the knife."

"The boat was getting bumped around a lot," I remember. "The sharks were coming in. At one point, we both went flying. I smacked my head against the hull. Luke got knocked off his feet. It was violent."

"When you climbed back on board," he says, "did you see the knife?"

I think for a moment. "No. I don't think I did."

"What kind of knife was it?"

"Fishing knife."

"Describe it."

"Steel blade. About twelve centimeters long."

"Yours?"

"... Yes."

THEN

I lunge for the boarding ladder, gripping the rail, hauling myself out of the water. I scramble up the stairs, pulling my feet up, darting glances over my shoulder as a fin ducks below the surface.

"Luke?" I croak out.

He's slumped in his skipper's chair, spitting blood, my knife stuck in his chest. I stand over him and wrench the knife out. The blood roars, gushing and gushing, its coppery scent filling the air. Even if I gun the engine and get him to the Pine Bay hospital, I doubt he'll make it.

And I'm not going to gun the engine. I'm going to wait here until he bleeds out.

Knife gripped in my palm I watch him die. His eyes are cloudy, unfocused. His hand flat against his chest, blood thick and heavy, seeping through the cracks in his fingers.

He speaks in a faint whisper, pausing between each word.

". . . Did . . . you . . . love . . . it," he pants, grimacing. "The . . . woods, Min?"

The violence. That pulse in the cabin. Hot and maddening. Blood boys and one blood girl.

His eyelids flutter, each breath a labored effort. I stare at the knife, thinking. I'm back in that A-frame cabin in the woods, the hot wind winding through, smelling like gore and new meat. Trav and I stand side by side, shoulders bumping.

I pull away the rabbit fur, the skin beneath pink and tender. I work my way down its body, careful not to tear. It's calming, intimate. Maybe this is what my father feels when he's sharpening his knife.

My father . . . Heath and I have been sleeping at the cabin on the weekends. Out of his hateful sight. But lately, Dad has been following us here to the Wicked Woods. Our woods. Our only refuge from him. He doesn't belong here. Amy didn't belong here, either.

Then I stop. And I decide. I know what I'm going to do. At home. Tonight.

And I promise myself that this time, I won't stop. I promise myself that if I succeed, I will never tell a soul what I did. That I will be the only one who knows.

I hand the peeled rabbit to Trav, and he calmly hacks the legs off with a cleaver. I want to pull his school collar down and kiss his neck, but Heath is watching.

Later, I lie on the creek bank with Trav, our hands entwined, blood under our fingernails. He asks me to marry him. I say yes.

Luke's labored breathing pulls me back to the present. The boat rocks gently beneath us as the wind stirs, salty and cold.

"I loved it, Luke."

"I know."

He reaches out in his final moments, his hand cold and unsteady. I let him. There's no urgency now. Just the fading rhythm of his heartbeat, the labored effort of his breathing.

His eyes flicker to my knife. He breathes in, lips moving silently. His voice is faint, almost lost. There's something he has to say. One final thing that he has to express before it's too late. I know what it is.

He squeezes my hand, eyes alight.

Luke Newton dies smiling.

The last thing he ever says is "I . . . know . . . that . . . blade."

THEN

The violence was worse after Mum was gone. There were no more warnings. My house was the ocean. My father, a shark on the hunt.
You're either the shark or the food.
The day Dad went missing, he was sitting around his homemade forge in the backyard. Heat-treating the black blade of his fishing knife until the flames were almost too bright to look at. He never knew I was there. Watching.
He always napped before night fishing. I crept to his room while he slept, removed his knife from his waders, and sliced long slits, one after another after another. Neat. Imperceptible. Then I crept outside to the forge and held the black blade to the fire until it broke away and only the handle remained.
Then I clipped the handle back in place.
Hours later, my father got dressed in the dark, pulled the waders on, unaware.
I watched him leave, his severed black blade warm in my palm, his words ringing in my ears.
Always take a knife.
Months later, I craft a handle made of kangaroo bone and fuse it to my father's black blade. The pieces slide into place like they've been waiting for each other.
Always take a knife.
I did.
I took his.

CHAPTER 35

My front yard smells like the daffodils my brother planted to honor our mother. My backyard smells like blood.

Sometimes I smell the flowers.

Sometimes the blood.

Sometimes both.

This morning, in my father's bedroom, the air is thick with the scent of flowers.

The room is empty. Colleen came over with her big rubbish bags, holding them open while I dumped in everything that belonged to my father. She gave me space when I needed it, letting me take my time with each object, an emotional anchor.

Before she left, she paused at the front door and asked if she could visit more often. I said I'd like that very much.

"I think Trav wants to drop by, too," she said carefully.

I don't tell her that he already does. That my windows are crowded with his love letters. That we meet in the Wicked Woods for a hot collision of teeth and flesh that leaves my brain fizzing. I don't tell her that he is patient and indulgent while I am sick with need. And I don't show her the teeth bracelet he made for me. Molars and incisors and canines all polished to a smooth shine.

I love it.

I bring my phone up to my face, re-reading the most viewed news article of the day, published this morning.

The outlaw ocean: Murder, illegal shark fishing, abalone poaching, and a thirty-year missing person case, solved

Kangaroo Bay: A Lawless Frontier
Trident Magazine
April 7, 2024

Jessie comes bounding in, football crammed in her mouth. I smile, slinging my arm around her, tucking my chin atop her head. I stare up at the windowsill where a trophy is set alight by sunlight.

HEATH GREENWOOD

SURF LIFESAVER OF THE YEAR

Maybe he's a villain in someone else's story. But he'll never be in mine.

Jess drops the chewed football in my lap, and I think of the fish postcard that arrived last week, and the two lines scribbled on the back:

I love you so much.
No trout about it!

Last month, I went back to Newcastle. Heath and I fished side by side on the back beaches as Jonah stood between us, clutching his rod with both hands, barely able to keep it steady. His line lurched, and my nephew instinctively pulled back, his movements jerky but determined. Heath coached him through it, and I cheered him on as he reeled the fish to shore. His first.

It meant a lot that I was there to watch it.

Actually, it meant everything.

There is no mention of my brother in this article. There never will be. They raided Terry's place and seized eleven thousand abalone, at an estimated street value of $250,000.

Terry Hargrave pleaded guilty to fourteen charges of possessing, receiving, and consigning abalone and three charges of illegally hunting great white sharks. He received a lifetime fishing ban Australia-wide and was sentenced to four years' imprisonment. He'll probably be out in two.

Soon enough, he'll be back, sitting at the bar of the Roo Bay pub, a hero to Heath and Trav because Terry took all the blame and never dobbed them in. I forgive him now for that. Whatever debt I felt he owed us has been paid. For good.

Heath's talking about coming home. Jonah starts school next year. Heath wants him fishing our beaches, diving off the pier with his mates, and learning how to skipper the *Deep Sea*. Tara's coming around to the idea.

I told him that as long as the shark fishing business is over for good, I'd like that. I'd like to be here to watch it all. Next week, I have an interview with the Pine Bay newspaper. I wish I could tell Chris.

I carry the heaviness of his loss with me. Sometimes it's a constant ache, a sadness that shows up without warning. Sometimes I wonder if it's all real. After Chris's death, the town faced a media flood. For weeks after, reporters parked outside the petrol station, snapping photos, standing breathlessly on the shore, gesturing sadly to the water. The town became a sort of morbid landmark.

The locals did what they always do. Closed ranks. Stopped talking. They wanted their silence back. Their town back. But with the VFA tightening its grip on the coastline, some of the blood men vanished overnight, forced to abandon their abalone trade before the law caught up. One of the men who left was Steven Newton, Luke's dad. The reporters camped outside his house every morning, shouted his name when he stepped outside. Shouted things like "How does it feel, having a killer for a son?"

He stopped opening the door after the first week. The phone rang and he never answered. It was fantastic. He'd spent his life lurking in the shadows, and now he was exposed and couldn't bear it. One night, he simply left. He hasn't come back.

It's a quieter town now, but the silence isn't as heavy these days. It's lighter. The shadows have shifted.

At the Geelong cemetery is Chris Cooper's grave. There's no body in it. I can't bring myself to visit him there. I like to speak to him on the shore, instead.

Yesterday I sat on the sand, wordless and listening to the wind. I finally told him about the article I was writing, and as I was leaving, I swear I heard his voice in the echo of a seagull: *Make sure to use the spellchecker.*

He's home.

And so is Donny Granger.

They found his body in the Wicked Woods, not far from Mum's. Dad is considered the suspect in his death. There's a warrant out for his arrest, but of course they won't find him. Dad drowned the night I took his knife. Only I know that.

Donny's mother released a statement: "We are deeply saddened and relieved to finally know what happened to our son. We ask for privacy so we can finally and fully grieve his loss."

Tomorrow I'm going to the shore again to speak to Chris. I'll read out the first few lines of my article and hope he likes it:

I want to acknowledge the contributions of Daily *journalist Chris Cooper, who went above and beyond for this story in the relentless pursuit of truth. His legacy will forever be defined by the difference he made in exposing the truth and bringing about real change.*

Chris Cooper was a fine journalist and friend.

I angle the phone screen to the trophy, then pan it around the room like a victory lap. I hope my mum sees this. I hope she's peeking down from the windows of heaven, watching. And I hope my father, wherever he is, can read the three words atop the headline that I can't stop staring at.

BY MINNOW GREENWOOD

I place my phone on the floor and take a slow, deliberate breath. My muscles loosen, and for the first time in what feels like forever, my mind stops sprinting. The light from the window stretches across the floor in soft shifting patterns, almost like the surface of the ocean from beneath.

I see myself as a child, diving into the water like a dolphin while Mum watches me from the shore, smiling. Heath's knee-deep in the water, calling out, "I got a fish! I got a fish!"

I surface, salt water dripping from my chin as he reels it onto the sun-warmed sand. Its scales flicker in the sunlight. Kingfisher blue, sunset pink, poppy red. You'd swear it contains all the colors in the entire world.

Heath crouches beside Mum, offering the fish to her like it's his whole heart.

Dad stands hatefully at the water's edge, salt water gushing from his ears and mouth. When he calls my name, the ocean roars.

I hesitate.

Then I swim toward my mum and Heath. Dad slips away like a falling star, burning as he leaves until not even a smear of him is left. I reach the shore and Mum pulls Heath and me into her arms. A cormorant glides above us, and its wings seem to stretch across the whole sky.

I stare at the news article again, smiling.

BY MINNOW GREENWOOD

My story. Finally. All of it.

Except for one thing.

I lean back on my elbows in my new bedroom, feeling like I've crossed a finish line nobody else can see.

Mum's silver fish pendant glints softly in the light, the delicate chain wrapped tight around my wrist. I like to feel it there at the base of my wrist. But what I like most is that each time my hand moves, the fish pendant responds with a subtle flicker. A flash of light that feels intentional. Like my mother's right here with me. Always will be.

My heartbeat slows down as I reach for the knife. The kangaroo bone handle, the sharp black blade.

I can never think of my father without a knife in his hand.

No, not anymore.

Now when I think of my father, he's drowning. Drowning in that dark ocean at night, all alone without a soul to help him as the water pulls and pulls, dragging him toward its hungry mouth. Roaring.

But it's not a call anymore.

It's a command.

He fumbles for his belt, grasps the knife handle, pulls it out. But the knife . . .

There is no knife. Only the handle.

He stares at it in shock, numb with terror. No knife.

Always take a knife.

A wave crests like a great black mountain—and then the crash, and he's under. I see his hands reaching up for help that never comes. I see the water rushing into his ears, nose, and mouth, swallowing him up like it will never let him go again.

And finally, I see him returning to the part of himself that was never truly gone.

Dad is the ocean now, elemental and ancient.

I let myself believe he knew it was me. That he knows I took his knife and him with it.

I let myself believe that when the waves throw themselves against the shore, curling and collapsing with a strange kind of desperation, that it's him. That he's reaching for his knife, but it will always be beyond his grasp.

That it will always be mine.

And I like to imagine that I hear the ocean calling, roaring and endless, repeating the same words over and over:

I can never think of my daughter without a knife in her hand.

ACKNOWLEDGMENTS

To my agent, Naomi Davis. I honestly don't know where I'd be in life without you—probably sad, unfulfilled, and eating cereal for dinner.

Thank you for EVERYTHING.

To my wonderful editors, Jenny Chen and Mae Martinez.

Jenny, I'll forever be grateful to you. Thank you for showing me how to get to the heart of a story and for making my craziest dreams come true. I'm so honored to have worked with you!

Mae, I'm indebted to how you shaped this book. Thank you for your incredible insights, and for being such a pleasure to work with.

For the amazing team at Bantam. No matter what comes next in my life, I'll always be able to proudly say "I'm a Penguin author!"

And that has meant everything.

Thank you.

Thank you to my family members and friends who continue to cheer me on.

To my mumsy, who now knows more about writing and publishing than she ever wanted to. Thank you for your fierce strength and endless belief in me, even when I didn't believe in myself—you're pretty awesome!

Thank you to Sissy, who taught me more about faith and strength these last few years than I ever expected to learn. Sissy is wise!

Thank you and Possum Lips for giving me a home when I had none. I wrote a lot of this book at your house, and I'll always be grateful. I know you miss me dearly, Possum Lips. Dry your tears—I'll be back.

DAN, THANK YOU FOR NOT blocking my number despite the endless fishing questions—and for stuffing my hands with books and rods since I was a kid. You've been teaching me longer than I ever knew. Thank you.

TO MY NEPHEW, NOAH. May you grow up to be smarter than your aunty and just as cool. Keep being awesome. We love you.

TO MY BEST FRIEND, Holly Strickland! For fourteen years of love, support, and snacks. Thank you for being a constant when everything felt uncertain.

Two years ago, during the worst time, you called me and said, "I'm right here. It's okay. I'm right here."

Thank you for always being "right here."

THANK YOU TO MY HEAD of security, Matty, for all your help and support!

BIG THANKS TO ALL MY Melbourne writer friends! Bridie Blake, Steph Huddleston, S. K. Stapar, R. E. Navan, Kat Turner, Katrina Toone, Tzeyi Koay, and Emily Nixon. It's been an absolute pleasure sharing our writing journeys together.

EXTRA SPECIAL THANKS TO Bridie Blake! Thank you for being a crisis hotline and cheerleader, and for letting me go absolutely rabid in your DMs.

TO MY #LLAMAQUAD! For seven years of laughing at my sexy toast GIF. Extra thanks to Ellie Blackbourne (Miep) and Susan Wallach for your support during some tough years.

To the lovely readers and Bookstagrammers! I'll forever be grateful for your feral support. I love this community so much. Special thanks to those who reached out to me about their mental health journeys. I want you to know I'm always cheering you on.

And finally, in response to the question I was asked on October 4, 2024:

My answer is Yes.

ABOUT THE AUTHOR

Lisa M. Matlin is the author of *The Stranger Upstairs*. She was a guitarist in a rock band before switching from songwriting to story writing. She lives in Melbourne, Australia, with her pug and golden retriever. She's probably rewatching *The Walking Dead* right now and trying not to laugh at her own jokes. Matlin is a passionate mental health advocate and your dog's number-one fan.

ABOUT THE TYPE

This book was set in Garamond, a typeface originally designed by the Parisian type cutter Claude Garamond (c. 1500–61). This version of Garamond was modeled on a 1592 specimen sheet from the Egenolff-Berner foundry, which was produced from types assumed to have been brought to Frankfurt by the punch cutter Jacques Sabon (c. 1520–80).

Claude Garamond's distinguished romans and italics first appeared in *Opera Ciceronis* in 1543–44. The Garamond types are clear, open, and elegant.